ENTER

TITLE

HERE

—Rahul Kanakia

HYPERION

LOS ANGELES • NEW YORK

First Edition, August 2016
10 9 8 7 6 5 4 3 2 1
FAC-020093-16169

Printed in the United States of America

Design by Maria Elias

Library of Congress Cataloging-in-Publication Data
Names: Kanakia, Rahul, author.
Title: Enter Title Here / Rahul Kanakia.
Description: First edition. | Los Angeles ; New York : Hyperion, 2016. |
Summary: High school senior Reshma Kapoor will stop at
nothing to gain admission to Stanford, including writing a novel.
Identifiers: LCCN 2015025229| ISBN 9781484723876 | ISBN 1484723872
Subjects: | CYAC: High schools—Fiction. | Schools—Fiction. | Authorship—
Fiction. | College choice—Fiction. | Perfectionism (Personality trait)—Fiction. |
East Indian Americans—Fiction.
Classification: LCC PZ7.1.K22 En 2016 | DDC [Fic]—dc23
LC record available at http://lccn.loc.gov/2015025229

Reinforced binding

Visit www.hyperionteens.com

SUSTAINABLE FORESTRY INITIATIVE   Certified Sourcing
www.sfiprogram.org
SFI-00993

THIS LABEL APPLIES TO TEXT STOCK

For every kid who's ever made a
beautiful effort to win an ugly prize

SUNDAY, SEPTEMBER 2

From: Linda Montrose <lmontrose@bombr.co>
To: Reshma Kapoor <rtkap@bombr.co>
Subject: Literary agent reaching out

Dear Reshma Kapoor,

I absolutely loved your column in yesterday's *Huffington Post*. Your voice was so brassy and articulate, even though the content had me shedding tears right onto my coffee table. I can't believe what your school tried to do to you. Thank God your parents were willing to stand up to them.

In fact, you're such an amazing writer that I can't believe you'll stop with just a column. If you were to someday write a novel, I'd love to read it. This is a matter of no small interest to me. I'm a San Francisco-based literary agent with Connor and Pavlovich. Although our firm represents all kinds of work, I mostly specialize in fiction for the children's market. I know that right now you're probably not even thinking about longer-form work, but please keep me in mind for the future!

Warmest Regards,
Linda Montrose

. . . .

From: Reshma Kapoor <rtkap@bombr.co>

To: Linda Montrose <lmontrose@bombr.co>

Subject: RE: Literary agent reaching out

Dear Ms. Montrose,

Thank you so much for your kind words! I worked really hard on that piece, and I'm so happy that it resonated with you.

It's actually very fortuitous that you brought up novels, because I have a secret project—a young adult novel—that I've actually been working on for years, and I think I'm finally about to finish.

When would you want to see it?

Sincerely,

Reshma Kapoor

· · · · · · · · ·

From: Linda Montrose <lmontrose@bombr.co>

To: Reshma Kapoor <rtkap@bombr.co>

Subject: RE: Literary agent reaching out

Fantastic! Please send it to me as soon as it's finished. Don't worry if it's rough, I can work with you! So excited to read!

—linda

'll begin my novel by saying that I was lying when I told you I had a "secret project."

The truth is that until yesterday I'd never in my life thought about writing a book. But when I got your message I felt compelled to reply immediately and say something that would keep you interested, because I knew your e-mail represented a can't-miss opportunity.

To put it simply: you are the hook that will get me into Stanford.

All successful people have a hook. In fact, you've probably been using one for years, although you might not think about it in those terms. Your hook is your tag line: the one accomplishment that sums up everything about you. People use their hooks to get the right college, job, internship, award . . . you name it. An interesting hook is what makes that one special application rise up out of a stack of thousands of near-identical ones.

Well, here I am, applying to college . . . and I'm still completely hookless. Yes, I'm going to be valedictorian, but there are thirty-one thousand high schools in America. That means (at least) thirty-one thousand valedictorians are competing for only sixteen hundred spots at Stanford. I have my op-ed, but *The Huffington Post* publishes a few high school students every year and, in my case, I got the chance because my dad has a friend who works at *The HuffPo*. Although I know you loved that column, any astute college admissions person could see it for the strategically placed thing that it was. And anyway, plenty of valedictorians have written plenty of bitty little columns that appeared in Slate or Salon or the *Wall Street Journal* or the *New York Times* or what have you. It's not hard, if you know how to exert the right pressure.

But an agent? That's a hook. Out of that thirty-one thousand, I doubt that more than two or three are being represented by a literary agent.

The only problem is timing. It takes years to publish a book, but my first app—I'm going to apply early to Stanford, even though Mummy thinks my SAT scores are too low for them—is due in less than two months, on November 1.

(Your best chance of getting into a school is to apply by their early deadline, but you can only apply early to one school, so you don't want to waste it on a school where you have no shot.)

However, I don't need to publish a book by that deadline; I only need to show that I'm capable of publishing one. The "secret project" might've started as a lie, but by the time you read this, it'll be true!

Since fiction—unlike a school paper—doesn't require any kind of research or preparation, I'm certain that I can finish in the twenty-seven days between now and October 1. Then, after you read it, you can sign me as a client and send a supplemental recommendation letter to all my colleges.

My main application materials will only barely allude to the novel I'm writing: it'd be too much like boasting, you know? But then, in your supplemental rec, you'll rave about my talent and precocity and emphasize the fact that I, at only eighteen years of age, am writing on a professional level. After that, we can publish this thing at our leisure.

Although, ideally, it would be good if it came out within four years, before med school application time.

Great! Now I just need to write it.

. . . .

To start with, I'm your protagonist—Reshma Kapoor—and if you have the free time to read this book, then you're probably nothing like me.

Since my second semester of freshman year, I've never gotten a grade on anything—test, homework, presentation, paper—that was less than an 87 out of 100.

And don't go thinking that I attend some soft private school where there are no class ranks and everyone gets an award for trying hard, because that's not how we do things here in Silicon Valley.

No. I live in Las Vacas, which is one of the richest towns in America. And it's full of engineers and entrepreneurs: people who constantly agitate for the school to become tougher and more competitive. Alexander Graham Bell High School has fifteen hundred Asian kids whose parents are top-notch researchers and engineers (or very upwardly mobile Dunkin' Donuts owners) and fifteen hundred white kids whose parents own the companies where the Asian kids' parents work.

The school's got a fifteen-million-dollar science lab, a theater that seats five thousand people, and a football team that's won State two times. It offers twenty-seven advanced placement classes, and over two-thirds of the student body will take at least one of them before they graduate. The average SAT score is a 2100 and 95% of its graduates go on to four-year colleges. Its alumni include two Nobel-prize winners, four billionaires, two pop stars, three film stars, and a National Book Award–winning novelist. Every year, at least one kid commits suicide.

And I'm its number one student. Not its smartest student. Not its most beloved student. But, by the numbers, the best.

· · · · · · · · · ·

I suppose I should set the scene. Don't novels begin by setting the scene?

I'm in my basement, sitting on the black plastic bench of the weight machine, with my MacBook Air poised on my knees and a big pitcher of ice water on the mat next to me. It's very early in the morning and the room's dark, but the blue light of my screen makes all the junk in the corner—a box of Christmas lights, a barely used carbon nanofiber bike, three old desktop computers, and a professional espresso machine that Daddy got shipped in from Italy after he got tired of standing in line at Starbucks—stand out like a pile of boulders. My heart is clicking irregularly, and the back of my brain is desiccated, and I have that cracked-out, numb feeling that I always get at the end of a long day. But it's okay. I can feel the tingles in my hands and arms. When I started writing this, I was pretty tired, but I popped an Adderall, and now I'm coming back to life. With each sip, I can feel the cold water pooling deep inside my chest.

George Trivandrum, the son of one of my dad's college friends, groans beyond the door. I hear him roll over. Then there's a loud sigh. He's registered as an occupant of this house so he can go to my school. This is borderline illegal, but my dad says it's okay because George actually *does* sleep here on most school nights. In fact, I think my presence might be keeping him up. Normally, George wakes up early for his track and field practices, but I guess today he's trying to sleep in.

Sometimes I can't even believe the two of us go to the same school, much less live in the same house. We have none of the same classes, and I almost never come down into the basement, so I literally never see him in either place. In fact, right now I'm a bit anxious that he might venture out here, but there's no help for me. Either I need to hide out down here and risk seeing him or go upstairs and risk facing Mummy.

(By the way, *Mummy* is a British/Indian term for *mother*. Not pronounced like the monster—it's Mum-Me, with a hard stop between the syllables.)

Of course, there are parts of this novel you'll never see. I'll maintain two versions of it, like I do for all my newspaper articles and school papers: an honest version and a pretty version. I suppose I could start with the pretty version, but when I do that, I get all mixed up and forget what I'm talking about. Eventually, I'll go back and prettify this and remove all the paragraphs—like this one—that would make you hate me.

Once people meet me, they start to hate me. That's because when I speak, I find it hard to create a pretty version.

I haven't read many novels, because reading is a waste of time, but I think they usually contain more than a girl sitting alone in her basement. God, I have no clue what this novel is about. . . .

. . . .

Before leaving the exercise room, I wedged my laptop into the piles of junk and ran in place for a little while in order to build up a sweat. When I opened the door, the hall was dark, and I picked my way across the floor very slowly, trying to not even breathe. I hate to disturb George. But I was only halfway down the hall when his door opened a tiny bit and he stage-whispered, "Goddamn it. Just go," so I jogged up the rest of the stairs.

Out in the hall, Mummy said, "Reshma, is that you? Reshma, where have you been?"

She was sitting in a corner of the living room in her shapeless beige nightgown and typing on her computer. Our first floor is a huge open-plan space that the decorator did up with the latest in European-influenced furniture: chairs that look like martini glasses; a couch that looks like cubes of red Styrofoam arranged next to each other; a glass table that's held up by a single titanium rod that juts from the wall. But Mummy prefers the battered, sunken love seat whose sides were clawed up by a now-dead cat she and Dad owned when they were in grad school.

Until two years ago, my mom and my dad swapped out responsibility for making breakfast in the morning, because they ran their own company and they had total freedom over their schedules. But ever since their company was stolen out from under them, my dad's been doing his own projects, and my mom's been too busy with her new job as a product manager for Google.

When I entered, she looked up over her glasses and said, "Have you slept tonight?"

"I was exercising," I said.

Mom's eyes flicked over me. "Exercising is good, but you should sleep, *ke nahi?*"

"I've been thinking about writing a novel," I said. "But I'm not sure where to go with it. I'm not a sympathetic main character. My quirks are not lovable. I am not clumsy. I am not overwhelmed by life. I am not unlucky in love."

"Love? What love?" She shook her head. "Is there some boy you've been seeing?"

"No. But if I wanted a boy, I could get one."

She snorted. "Life is not so easy as you think. You can't conjure up love."

"I know. That's my problem. The readers are not going to love me."

"Come now. Are you depressed? I can call Dr. Wasserman."

"I'm not depressed. I was *never* depressed."

"You were very much not yourself after your SAT scores came back, but I had thought we were past that."

I took the SAT three times and never got higher than a 1710. My mom keeps trying to tell me that's a fine score, since it's better than 75% of people who take the test. But it's actually terrible: only 2% of admitted Stanford students have scores that low, and I bet they're mostly athletes.

"I already told you: I'm not worried about my SAT anymore. I have another plan for getting into Stanford."

"Please, *beta*, all this silliness with hooks and lawsuits and class ranks is meaningless. You will simply apply to a number of colleges and the one that can see your specialness is the one that will be right for you."

Mummy reached out for me, and I backed up to stop her from getting ahold of my hand. "Even without Stanford, I know you will be a success," she said. "By God, you know how to work hard, and that is the most important thing. When I remember your effort with the dictionary, well I—"

"Can we please not talk about that?"

My mom's fingers pulled and plucked at each other. "Why not? Why do you always treat me like I am your enemy?"

I felt a single Adderall pill floating around in the pocket of my pajamas. My mom is energetic and smart and creative, but, fundamentally, she's a sucker. Which is good for her, I guess, since that *hard work will win out in the end* thing is what's stopped her from becoming bitter like my dad.

I clicked my tongue. "I've got it," I said. "You're the villain. People will really sympathize with a girl who had a crazy tiger mom that forced her to work too hard. You messed me up. That's my angle."

Mummy's feet slipped onto the ground. "What is this? What are you blaming me for? This is not good. I have only ever—"

I made tamping-down motions with my hands. "Don't worry. It's no big deal. It's for the novel."

She tried to argue with me some more, but I ran upstairs and through my door and collapsed onto my bed. I've never cared about decorating my room. What would be the point? No one is ever going to see it. But when I was eleven, my mother hired a decorator: a woman who wore perfectly creased white slacks and pink blouses and horn-rimmed glasses.

The resulting bedroom is dominated by a huge four-poster bed. The walls are tinged with pink and my bedspread has a profusion of purple flowers. My closet is a full, lush walk-in with floor-to-ceiling mirrors and smaller ones, angled at the floor, for trying on shoes. It's half-empty.

But lying on the bed wasn't going to get me anywhere. I needed to work!

When I got up, a dizzy rush made everything go white. But that passed in a few seconds, and now I'm at my bedroom computer (it syncs automatically with my MacBook), still trying to figure out what to put in my novel. In search of inspiration, I've been opening drawers and wading through the pile of old notebooks, journals, assignments, papers, textbooks, etc., etc.

. . . .

Just now, I picked up a black journal and flipped to a random page.

It says:

Things I Must Never Ever Do Again

Fall when I wear socks on the stairs
Eat more than three Double Stuf Oreo cookies at a time
Put one of my bears back in its bocks [sic] without checking it for rips

I actually remember this day. I was clambering down the stairs, while wearing socks, when my foot hit the edge of the stair and I slipped. Not a big slip: I caught myself and didn't fall. But Mummy clucked her tongue and said she wasn't going to tell me again to take off my socks before going on the stairs and that if I fell, then it'd be my own fault.

Just to prove her wrong, I swore to NEVER take off my socks before going down the stairs and to MAKE SURE that I NEVER EVER fell.

And I never did, because that's who I am. Once I decide I'm going to do something, then I do it. My mom has never understood that. She thinks, *Oh, you know, if you want something, then you try your hardest, and if you're good enough, then someone will give it to you.* I know she's down there thinking, *Oh, Reshma tried really hard, but she just couldn't hack it on the tests, so I guess she doesn't deserve to get into Stanford.*

But she's got it backward. You start by saying, *I deserve it. No matter what anyone else thinks, I deserve it.* And then you do absolutely everything it takes to make it happen. And I did.

At school there's a group of otherwise smart and hardworking kids—the perfects—who weren't willing to make the sacrifices, weren't willing to give up boys, popularity, the respect of their parents and teachers. And that's why they've always been in second place.

Although, ugh, if I'd paid just a little more attention to those things, then writing this novel would be a lot simpler.

Oh God, just had a brainstorm.

Novel Synopsis: *In order to get more material for her novel, an introverted, studious Indian American girl decides to break out and become one of the popular kids. She starts doing all the regular American girl stuff that she always used to ignore: making friends, going to parties, drinking, dating, falling in love, having sex, etc. Although she begins the project in a cynical manner, she eventually realizes that human relationships are the most important things in life.*

I bet you love this, don't you, Ms. Montrose? White people like to think we're all emotionless study machines. They tell themselves that their kids might not do as well in school, but at least they know how to enjoy life.

Well, I'll spend a month enjoying life and then, oh, I expect it'll "transform" me. I learned in English class that stories often end with the character having a staggering realization: an epiphany. And I expect to have one sometime right around September 28.

I'll realize that life is only a series of moments. And that I've wasted a dozen years of those moments by constantly looking ahead and wishing that some other moment would arrive. I'll realize that I never got to enjoy the things I had because I kept wishing for things that I didn't yet have. And I'll realize that even if I get everything I want . . . I'll immediately find something new to want. I'll realize that I've wasted my life.

By the end of the novel, I'll turn into a whimsical girl who harvests all the possible joy from each moment and lives a carefree existence and lets the future take care of itself and all that other bullshit.

I don't mind calling it that because, you see, we're still at the beginning of the novel, and right now I'm still my cynical old achievement-obsessed self. But in three hundred thirty-two pages, you and I are going to look back on that "bullshit" and laugh at the naiveté of my hard-bitten pose.

RESHMA KAPOOR'S SEPTEMBER TO-DO LIST

Needed in Order to Complete Novel

___ Make a friend

___ Go on a date

___ Go to a party

___ Get a boyfriend

___ Have sex

Journalism-related

___ Check layouts

. . .

. . .

· · · · · · · · ·

Today was not a good day.

You know, the way I got to be valedictorian was by knowing the unspoken rules. I know what teachers are looking for, and I know exactly how much work it takes to get the highest grade they're willing to give.

But sometimes teachers break the rules.

I never wanted to take Ms. Ratcliffe's literature class. For more than three years, I've tiptoed around her down at the newspaper, where she's constantly interfering and lecturing and playing favorites. Do you know how many times I've put together a comprehensive and well-researched story, only to hear her say: "Come on, Reshma, can't we go deeper?"

Even though she's thirty-plus years old, her brunette hair is buzzed almost to the skull. She paints her nails black and wears colorful peasant skirts that swirl around as she bounces back and forth across the room.

When I first met her, she told us, "My last name sounds so severe, doesn't it? Please, just call me Tami."

Ever since then, I've never called her anything but Ms. Ratcliffe.

Everything I'd heard about her class made it sound even more insufferable than the woman herself. And guess what? All of it is true! For instance, she teaches in front of a huge poster that says QUESTION AUTHORITY in bulbous purple hippie-type lettering.

Why can't she understand that she *is* the authority?

But since the school wouldn't let me use this period to take AP Mandarin at the charter school down the street, her class was literally the only Bell High AP class that fit into my schedule. At Bell, AP classes get additional weight when they calculate your GPA, which means every semester I need to take eight APs if I'm going to stay at number one.

Still, I thought I'd be fine. This is an AP literature class, and I know how to write about literature. But, on the first day, she asked us to pick something that mattered to us and write a poem about it. And she only gave us two days to write it. The short deadline was so it'd sound "fresh."

Well, what do I know about poems? I have no idea what an A+

poem looks like. I had to go to the library and check out a book about poems. And when I asked her to give me some more guidance, Ms. Ratcliffe said, "Oh, do your best. Write what you feel. . . ."

I know that means I'm being set up to fail. Teachers always try to game me. She thinks if she gives me a bad grade on the first assignment, I'll try harder on all subsequent ones. But in order to stay at number one, I need as many A+'s (not A's, not A–'s) on my report card as possible. And getting an A+ for the semester means never getting a single bad grade, ever.

Immediately, I understood that I couldn't write a regular poem with line breaks and whatnot. I had no idea where the line breaks were supposed to go: they all looked pretty random to me. No, I needed something clever. I was flipping through the book, almost too tired to read it, when I opened it to a section on "prose poems."

These are basically long, beautiful sentences that are full of flowery words and complex metaphors. Well . . . I know how to do that. My poem was:

"To a Gas Lamp"

The dark blots in the gas lamp move frenetically for a time, battering against the glass and trying to find the paper-thin ingress that'll allow them entrance to the chamber of their despair, but soon enough the miasmic air, sweetened by fire, lures them down onto a bed of silky moth-wings.

But today she returned our poems, and I immediately sensed that something was wrong. My throat went dry when she dropped it facedown on my desk, and my hand shook as I flipped it over.

Not even a straight C. A C–. The only note was: *Please come see me.*

During class, I read it over and over. She lectured us on the first pages of *A Tale of Two Cities* (which starts with a poem), and though my hand was automatically taking notes, I couldn't concentrate. Ms. Ratcliffe always organizes the classroom desks in a big rectangle, and she sits at one corner, as if she's juuust another student.

After the first week of class, I realized she wasn't going to call on me unless I sat directly opposite her and waved my hand right in front of her field of vision. But that meant she saw everything. After I wiped a tear away with a flick of my jacket cuff, she shook her head, and her bloodless lips twitched up into a slight smile.

Even worse, Chelsea had caught onto the same trick, so she always sat next to me. I glanced over. Her poem had gotten an A. Of course. Ms. Ratcliffe loved her. During the newspaper elections last year, she told a bunch of the freshmen and sophomores that Chelsea was the most energetic and knowledgeable staffer she'd ever taught.

The perfects don't have an official leader. That's the point: they're all perfect. But if there was one, it'd be Chelsea. She went to the same elementary and middle school as me, and we've always been in the same advanced classes. For a while, in middle school, it looked like she'd get ahead: we used to duel on tests, competing to get at least one point ahead of each other, and although our middle school didn't rank people, I remember that when we compared final report cards, she ended up ahead of me by a sliver of a percentage point. But during freshman year, she decided that maintaining appearances was more important than doing well in school, and now she struggles to stay in second place.

That day in class, her sunglasses were cocked on top of her brunette hair. Sometimes, when she moves too suddenly, they'll flip down onto her face and then she'll tweak them up again with two fingers.

I craned my head to look at her poem. "What did you write about?"

"Oh, just something silly." She smiled. Her poem was entitled "Storefront."

I tried to read the first line, but she hurriedly slid it into her notebook.

"Come on, I'm sure it's brilliant."

I wanted to tell her that a literary agent had contacted me, but I wasn't sure how to do it.

When she turned her head, her sunglasses flipped down again, so she took them off entirely. Up front, Ms. Ratcliffe was saying good-bye to everyone by using big operatic sweeps of her hand.

"Hey." Chelsea tore out a scrap of notebook paper and handed it to me. "Write down your e-mail. I have something to send you."

"What's happening?" I said.

"Oh, it's not a big deal," she said. "You'll see."

I scrawled my e-mail on the paper. She stashed it in her bag, then smiled and said, "By the way, Resh, I meant to tell you: I saw your article online, and I thought it was so great, and, you know, just absolutely true." The corners of her mouth came up slowly and fitfully, as if she was cranking up her smile with a winch. "I mean, I hope by now you know me well enough that this goes without saying, but . . . I *never* supported Colson's scheme."

I didn't buy it, but I nodded anyway. What can you do with a person who *never* says what she really thinks?

. . . .

After class, I approached Ms. Ratcliffe with my paper in hand. "Excuse me," I said. "I'd like to talk about this assignment."

She looked up at me. "Oh yes, Reshhhma."

Ms. Ratcliffe always pronounces my name with way too much emphasis on that *h*, as if she's so much more enlightened than all the other stupid Americans who can't recognize that my name contains some crazy-sounding Indian phoneme. Except, umm, she's wrong.

The *sh* sound in my name is pretty much the same as in English. It's the first syllable that actually ought to sound different.

"Look," I said. "I've never gotten a grade this low before."

"Hmm, right . . . Why don't you come and see me in my office after school?" she said. "We can have a good long talk about it."

My lips made a noise as they pulled apart. "You can't write '*Please see me*' and then refuse to talk to me."

She rubbed her stubbly head with one hand and looked at the exit. No one was coming in. She reached down—exposing the red hint of a tattoo on her upper arm—and raised the doorstop. The door crashed shut as she stood up.

"It's unusual for a creative assignment to get a grade like this," I said. My heart was tap-tap-tapping against the inside of my chest.

She tucked herself into one of the student desks and said, "It's the creative part that I wanted to talk to you about. I know you're smart. But I've seen a lot of your writing over the years, with the newspaper. And you never seem to go as far and as deep as you could."

"You're supposed to prepare us for the advanced placement test," I said. "Writing poems isn't part of the curriculum."

She cocked her head and spoke softly. "Where did you get the idea for your poem? Gas lamps are an odd subject for a modern teen."

I rocked up and down on my toes. "I was looking at a bug trapped in a lighting panel. I changed it to a gas lamp to be more poetic."

"Oh, well that's what isn't working. It's too artificial. Not authentically yours. Not your background, your experience. I know you like to win at everything, but I can't promise you that you're going to win at this assignment. The problem is that in the entire three years I've known you, I can only think of one time when you've been honest with me." God, how many times would I have to pay for confiding in her that night? "You're always trying to tell people what they want to hear. I wish you'd stop worrying about your GPA and start worrying about how you're living your life. I think if you looked into your own life and family and culture, your writing would be different and more interesting."

Let me tell you, it's true. When you get super angry, you do see red at the edge of your vision. I think it's because of increased ocular pressure. So much pressure. My body felt like it'd been pumped full of air.

I stood totally still, except for the quivering, and I said, "I am one hundredth of a grade point ahead of Chelsea Blahnik and two hundredths of a grade point ahead of Jeremy Ozick. Every point on every assignment counts. Maybe you know that over the summer, Mr. Colson tried to revamp our grading system so Chelsea could be valedictorian instead of me. But I stopped him. I stopped the vice principal. Don't you think I can stop you?"

She rubbed her fuzzy head and let the hand fall down over her face. From under that shield, she mumbled, "Well . . . all my grades are final. What you handed in was generic and the sentiment was cliché. Nor did it have any poetic form. It's a stretch for me to even call it a poem. . . ."

"Fine." My heart quieted. I'm always prepared for a fight. "This will keep going. We'll argue about it day after day. You'll have to meet with my parents, with the principal, with my lawyers, with the school's lawyers, with your own lawyers. . . . The meetings will go on and on and on and each one will cost you a fortune in legal fees."

I grabbed my backpack and put a hand on the door.

She said, "I know you're under a lot of pressure at home. But at some point you have to begin charting your own course in life."

We locked eyes for a long moment. And she sighed. Thank God. Most teachers will back down after putting up a show of resistance, but occasionally I encounter someone who doesn't understand what I'm capable of. I'd been worried that Ms. Ratcliffe might force me to go ahead and destroy her life, but I was glad to see she was no different from the rest.

I don't enjoy destroying people. Or, well, I suppose that's not strictly true. But still, I try to only do it when I have to.

"All right," she said. "I'll take another look at the assignment."

Before closing the door, I added, "By the way, you're still saying it wrong," I said. "My name is pronounced Raysh-ma. That's a long *a*; not a short *e*."

"That's fine, Rice-shma," she said. "I'll try to remember."

When I left, she was still hiding behind her hand.

WEDNESDAY, SEPTEMBER 5

On Google Earth, Bell High looks like a huge smiley face. It's a cluster of buildings that are organized around three huge courtyards. The biggest one—the mouth—is the south courtyard, near the main entrance, and it's flanked by two jowls—the gym and the auditorium. The eyes are the east and west courtyards. In the center, the cafeteria rises up like a bulbous glass nose. Painted on the roof of the caf is a stick figure wearing a huge sombrero. It was put there years ago by some students who understood the potential humor value of this whole satellite imagery thing. Every spring, the seniors like to sneak up there and arrange random stuff near the stick figure's midsection so that it appears to have a penis.

The school is built in a Spanish style, with red shingle roofs and walls that're painted a faux adobe brown. Arid-climate plants— cactuses and shrubs and fruit trees—live in the planters around the school. We don't have too many internal hallways, since classrooms usually open right into the courtyards. Around the edge of each yard the roof overhangs a little to keep out the rain, but that's about it. In a lot of places, greenish lockers line the yards. So the courtyards are hallway and dining area and hang-out spot. It's a bit miserable from November to January, when it rains all the time, but during fall and spring, it's glorious. The wind rushes through the courtyards at exactly the right speed to wick away the sun's heat. It's like being at a tropical beach.

The three courtyards are distinctly different places. I don't know much about the south courtyard and the east courtyard. The south has all these white plastic tables with umbrellas on them and the ground is made of these wooden planks, like a boardwalk. The athletes hang out at one end, near the gym and the playing fields, but mostly it's freshmen and sophomores mingling around down there, since that's where most of their classes are.

The west courtyard belongs to that undistinguished rabble of juniors and seniors: people who don't matter—the ones who never spoke to anyone but the three friends they'd made on the first day of freshman year; the ones who found a boyfriend during sophomore year and stopped talking to everyone else; the ones who've been playing video games on Saturday night with the same two guys for the last three years; the ones who don't *do* anything or seem to *want* anything.

I call them the invisible two-thirds.

But most of the school's advanced classes—the classes I've been taking since freshman year—are clustered around the east courtyard, where we have three sorts of people:

- *"Study Machines"* want to win. They get good grades because they work all the time and have a relatively limited social life. They're rescued from the invisible two-thirds because they're usually also pretty involved in extracurricular activities (although they rarely rise to the highest leadership positions).
- *"Smart Slackers"* pretend they don't care about winning. They take advanced classes and appear to be intelligent, but don't get good grades. Half are white and half are Asian. They tend to put most of their energies into extracurricular activities and, on occasion, they'll rise into leadership positions.

- *"Perfects"* are afraid of losing, so they pretend the game doesn't exist. They're preppy kids, mostly white or halfie, who dress well, party hard, get good grades, take advanced classes, and attain most of the leadership positions in our school, i.e. school president, newspaper editor, lead in the school play, honor society president, etc., etc. And they're pretty much the rulers of the hagiocracy that is Bell High.

As for me? There were, like, thirty seconds during freshman year when I tried to be a perfect, but I eventually realized that all of that *I'm so perfect* posturing was preventing me from getting ahead. So instead I'm the queen of the study machines, obviously. First in terms of grades, but runner-up in everything else. Layout editor instead of editor-in-chief. Honor society secretary instead of president. The one who organizes canned food drives and leadership conferences and essay contests, but never the one who gets the credit for them. Always the mule, never the driver.

· · · · · · · · · ·

I realized I'm never going to finish my novel if I only work on it at home. And, unlike all of the rest of my work, this doesn't require textbooks or computers, so I'm writing this in English class while pretending to take notes. Why would I want to take note of anything Ms. Ratcliffe says? I hate her so much.

So yeah, let me take you back into the unfathomably distant past of . . . this morning, when I was in chemistry class.

I love chem. Actually, I couldn't care less about the subject itself. But I love my chem teacher.

Most of my teachers don't like me, because I am very vocal in my opinion that A+ work deserves to get an A+, but Ms. Lin is the exception. She's a tiny Taiwanese woman with big bouffant hair and gnarled little hands. At the beginning of class she struggles up onto a tall stool—her feet dangle a foot above the floor—and never comes down. She doesn't write equations on the board or conduct showy experiments. She talks in a whisper-soft voice, so you're always leaning forward to hear her. And she waves those stubby arms in a choppy, impressionistic way, like she's sketching out particle flows in the air in front of her. I think her husband used to be a government minister in Taiwan, but, for some reason, they were forced to leave.

And then she points at you and whispers a question like, "How many covalent bonds are in a CH_4 molecule?" If you don't answer correctly, then you get extra homework. And if you do answer correctly, well, then, you get those A+'s.

I always answer correctly.

Anyway, this morning, I was having trouble concentrating because I was sitting at the front of the class, with my knees crossed, hoping that nothing was showing.

I blame the denim skirt I was wearing, which I'd bought at Hollister last night. I'd blushed bright red as I paid. It's so short! And my T-shirt—also from Hollister—is tight and pink. It says HAPPY IS and then a picture of a seagull. Happy is a seagull.

When I came downstairs this morning, Mom raked me over with her eyes and said she was making an appointment for me with Dr. Wasserman.

I was also wearing ninety-dollar Sperrys that I bought after typing *"What shoes do girls wear?"* into Google. Usually, I wear flip-flops everywhere. My toes felt constrained, even as air brushed past parts of my legs that were normally hidden by any of my twelve identical pairs of blue jeans. At least the denim of the skirt was heavy enough that I was somewhat sure I wasn't going to be exposed by a random gust of wind.

But this ridiculous outfit was serving its purpose, because my potential boyfriend had just flipped me another sidelong glance.

I turned my head in time to see Aakash look away. Ever since I'd met him—he's a copy editor on the paper—he's done his best to sit next to me in all my classes. Aakash is an Indian guy, who wears his shirts with two buttons undone and constantly taps at his protruding collarbone in a way that produces an audible sound. He's not exactly ugly, but he is a little scrawny and an inch shorter than me.

A year ago, he signed a red heart and slipped it into my locker on Valentine's Day. I've never acknowledged it.

And now I had to get him to ask me out.

All the Indian girls at Bell are the target of at least one silent Indian nerd-boy crush. Most of us—even the ones who are desperately lonely—know, with unspoken female intuition, that if we were to acknowledge one of these boys for even a second, we'd end up trapped in the mire of their saccharine devotion for years. Which isn't really that appealing. But I only have twenty-six days to get a boyfriend!

Even so, it was hard for me to smile and brush his elbow with my fingers and ask him if I could borrow a pen. I was marking myself as someone who couldn't do better than an Aakash.

And Alexandra Sorenson, one of the founders of the perfects, was sitting in the back of the class and watching everything from underneath her perfectly plucked eyebrows. I glanced back. She collected her blond hair in the cradle of her thumb and forefinger and threw it over her shoulder. Her nails were long and pink, with little white stars painted into the corners. Alexandra is probably the closest thing I have to a friend. Which isn't that close, because she's not actually my friend at all: she just sells me Adderall sometimes.

I looked back at her and raised an eyebrow. Then she smiled with half-lidded eyes, as if she'd just taken a large, fiber-packed shit.

When the bell rang, covers slapped against covers and pages were torn free. Aakash threw his books and his notes into his bulky black backpack. He zipped it up and rubbed his forehead with a hand. Damn. He was about to bolt.

"Hey, Aakash," I said.

He threw his head back and his chin outward and looked all around like he wasn't exactly sure where my voice was coming from. "Umm." I held the pen out to him. "Thanks for letting me borrow this."

Chattering people flowed out of the room around us, but Alex hung back, standing by the door. The world was fuzzy, like I was viewing it through a layer of plastic wrap. And it was good. The plastic wrap was the only thing keeping my insides from spilling out. The room was empty and almost quiet, except for Alex, laughing by the door with a junior perfect—she looked like she was 70% composed of skinny jeans—who'd been summoned to her side.

Aakash's voice emerged from somewhere down deep in his stomach. "That's . . . err . . . no. You keep it."

I reversed the pen and stuck it behind my ear. Was that sexy? I'm still not sure. My instinct is no.

He put a palm on the desk, and shifted upward, like he was about to lever himself out, but then said, "Hey . . . I've been meaning to tell you that you did a great job laying out Rachel's article the other day."

"It was a thoroughly ordinary job," I said. "But thanks."

He leaned in. "No . . . I, uhh, it looked beautiful," he said. I could hear the staccato tapping of his index finger on his chest.

Then the room changed. The laughter got louder and rougher. Shoulders slapped against each other. A boy in a letter jacket tussled with another boy, and when he broke free they chased each other around the room. Ms. Lin's forehead acquired a slight crease. But then one of the letter jackets—a three hundred pound guy in a 49ers shirt—jogged up to her and tried to coax her off her chair to stand next to him while a girl—her breasts almost bouncing out of her halter—laughed and pointed her phone's camera at them. Ms. Lin pursed her lips in a way that was almost like a smile!

The athletes were always around. I mean, they were so big that you couldn't help seeing them in the halls. But I never saw them in class. I have my set paths through the school, from AP class to AP class. And I mostly see other people—study machines like Aakash or perfects like Alex—who are on the same trail. But there's a shadow trail and a shadow set of classes that I'd slipped over into. This must be regular chem—not even honors.

Aakash was still talking. I took his hand. I thought it'd be sweaty, but it was surprisingly cool and smooth. His skin was a few shades lighter than mine.

"I need your help," I said. "I'm not getting this covalence stuff." Ms. Lin glanced up at us. "Do you think you could come over to my place sometime and explain it to me?"

"Sure . . . I . . . It's pretty ea—" Then he fell silent. Aakash knew that twenty minutes ago I'd correctly answered a question about this.

A strand of hair caught in the pen when I pulled it out with my other hand. I extricated it and pressed the tip to the back of Aakash's hand. The ink didn't want to flow onto skin. I pressed harder and he winced slightly. Then his eyes flicked down, for a second, to my exposed thighs, and it hit me. My first time was going to be with this . . . this geek.

And why? So I could get into Stanford.

After moving the pen in a series of straight lines, I finally managed to write out my phone number in a blocky, childish script. "Call me," I said.

The bell rang.

Aakash grabbed the neck of his backpack and ran off without even zipping it. Alex looked down the hallway at Aakash's retreat and swung her eyes back toward me. Then, incredibly, she smiled—a huge, open smile—and gave a big wave!

Shocked, I waved back, but I realized she wasn't looking at me. I glanced over at the guy to my right.

The wiry athlete sitting next to me? It was George! He waved back at Alex—how did they know each other?—then ran a hand through his hair, which went down past his ears. The corner of his mouth twitched.

"Hey, Resh," he said. "Who was that guy?"

"I, umm, no one."

"No one. Got it." His eyes lingered on my skirt for a moment, and he gave me a quick wink. "I understand how to maintain the party line."

I could feel the warmth spreading across my face and shoulders as I headed out into the hall. Was I blushing? I couldn't *believe* he'd seen me in these clothes. Why was he even here? Why didn't he go to his own school? I tried to zip up my bag with some of the savagery of emotion that I felt, but the zipper got caught on the hem of the backpack and I had to saw it back and forth a few times before it popped free and I could finally get the thing closed.

THURSDAY, SEPTEMBER 6

Today was a complete failure.

I spent the whole of chemistry smiling at Aakash and asking him questions about the material and tapping him on the back of the hand to show him I was just so interested. When class ended, I stood very close to him and looked into his brown eyes, and I was absolutely sure that he was going to ask me out right then and there. But instead he quivered and ran for the door.

Later on, I saw him in the hallway and tried to get closer, but he dashed away.

Then, during lunch, Alex yelled, "Hey, Resh!"

I tried to ignore her, but she raised her voice.

"Loving your nerdy little courting rituals."

She was sitting with Tina and Chelsea at their table in the cafeteria, looking down at me from a raised dais, as if they were lords of the school.

Alex tapped her pink fingernails against the table. "And don't worry about wearing the same skirt two days in a row," she said. "Aakash isn't the type to notice."

I blinked and searched for a comeback, but all I could think to say was "Mind your own business."

"Oh, is that how it is?" she said. Then she shifted positions and I could see what was in her hand: her keychain. There was a little pill dispenser on her key ring. With a careful twist, she uncapped it and shook one orange pill out onto the table, right within sight of everyone.

For me, owning that pill would be illegal, but Alex has a prescription. She was warning me that she could cut me off whenever she wanted, so I turned on my heel and stalked away from her while she laughed.

The perfects are always nice. That's part of what makes them perfect. But Alex has always had trouble with that, and this year she seems to have lost control and become completely evil. Which is not necessarily something I disapprove of, except when it's directed toward me.

When I got home, I spent a few hours brainstorming who I could get to be my friend. I do know a few people, I guess. I'm not completely pathetic. But they're so uninspiring. Does anyone really want to read a novel about an Indian girl who becomes friends with Jenny, the girl with the gratingly harsh voice who serves as secretary of the World Leadership Council? Or with Eileen: the completely nondescript girl who shared a room with me at math camp when I was in eighth grade?

No, because the truth is that a friend isn't just someone who hangs out with you. A friend is someone who understands your real self. And that wasn't going to be Jenny. If I ever showed my real self to Jenny, she'd run screaming.

And then, as I was sitting in my room compiling lists of potential friends, I got this weird e-mail from Chelsea:

From: Chelsea Blahnik <cblah@bombr.co>
To: Reshma Kapoor <rtkap@bombr.co>
Subject: Coordinating early action / early decision choices

Hey, Resh—
I've been talking it over with a few of the other top-ranking kids at Bell, and we've come up with a really simple system for avoiding last year's Princeton

pile-up disaster. Basically, only one person is going to apply in the early lottery to each college. That way, we avoid getting in each other's way. This doesn't really constrain you, since as valedictorian you would of course get the first pick: if you tell me which school is getting your early application, I'll make sure no one else applies there. We're hoping to settle this at lunch on Tuesday. Do you think you could give me an answer by then?

—CB

. . . .

From: Reshma Kapoor <rtkap@bombr.co>

To: Chelsea Blahnik <cblah@bombr.co>

Subject: RE: Coordinating early action / early decision choices

I'm sorry, but that's private information.

. . . .

At first I couldn't believe it. I mean, I knew what she was talking about. Last year, for some absurd reason, eight of our top ten kids applied early to Princeton, which only took one of them and left the rest to fend for themselves in the spring regular-decision pool. And of course the perfects would be traumatized by that kind of uncertainty. They like things to be tidy and straightforward and rule-bound, and the idea of not getting into a top school because of some fluke confluence of factors would be intolerable to them.

But why would they think I'd participate? I don't care how many of them apply to Stanford: I'll beat them all.

After stewing on it for half an hour, I heard the front door open, and before my mom could put down her laptop bag, I stormed down to show her the e-mail.

"Can you believe her?" I said. "I mean, she has to know that I don't get anything out of this. She's just trying to neutralize me."

"Why play such games? It doesn't matter if two or three or five of you apply to the same school. If you are good, then colleges will take you. There's no need to worry about competition from Chelsea."

I grunted. Why was she always *so* obtuse? "Come on, Mummy. Do you really think I'm afraid of Chelsea? I'm not afraid of Chelsea! I'm better than her! And she knows it! This is what they always do. She wants to make sure that she never faces me in a head-to-head matchup, because that way I can never say I won and she lost."

"Please, *beta*. You and Chelsea will *both* be very happy and successful in life, because you are *both* very smart and very hardworking, and that is what truly matters."

I stared at her. I just . . . There was *so* much that was wrong with that statement.

"Come on, Mummy. You know that's not true."

I explained myself very slowly, in very quiet words, as if I were talking to a child. I knew it was insulting, but I didn't care, because I couldn't believe that after all I'd done, my mom still thought I was worried about Chelsea.

"Mummy. I'm not worried about anyone else at Bell High. If I wasn't the best at Bell, do you think I'd have even a hope of Stanford? No. I'm worried about all the other kids at all the other schools. The other Bell High kids are nothing. They are beneath me. This is just a ploy to make sure no one else will ever know how badly I've beaten them."

I hoped I might get through to her, but as I spoke she looked more and more shocked, until finally she said, "But is this truly how you think? This competitiveness is not right. What matters is to do good work."

And that's when I almost lost it and told her that I'd learned from her mistakes, and that I was going to make *sure* that what'd happened to her and Daddy wasn't ever going to happen to me. They'd trusted the wrong person, and she'd stolen their company right out from under them. And I wanted to tell my mom that it made me sad— like, really fucking depressed—when she said or implied that people got what they deserved in life, because she knew that wasn't true.

But then she said, "Come now, perhaps Stanford won't be able to look past your SAT scores, but there are many other schools which could—"

I ran upstairs, threw on a gray hooded sweatshirt, and grabbed my keys. When I stormed down the stairs, my mom just said, "Please don't upset your father with this," but I was already forwarding him the e-mail.

. . . .

My dad works in a start-up incubator on the outskirts of Sunnyvale: a place where people rent a workstation or two while they're still getting their companies off the ground. It's a huge warehouse filled with desks. My flip-flops slapped against the concrete floor as I made my way between the empty cubicles. Even this late in the evening, a bunch of people were working.

One kid—he looked like he was still in college—was resting his cheek against the gray laminate surface of his desk. His chair was shoved out all the way across the aisle and I had to pick my way past him as he stared at me. It's always like that in the incubator; there aren't many girls in the tech industry, and almost none in that building.

My dad pays a little more so his workspace can be a bit fancier: it's surrounded by chest-high office partitions.

When I knocked on his cubicle partition, he looked up at me and blinked. He has fierce eyebrows that are entirely white, and they meet in the center of his face whenever he's angry.

He slammed a hand down on his desktop; his coffee cup shook

and I grabbed it before it could fall. The coffee was cold, and an oily scum had built up on its surface.

"You . . . you got my e-mail?" I said.

"It is silly. Absolutely silly. And it is one more reason to be glad of our lawsuit. Clearly this Chelsea person does not deserve to be valedictorian."

I shoved my fists into the pockets of my hoodie and held my elbows in close at my side. Suddenly, my body was cold. The whole reason I'd come here was because I'd known my dad would see my point of view. But now that we were face-to-face, my dad's intense stare was unnerving.

"So . . . what are we going to do? We're going to stop it from happening?"

"What? No, no. You must go in there and make sure they give you the first pick so that no one else can apply to Stanford."

"But I'm not worried about Chelsea. I can beat her."

He was silent for a long time. His fingertips were drumming against the countertop and he was staring off into the corner, as if he was doing some calculation in his head. This cubicle was all that was left of KapCo: the company my parents had started five years ago in order to pursue a major breakthrough in image recognition technology that they had discovered. However, a few months after my dad finally perfected the algorithm—among other things, it allowed computers to recognize ice on the roads with almost perfect accuracy—his chief investor and board chairman, Susan Le, sneakily forced my parents out, then turned around and sold the technology to Apple in a billion-dollar deal.

"You have already beaten her, and with this proposal she is signaling her defeat," he said. "Now it only remains to ensure your victory."

"But—"

"Remember," he said. "You must always be careful with these people. It is best to go and learn the details of their plan. If they truly intend to not apply to the same college as you, then so much the better! Stanford will certainly take at least one student from Bell High, and if you are the only one who applies, then it will be you who they take!"

"I just—" I felt like I ought to object. This wasn't . . . When I imagined getting into Stanford, it always came with the look of disappointment on Chelsea's face when she didn't get in. I wanted her to *see* what all her pretend-perfection had cost her.

"Come now," he said. "I agree that this is silliness. And if you were in even the second place, then I would advise you to fight it to the end. But you are first. You will get what you want. Isn't that what matters?"

I was going to object again, but instead I took a deep breath, because my dad was right. Beating Chelsea wasn't what mattered. What mattered was getting into Stanford. And if I didn't use every single tool at my disposal, then I'd be no better than the perfects.

Giving up my desire to humiliate Chelsea was almost physically painful, but I eventually said, "You're right."

"Yes. So it is settled. You will take the first place." My dad squeezed my hand. "And justice will win out in the end, as it always does."

I should've left that statement alone, but something compelled me to say, "Come on, Daddy. We know better, don't we?"

His face had gotten so pouchy and old, and when he squinted at me, his eyes disappeared behind the flesh. And I thought for once he was going to be honest with me, but instead he said, "You've done well, *beta*. Don't give up now. You are almost there." And then he went back to his computer.

. . . .

The thing you need to understand about my parents is that they are the biggest study machines who ever lived.

In the year my mom and dad graduated from junior college

(i.e. the Indian version of high school) something like one hundred thousand of the smartest kids in India took the entrance test for the Indian Institute of Technology—India's top engineering college. Out of that group, maybe one thousand five hundred would get spots at a good campus in a good program. In India, there's no second place: the only people who are really securely middle class are the country's most educated professionals. Which means that if you want to be able to afford proper medical care and a place of your own, then you need to be in the top 3% on a test that's already only being taken by the top 5% of India's kids.

Growing up, all my parents did was study. School in India is six days a week. And if you're going to keep up, then you spend all of your "free" time going to extra classes—they call them "tuitions"— so you can have an edge over everybody else. Extracurriculars are nonexistent, and if you go on a date, then your whole town'll be scandalized. Instead, your entire high school life centers around one test.

It's clean, simple, and pure. Because that's what life is like in India: if you study hard enough, then you get what you want.

My dad got 781st place. And my mom got 11th. Eleventh out of two hundred thousand. She was one of only three women to matriculate at IIT Bombay in her year.

And, really, that was the high point of their lives. Afterward, they came here and tried to do the same thing. They worked hard in graduate school and, later, at their jobs. They studied their industry and identified a gap in the prevailing knowledge, and, after starting their own company, they worked sixteen-hour days to fill that gap.

Then they took money from the wrong investor, and she stabbed them in the back and stole their company.

Because my parents don't understand that in America it doesn't matter how hard you work. What matters is that you learn all the tips and tricks and do everything in the right way. And you know why? Because white people know that if hard work was all that counted, then my family would destroy them. We would own this country.

So instead they shifted everything and made it so other things counted: extracurriculars and playing well on the sports field and helping other people. And when we Indian people started to do that stuff, too, then they changed the system even more so that what mattered became intangible stuff: leadership and charm and attractiveness and being able to impress people at interviews.

And even after everything that's happened to my parents, they still don't understand. Whenever I have any kind of trouble, my mom tells me to buckle down and do my best. And whenever I try to argue with her, she sighs and looks away, as if I'm some big disappointment.

My dad is a little better, though. The frustrating thing about him is that he almost gets it; he almost sees the truth about how the world works. And although he's not willing to talk about it, sometimes he hints at how he respects me for not making the same mistakes that he did.

For instance, I remember way back in freshman year, when I'd just started at Bell. Even then, all of us smart kids were grouped together. We were only a small subset of the school, but everyone else was invisible: they were the people I saw in the halls but never in my classes. Even back then I was taking honors physics and AP European history and precalculus.

So from the very beginning I was spending a lot of time around people like Chelsea and Alex and Aakash.

And of course we knew we were competing for the best GPA, but it was all right, because we all understood the system. We would spend our lunch periods talking about how many AP classes it was logistically possible to take by the time you graduate, and which AP classes were easiest and which ones we should avoid at all costs because the teachers were hard graders. And it was apparent, even from really early in the first semester, that I was getting better grades than everybody, and that I was probably gonna end up as the valedictorian.

But then, one day—it was maybe about two months into the year—Chelsea went around the lunch table and shut everyone's books. "No school talk today!" she announced. And then she began asking us which guys we liked. Every time someone brought the conversation around to school, she'd stare at them silently until they quieted down.

And sure, I had fun and I went along with it, because it was good to talk about something other than school for a bit. What did I know? I was only in ninth grade. I was bright and shiny and innocent, and I still thought we were all playing the same game.

Over the next few weeks, she and Alex and Tina Huang codified ten rules.

The Rules of the Perfects

1. Always take the hardest classes.
2. Never do the extra-credit assignments.
3. Never do the reading.
4. No talking about class, homework, or tests.
5. Never raise your hand or contribute to class discussions, unless class participation is a major part of that teacher's grading.
6. Homework has to be done *at* school—preferably in the five minutes before class.
7. The weekend before a midterm, you *have* to party.
8. On a party night, you *have* to drink and/or smoke.
9. Never wear sweatpants, flip-flops, ponytails, polo shirts, or any skirt or dress that goes below the knee.
10. If you violate one of these rules, you can't eat lunch with us for a week.

And they started talking about sisterhood. About how we'd be better than all the other kids, because we'd take the hardest classes and get the best grades without making a fuss about it. Which seemed weird, and maybe a little frightening, to me, but whenever I complained about it, Chelsea and Alex said it was just a game, so I went along with it. And during that first semester I could almost convince myself that it was possible, since most of my classes were so easy that I didn't need to study or spend much time on the homework.

But then it happened. On the honors physics final, I got a 75—my lowest grade of the semester. But I wasn't alone. The class was impossible. Chelsea got an 82; Alex got a 71; and everybody else got a 65 or below.

At lunch, after we got the tests back, I remember I said something about transferring to AP environmental science next semester, since it was an easier class and also it was an AP, but Chelsea stared at each of us and said, "No school talk."

That night, I showed my parents my grade, and my mom was confused: she asked what had gone wrong. And when I told her that I'd gotten the second-highest grade in the class, she said okay, I should stay in the class and learn as much as I possibly could, and if the best I could get was a B then that was fine.

My dad was quiet. That was right after their company had failed. My mom had gotten her job at Google immediately, but my dad was still sitting around the house all day. As my mom talked to me, I kept looking at him to see what he wanted, and he gave me a little smile.

When I finally said maybe AP enviro would be better for me next semester, my mom went ballistic. She said it was absurd that one test was enough to make me run away and quit.

But my dad put his hand on her arm and said, "No. We should discuss this."

And the next morning he came down and said to me that I could transfer if I thought it was best.

Something passed between us at that moment. He couldn't come right out and say it, but I knew he admired me for being savvy and adaptable and doing what needed to be done.

The next day, I transferred into AP environmental science for the spring semester. Somehow the news got out, and when I sat down to lunch, Alex said, "You can't sit with us, Resh."

Chelsea looked uncomfortable and tried to say something about how I could come back in a week, but Alex cut her off and said, "I'm sorry. No offense, but you betrayed our pact, and traitors aren't allowed at this table."

So I walked out to the edge of the courtyard, and I cried about it. What hurt the most was this idea that they were somehow better than me. They knew I was the smartest. They knew I was the hardest worker. But because they were willing to sacrifice their grades, they were entitled to look down on me? It was a vile and stupid stance, and even though I went back a few times, over the course of the semester, and tried to explain that to Alex, she never changed her mind.

But it doesn't matter. At the end of the spring semester, my 5.3 in AP enviro had propelled me into the top spot in the class—Chelsea, Alex, and Tina were knocked out of the running by a 3.3, 3.0, and 2.7 in physics—and I've been number one ever since.

FRIDAY, SEPTEMBER 7

Finally heard back from my would-be suitor.

> Hey, you wanna hang out sometime?

> Sure. When?

> Sat night? You want to see a movie? "Total Kismet" looks good.

> K. Works for me. =]

> Cool. Pick you up at 8.

That made me smile a little bit. I'd wondered if I would need to do everything for him, but he stepped things up. Of course, his next text to me was:

> OMG, everyone! She said yes! #CrushedIt #TotalVictory #ThanksForAllTheFish.

A second later, he texted me:

> Uhhhhm sorry that was meant for someone else. ;)

So I wrote back:

> No problem.

A quick search led me to what I guess Aakash thought was his "anonymous" Bombr account: @AardvarkPatel. Personally, I don't even have a Bombr profile. Every day, you read about colleges using people's online postings to reject them. Why run the risk?

Clearly Aakash wasn't so cautious. He'd thrown 10,541 bombs, and he had 713 followers. As I watched his feed, he replied to dozens and dozens of congratulatory bombs:

@Thriptych
Yep, did it by text message.

@Prozblem
Thanks! Yep, just now! I followed your advice. Totes great.

@Azblyni
I went with a chick flick. Seemed like the simplest thing.

Wow. Even Aakash has managed to find a few hundred people who care about him.

. . . .

This morning I realized I had skipped one of the steps in my novel-writing plan. I was well on my way to going on a date, securing a boyfriend, etc., but what about the very first item? What about making a friend? For the last week, I'd gone around and around on this one, but in the end I had just one real option: Alex was the only girl my age whom I regularly interacted with outside of school.

I was sitting at my computer, rubbing at the sides of my head as if I could physically push another friendship possibility into my brain, when I saw I was about to run out of Adderall.

That settled it. I needed to see Alex.

I wanted to wait until school hours to talk to her, but by 7 A.M. I was so antsy that I texted her and asked if we could meet today.

She wrote back instantly.

> What happened to "mind your own business"?

I wrote back right away.

> Sorry about that.

> I don't need the hassle.

Alex has access to plenty of money: she drives a silver beamer and carries a thousand-dollar handbag. But it's all on her credit card, which means she can't use it to buy . . . well . . . other things. For that, she needs cash. Which is where the Adderall comes in: five dollars a pill, except during midterms and finals, when it's ten.

> Come on. Stop playing games.

> Should've thought about this before you went after Chelsea last summer. She never did anything to you.

> You don't want to do this.

> We're done.

And that was that. I was left in the basement, staring at my phone. I put my last remaining pill into my desk drawer, since I knew I'd need it for finals, but by 8 A.M. I was feeling so cracked out and empty and exhausted that I took it.

But even then, my energy didn't come back. My heart just started to race and my fingertips tingled and the whole world felt distant and blue and when Aakash tried to talk to me during class I looked at him with faraway eyes, because I was just not in the mood for this.

And when I tried to do my homework during lunch, I couldn't write one coherent word because my fingers were shaking so hard, and I could feel the blood pulsing through my wrists. I'm not addicted to Adderall. I go off of it for a few days each month, just to prove I don't need it. But most weeks, I sleep so little that normal life becomes really difficult when I don't have it.

I couldn't think. Whenever I closed my eyes, I saw circles inside circles inside circles, all vibrating rapidly. I closed my books and opened my phone. I had less than three weeks to write this book, and I *needed* a friend. And if Alex refused to see me, who did I have left?

I scrolled through the names. I'm not a complete loser. I do have a certain austerity that the other study machines admire. They band together for support and friendship, gathering in their sad, battered geek klatches that meet in libraries or basements or the corners of the cafeteria. They sit around and whisper to one another that they are the smart ones and the talented ones and that someday the world will belong to them. Maybe some of them are even right. But right now, at this moment, their lives are just so unbearably sad. And I knew I could work my way into one of those circles. It'd be easy. All it would take was a call. But what would be the point? I wasn't actually trying to make a friend. I was trying to write a novel. And not a sad novel: a novel about some poor girl who was bravely able to soldier on and carve out a nice little friend circle for herself even though the world didn't care about her.

No. My novel will be bold and triumphant. It'll be about

someone who wins and wins and wins until the entire world begs to be her friend.

So, I texted to say I'd pay twenty dollars each.

I stared at the little three dots that showed she was composing a message.

Fine. You know where to meet.

Within fifteen minutes, I'd transported myself to her surprisingly filthy silver beamer, which was idling in the little parking lot on top of the CVS on the other side of El Camino. From up there, we looked down on the big, complicated T intersection where El Camino flew over the Embarcadero expressway. Bell High was off to the left, on one side of the expressway, and I could see tiny clusters of people sitting around at the picnic tables in front of the cafeteria.

Alex rummaged through all the trash at our feet: old scarves and sandwich wrappers and Starbucks cups, until she came up with an orange pill bottle. We conducted our business without talking. Alex sold her prescriptions to a bunch of other kids at Bell, but I was probably one of her biggest customers.

After the pills were in my hands, I took one and popped it into my mouth—not even caring about how it'd look—and crunched it into powder so it'd dissolve into my bloodstream quicker.

After I swallowed, I ran my tongue through my teeth to pry loose any bits of the pill that might be stuck.

Alex cleared her throat, trying to get me to leave, and my words came out so fast that they tasted jagged and sour in my mouth: "What was that about, this morning? You don't honestly care about my lawsuit, do you?"

Alex cocked her head at me. "No matter what the court said, Chelsea deserves to be valedictorian," she said. "She took harder classes and did better in them than you would've."

"She knew the right classes to take; she just chose not to do it."

"Chelsea is too nice to confront you," Alex said. "But I'm not going to pretend like you didn't screw over my friend. Did you ever stop to think what you were taking away from her? Your parents aren't poor. You'll get into a good school, and they'll have no trouble paying for it. You don't think being the valedictorian would've helped Chelsea a lot more than it'll help you?"

I squeezed my eyes tightly together. When I opened them, she was still looking at me. "I earned—"

"No, you didn't!" Alex said. "I already know that you're a cheater and a liar, but it would really make me happy, just for my own sake, to know you're not lying to yourself. We're alone. No one's here. No one's listening. Just admit to me that *you* know, in your heart, that Chelsea is smarter and more deserving than you."

"No." I rubbed the heel of my hand against my aching head. I didn't want to get bogged down by all this talk about Chelsea. "If she was better, then she wouldn't have lost."

I felt myself balancing on the edge. Once I spoke the next words, I'd be committed. "You shouldn't be friends with her," I said. "You should be friends with me."

Alex shook her head slowly. She chuckled a few times, and then the laughter trailed off. "You can't be serious." When she raised her thinly plucked eyebrows they looked like a pair of apostrophes.

"Don't you see it, though?" I said. "We always should have been friends."

"Umm, you never cared about being my friend," Alex said.

I squinted at her. I guess that was true, in a way. "Yeah, of course," I said. "But not because we didn't have compatible worldviews and social backgrounds. It was because I had better uses for my time."

Alex blinked. "Oh wow, thanks. You're making an amazingly strong pitch for my friendship right now. So you're saying now you *do* have the time?"

"Well." I mentally slid my schedule around, trying to figure out when I could hang out with Alex. "Not really . . . But I'll find space for you."

"And what's changed?"

I wouldn't have told just anyone about this, because I know that making friends for the purposes of a novel would strike most people as, well, strange. But Alex was different. She was ruthless and canny, and I knew that in some way she'd appreciate it. So I told her about Ms. Montrose and the novel and how I needed a hook.

Alex glanced across the street, and I followed her eyes, trying to see what she saw. "Riiight." Her voice was slow and distant. "Got it. And, umm, how exactly do you see this playing out?"

I calculated what I'd need for my novel. "I want to sit with you at lunch. I want you to respond to my texts, within three hours, with a message that's of equal length. And I want you to invite me to at least one of your parties."

She twisted around in her seat to look at me. Her face had narrowed and I could see her mind working. "I think I'm going to pass," she said. "I honestly . . . I cannot believe the ridiculous story you just gave me. You don't want a friend. You want something weird and sick and artificial."

"I wouldn't make this offer to anyone. But you're not like Chelsea. You're like me. You're maybe the only other person at school who's like me. You don't believe in rules. You believe in doing exactly what you want. And that's why we ought to be friends."

"No," Alex said. "We are not alike. You are a liar. And a cheater. And a manipulator. And I've never seen you think of anyone who's not yourself."

She looked right into my eyes.

I didn't look away.

You know what? This is what life was like. You could give people the opportunity to be your friend, but they wouldn't respect it. No. To them, any friendly overture was weakness. Which meant the only real way to make friends was from a position of strength.

I love those moments when I can feel the power collecting inside me. They don't come very often, but when they do . . .

"I know how to get what I want, Alex." The ice had crept back into my voice.

"Get out of the car. Our business is done."

"Look, you can either fall into line, or I can force you into line," I said. "But in the end, you *will* become my friend."

She tried to laugh, but the sound died in the back of her throat. I closed my fingers around the pills and dropped them into a side pocket of my bag, then searched the floor of her car and came up with an orange bottle that had her name on the side. "Do you know how many of these I have? Enough—more than enough—to prove you've sold me a serious felony-level amount of Adderall."

"You don't actually think you can report me to the police, do you?" Alex said. "Because you'd go down, too."

"Maybe, but I'm just a victim here. You're the drug dealer. Somehow I think you'll go down harder."

"Reshma, this is unbelievably sad. Seriously, you should get help."

"I am serious," I said.

And in that moment, I tested myself and found that I was telling the truth. I didn't care about the consequences. I needed to be friends with Alex in order to write this novel, and I needed to write this novel in order to get into Stanford, and I needed to get into Stanford in order to live. Ergo, my life depended on this.

Her smile flickered in and out of existence. "Just what are you . . . ?"

"Look at me, Alex," I said. "You're rich, so you won't go to prison, probably. But you will be arrested. You're eighteen, which means your name will be in the police blotter. There might even be newspaper articles. Your parents will hear about this. And so will Princeton. I'll tell them about it if no one else does. Your life will be ruined, and you will be *nothing*. So do we have a deal?"

Her mouth was hanging open. "Get out of my car, you crazy bitch."

"Okay." I opened the door and put one leg out of the car, then looked back. "Let's do it this way. I've told you my terms. And if you fail to meet them, if you don't respond to my texts, or ignore me when I talk to you, or refuse to let me sit with you at lunch, or throw a party without inviting me, then I *will* go to the police."

Before she could answer, I hopped out into the parking lot.

I stood on the asphalt in the noontime light at the tail end of summer. The wind brushed past my sides and tickled the trees that grew along the side of El Camino. And, for the first time in days, I felt truly happy.

SATURDAY, SEPTEMBER 8

All day, I kept thinking, When can I finally go to sleep?

But school is in four hours and here I am, still awake.

I thought I was going to relax this year. I was going to apply to colleges, do my activities, turn in my assignments, and let my momentum carry me through. But my unconscious saw that I had an easy month ahead of me and said, Welp! Why not write a novel?

Is this an insane plan?

I got home at 4 P.M., long before either of my parents. I tried to nap for a bit, but my heart and mind were racing. My novel had only one thing I couldn't control: the romance. Without a romance, I was sunk. If being forced to read *Pride and Prejudice* in the tenth grade had taught me anything, it's that I actually needed two guys: a stolid, mildly rude one—Aakash—and a dangerous-but-charming one. In the end, I'd go for the former, of course. But what if it didn't work out with either one?

In a movie, this is where I'd go to a salon and get a makeover. But that was bullshit. School is full of vaguely pretty girls with their hints of lip gloss and their painted nails and their brand-name jeans, and they get even less attention than me. If there's one thing I know, it's that if you want competent work, you either have to pay for it— and pay a lot—or you need to do it yourself. I grabbed my computer from the bedside table and YouTubed *"How to make guys notice you."* A somewhat overweight British woman reeled off the names of various cosmetic products. Halfway through her spiel, I popped an Adderall and started taking notes.

I dropped the computer on the countertop of my bathroom, set up a stool in front of the mirror, and collected an armful of Mummy's cosmetics from the master bathroom. I was the only one who used the hall bathroom nowadays, but there was a time when my sister, Meena, and I had to share it: our rooms were clustered around one end of the hall and my parents' room was at the other. The cabinets still held remnants of my sister's presence: Meena's curling iron and her facial creams.

There were a whole series of videos online. I began with lipstick.

Four hours later, night was seeping into the bathroom. Goose pimples were rising on my arms, but I did not feel cold. A bird sat on the windowsill, still and silent.

"What are you doing?" Mummy said. "We can hear voices."

"I'm busy."

"Were you in my bathroom? If you want to learn cosmetics, then at least let me teach you."

I took a deep breath and moved the eyeliner pencil closer and closer to the edge of my eyelid. My hand was shaking so hard that I thought I was going to stab myself in the eye, but I stared at my fingers and concentrated on them until they went still.

"Go away, Mummy," I said. "I don't need you right now."

The door sighed as my mom stopped leaning on it. My eyes stung when I blinked. Where was I? What was I doing? Out on the street, my Explorer was parked next to Dad's Corolla and Mummy's Passat in the semicircular drive. A young couple—holding hands—phased in and out of view as they passed behind the intermittent foliage of our hedges.

I was starting to crash, so I took another pill.

An hour later, my phone rang.

"What crazy stunt are you pulling now?" my sister said. Meena graduated near the top of her class and went to Yale. Now she earns a half a million dollars a year as a trader for Morgan Stanley.

"Right now? Applying foundation."

The words were cracked and painful. My throat refused to swallow—not enough saliva. A glass of water, its rim stained with lipstick, was on the counter in front of me, but I couldn't glance down at it, much less raise it to my lips.

She laughed. "God, I bet you look grotesque. I understand why you didn't want to go to Mom, but you should've at least come to me." Meena lives an hour away, in San Francisco. But since she works a hundred hours a week, we don't see her very much.

"I can do this, you know," I said. "It's not hard. I just never cared about it before."

"Fine, then send me a pic."

I ended the call.

My face was mottled with browns and reds and pinks. My lips looked like a child had colored them in with crayon. At some point I must've been crying, because my tears had etched a trail of black down my face. I wet a paper towel. Then I removed everything. Back to square one. I keyed up the first video again.

And then, suddenly, I was calm. My face and hands were the world, and I finally understood everything there was to know. Euphoria snaked through the dry sands of my back-brain. I would not be unhappy if this moment never ended.

At midnight, Daddy knocked on the door. "I know that you were unhappy with your SAT scores," he said. "But this is not the time to give up. We know that if you work hard, you can get into a good school."

"Leave me alone," I said. "I've almost got this."

The click of a key. The bolt slid back, and the door sprung open. Another stroke through my lashes. The trash can next to me was full of powder-stained paper towels. Both the sink and my white T-shirt were a mess of dark splotches. The British woman droned on.

"Oh," Dad said.

He was kneading the ridge of bare scalp above his forehead. He was wearing a wrinkled maroon-colored polo shirt. My mom peeked out from behind him. I rinsed out the head of the mascara wand.

"When did you learn to do all of this?" Mummy said.

"Do you mind?" I said. "I still need to do my nails."

At 2 A.M., I sent a selfie to Meena. All she texted back was:

I wasn't sure why everyone was so surprised. In the pic, my eyes are a bit larger, my face is a bit smoother, and my lips are a bit fuller. Minor changes: maybe a 3% improvement. But 80% of the effort is in going from an A to an A+.

Afterward, I think I felt happy for a while, but my heart was beating so loud and fast that I couldn't fall sleep even though I lay in bed for hours.

. . . .

It occurs to me that my readers might not've heard of the lawsuit. Honestly, though, it wasn't a huge deal.

At the end of last year, Vice Principal Colson took me aside at school. He said he was going to e-mail the whole student body about this, but he wanted to talk to me privately so I wouldn't be surprised. Really, he said, it was a minor adjustment: the school was changing the formula that they used to weight the grades. He said some of the teachers had been agitating for some of Bell High's tougher classes to be redesignated as Professional Track classes.

There wouldn't be many PT classes, but they would be worth 1.5 additional GPA points. The change didn't affect many people, but there was a chance that my final GPA would shift by a few hundredths of a point.

Basically, they were changing the system so that Chelsea would be the valedictorian, and not me.

About fifteen seconds into our talk, I hit RECORD on my iPhone. When I played the recording for Daddy, he went quiet and forwarded it to Arjuna Rao: a college friend who had become a very famous lawyer. Because Chelsea is white, Arjuna filed a racial discrimination suit, saying that the school didn't want an Asian valedictorian. During the discovery phase of the lawsuit, we found out that they'd only redesignated classes that Chelsea and Alex and the rest of the perfects had taken and which I hadn't. That honors physics class, for instance. And, because of that, the primary impact of the change would've been to shift me from first place to fifth place. Chelsea would've been the new valedictorian.

Anyway, after a ton of very tense depositions, we arrived at a settlement whose terms are sealed.

But the upshot is that I'm going to be the valedictorian.

. . . .

I finally collapsed into bed around 5 A.M. but only slept for an hour. Woke up with pins and needles all over my body. I put on my tennis shoes and started running up and down the first-floor stairs, trying to calm myself, but George came out from the basement and said, "Come on, I'm right underneath you."

I shrugged and kept running. "The steps are carpeted."

When I tried to squeeze past him, he barred my way. His chest hair formed a thin black T whose bottom end disappeared under the waistband of his plaid boxers. I feinted to the left and then to the right, trying to slip around him. But he caught my wrist. I pulled away, and he squeezed, rubbing my wrists together.

"Christ, you have a huge case of crazy-eyes right now," he whispered. "Ecstasy?"

My face got hot, and I felt needle pricks of heat all over my cheeks and arms. For a minute, I thought it was a weird drug reaction, before realizing I must be blushing! God, I hope I didn't actually turn red.

"Why don't you ever go home?" I said.

"Why don't you ever sleep?"

"You don't belong here."

Locks of long black hair swished as he jerked his head backward. And when he spoke, his voice was quiet.

"You're right," he said. "I, umm, I know you've been trying to work on stuff down here, and, if you want, I could start sleeping at my mom's apartment, and you could work in the guest room. My mom is always telling me not to get in your way and—"

"What?" I said. "Really? That'd be great! Thanks so much! Yeah. No. It's wonderful. The exercise room is . . . There's no chair. It's a bit cramped. Your room has a desk, right?"

"Are you . . . ?" He cocked his head and looked at me out of the corner of his eyes. "Are you serious? You're gonna make me go back to Fremont every day?"

"Umm . . ." I said. "I could really use a private place to work."

He didn't look away or blink. "I'm . . . I'm writing a novel. And it's about my life. And when I try to write in my room I feel too close to everything. Too—"

"I was being nice!" he said. "I was expressing concern. I was trying to defuse tension. But my parents' place is twenty miles away! Jesus, what is wrong with you?"

I shrugged. I was too tired. I didn't know or care what was happening. "So now you don't want to leave?"

He let out an exasperated breath, but whatever he was about to say was cut off when our maid, Maria, began trudging up the stairs with the vacuum cleaner. She looked down, pretending she couldn't see us. As she passed, George and I pressed ourselves to the side of the stairs. I could feel the moisture coming off my body and sticking to the wall.

And that's when I had a weird inkling. My thing with Aakash was already well under way, but I did need another guy to complicate things. A dangerous-but-charming one.

"Hmm," I said. "All right. You can stay. I'll write in my room from now on."

I'm still not sure exactly how I'll use George, but if I keep him around, I bet I'll eventually find a place for him in the novel.

. . . .

Okay, I just spent twenty minutes trying to think of a joke about how I'm an Indian and Indians know how to use all the parts of the buffalo (where, in this analogy, the buffalo is my life, and George is a particularly weird indigestible part like the hoof or something), but I couldn't figure out how to phrase it, so I'm just going to plop this down here and move on.

SUNDAY, SEPTEMBER 9

A day of many meetings.

Yesterday, I looked on Yelp to find the best hair salon in Silicon Valley (even I'm not confident enough to attempt to cut my own hair) and made an appointment for a four-hundred-dollar haircut. Mummy flipped out when I told her about it. She keeps saying that I'm having "my troubles" again. Mummy projects these "troubles" onto me whenever she's feeling particularly stressed-out by her work. Over the summer, she became obsessed with the notion that I was secretly very unhappy. She'd hold my face in her hands and stare into my eyes and say, "Oh, poor child," and then make another therapy appointment for me.

So I also had to go to Dr. Wasserman's office: an old house on the outskirts of Mountain View. Although I've never seen anyone smoking in it, the place always smells like cigars. The black lacquer of the tabletops is covered with a complicated Venn diagram of coffee rings, and the dark greenish wallpaper has a raised design that looks like a bunch of spades. Since Mummy picked him out, it's no surprise that all three diplomas on the wall are from Harvard. He's a huge, rangy guy with scraggly hair and a narrow face.

When I walked in, he raised an eyebrow: I was wearing a T-shirt that showed four inches of midriff above the waist of my skirt. Then he started asking me all kinds of questions about whether I was feeling unusually good about myself or experiencing a surge in sexual behavior. Finally, I explained to him about the stuff I needed to do to write my novel.

"See? I'm not crazy. I'm just an artist," I said.

"Interesting. What's your inciting event?"

"What?"

"It's one of the basics of any narrative: in the middle of the first act you need an inciting event that'll drive the rest of the plot."

"Deciding to write this novel wasn't enough of an event?"

He sucked in his breath. "Well, okay. Stories should have an internal arc—the way the character changes over time. Your book's internal arc is about the character's secret worry that her all-consuming ambition has robbed her of her girlhood, and that arc plays out through the 'I'm writing a novel that requires me to do things that I unconsciously want to do anyway' metafictional conceit. And for a very literary novel, it might be sufficient to only have an internal arc. But I think you want to produce a more commercial book, right?"

For the first time, I noticed all the detective novels—hundreds of paperbacks—on his shelves. "I don't care about its genre. All I want is to get into Stanford."

"Well, almost all popular novels have an external arc—some outside obstacle that the hero must confront. Usually, the internal and external arcs are related. In order to defeat the external obstacle, the hero eventually has to confront the internal demons. Audiences don't want a character who just thinks and thinks and thinks. They also want a character who *does* things. That's why, in each of my own books, Dr. Nathan West solves a murder which thematically echoes whatever neurosis he's currently afflicted by."

"Are these books published?"

"I'm, uhh, I'm currently looking for an agent."

I picked up my bag. "You better not charge my mom for this session. You don't think I have an external arc? Every single day I have to struggle against bullshit obstacles like this meeting. You know my mom forced me to come here."

The doctor lifted his face from his hands. "Mmmhmm," he said. "As one artist to another, I sympathize. But, umm, your ambiguous relationship to parental authority is part of that selfsame 'stunted girlhood' internal arc. Don't worry, though. As I understand it, you still have a few thousand words left in the set-up phase of your novel. That's plenty of time for your external arc to appear."

God, that guy was crazy. I understand writing a novel to get into medical school, but why would a certified doctor waste his time writing unpublished, and probably unpublishable, novels?

Still, he unsettled me. I'd rushed into this novel-writing business without doing enough research. And I only had twenty-one days left.

The hairdresser gushed about my beautiful complexion, because, yeah, four hundred dollars ought to buy you some flattery, too. But it still left me smiling. And when he was done, my hair was perfectly layered and highlighted with subtle tinges of brown. I couldn't afford to do this all the time, of course. But it only needed to last until the end of the month.

. . . .

I don't know what Wasserman was babbling on about. The secret to succeeding as a writer is pretty simple: in general, people don't try to understand anything; they judge a work by how smart it sounds. So, after I finish an article or essay, I go through my work and rewrite every sentence to make it sound more complex. I increase the register of the diction—using weirder and more sesquipedalian words—and make the syntax a bit more complex: often through the addition of parenthetical asides—(this is one of them!)—and dependent clauses. The result is prose that sounds a bit more complicated and beautiful than it needs to be. I call this the prettification process.

Teachers eat this up. They're lazy. They have ninety papers to grade. They want the external markers of intelligence. I figure that you, Ms. Montrose, will be no different, so I have to remember to allocate some time at the end to prettify this novel.

. . . And take out a few passages, like this one, that are too revealing. The perfects have taught me that it's not enough to look smart; your intelligence also has to look effortless.

MONDAY, SEPTEMBER 10

W hen I first told Mummy about the perfects, she laughed and said, "No one can be perfect."

People say that all the time, as if it's obvious.

But is it?

That's the problem with people. They think perfection is about things you can't control: your intelligence or your wealth or your beauty. But if they thought of it as avoiding mistakes, they'd understand how achievable it is.

We all know that it's possible to go one hour without making a mistake. And if that's possible, then it must be possible to string together twenty-four consecutive mistake-free hours into a perfect day.

Having an entire mistake-free day is difficult, but it's doable. I've done it for more days than I can count. Yesterday was a mistake-free day: I got a haircut, calmed down my doctor, did my calculus and chemistry problem sets, finished reading *A Tale of Two Cities*, made flash cards and memorized vocabulary for Latin and Spanish, studied for my econ test, ate less than twelve hundred calories, made progress on my novel, started writing my newspaper column, called hotels to make arrangements for the World Leadership Conference I'm organizing, made a set of flyers for the Halloween Charity Auction, and slept for more than four hours.

And if I can have one mistake-free day, then I can have two, and three, and four, and eventually whole weeks and months and years will pass without mistakes. Is that so insane?

. . . .

God, I've been having trouble sleeping. I finish my writing for the day and lie awake with my skin buzzing and think, I'm writing it. I'm writing it. I'm actually writing it.

It's the same way I felt over the summer, after the lawsuit, when I realized that I'd clinched the valedictorian spot. During my whole first three years of school, I was convinced that I was about to lose the top spot. But after we won the case, I let myself believe that I was actually going to get it.

I started spending hours staring out my bedroom window at the vines sucking the life out of our elm tree and mentally composing valedictory speeches.

I know, it's dumb. We're one of the last Silicon Valley schools to have a commencement address by the valedictorian: everyone else has moved to elected class speakers. But that speech will be the first time in all of high school that I'll be publicly acknowledged as the best. I want to pierce the bullshit and let some air into that auditorium. I'm thinking of starting it:

> In your life, a lot of people are going to tell you that if you just do good work, then the world will recognize you for it, and I honestly can't tell if those people are lying on purpose or if they're just deluded. . . .

They all need to be told that if they're going to indulge in that "I'm so high above everything" posturing, then they'll be defenseless against people like me who're willing to swoop in and take whatever we want.

TUESDAY, SEPTEMBER 11

O ur cafeteria is an octagonal building whose whitewashed walls are covered with huge splatter paintings: pseudo-Impressionist pictures of trains and canyons where the neon colors run together like an oil slick. They were donated by Susan Le, the CEO of Bombr. She only graduated in 1999, but she's already worth $1.8 billion.

(And she stole a few hundred million of those dollars from my parents.)

The biggest painting is a forest of floppy purple trees—if it wasn't fifteen feet tall and framed in gold leaf, it would look like a child's finger painting. My mom said that since the artist committed suicide last year, it's probably worth millions. It's kept on a raised platform, under glass, and sometimes students come from Stanford or Berkeley or the Art Institute to sit there for hours amidst the tumult and sketch it. The one cafeteria table that's also on that dais is, thus, above and apart from the other tables. Whenever you enter the caf, your eye naturally flits to that vomited-upon canvas. And then it travels downward to that lone table.

The remaining perfects are the only seniors who still eat at school. Almost everyone else goes off-campus or, if they want to be seen, they lunch on, in, or near their cars. But since almost all the perfects are taking classes during both lunch periods, they can only eat during the twenty-minute intersession.

Ever since switching to AP environmental science, I've lunched on protein bars in the hallways or at the newspaper offices.

But not today.

. . . .

The moment I stepped onto the dais, I felt a hundred eyes snap onto me. I hovered there for a moment, debating whether to bolt. But then Alex sneered at me, and I steeled myself. No, if I was going to write this novel, then I needed Alex to be my friend, and I needed for that friendship to begin right now.

When I slid into the seat next to Tina, she didn't even nod. Her hair was so straight, black, and shiny that it rippled at even the slightest movement.

Alex looked up from her phone, though her fingers never stopped moving. "What are you doing here?"

"We're doing that dividing-up-the-colleges thing today, right?"

Tina looked up. "Chelsea said you never got back to her."

"Well, yes," I said. "But then Alex convinced me that I ought to drop by. I know, right? She's such a good *friend*."

Alex's phone went down, and she blinked a few times. I looked at her. If she told me off, I'd call the police right away. I wouldn't even wait until I was out of the cafeteria. All of my actual pills were hidden away in an Altoids tin that I'd buried behind our house, but I had five of Alex's empty pill bottles in my bag. Hopefully, that would be enough to put her away without necessarily threatening me.

I said, "Don't you remember, Alex? You said it would be in my best interest to cooperate." Then I leaned over, slightly, so my bag was behind Tina's chair, where only Alex could see it, and opened it up a bit. She glanced down, and I knew she was seeing the orange pill bottles inside.

She sighed, and said, so quietly that I almost missed it, "Yeah. Fine," and the moment was over. As she went back to her phone, I felt a weird pressure build up in my chest. I'd done it. I'd come back.

Jeremy Ozick nodded at me. "Hey, you're looking good today, Resh."

I let out a nervous laugh.

"Yeah," said Tina. "What happened to you? Alex said you were *all* over Aakash in class the other day."

I froze. Two years ago, Tina relentlessly mocked me for coming into school in a pair of skinny jeans. She said I'd be a millionaire after I patented whatever machine I'd used to load my fat ass into them. I stared at a red blotch in the corner of the painting. Whatever they said, I wouldn't react.

Jeremy drummed the side of his head with two fingers. "Yeah, and I don't think I've ever seen you in a skirt."

"Just following rule number nine, right?" I said.

Tina was silent for a moment. Then a loud exclamation erupted from the back of her throat. At a nearby table, a junior dropped his fork and looked up, startled. Tina's hair danced as she shook with laughter.

"My God. I can't believe you remember that!"

Raymond Lodge dropped a soggy SUBWAY sandwich onto the table. "What? What're we laughing about?"

"Resh reminded us about these rules we made up when we were freshmen," Tina said. "Like . . . you had to drink on the night before tests and stuff like that."

My face burned with embarrassment. I normally never thought about those rules. She was the one who'd created them.

"You got drunk before your tests?" Ray said.

"No. Well, maybe like a sip," she said. "We broke all the rules all the—"

Chelsea took the seat next to me. Every eye turned to Jeremy. He nodded and twisted the dial of his watch.

"Oh, hi! You're here!" Chelsea said. "Look, everyone. Resh came, too!"

"Really?" Alex said. "You're still going to be nice to her? Even after she—"

"Alex." Chelsea frowned. "She's part of this, too. Now come on everyone, give me your phones. I hate how everyone's always going tap-tap-tap on their phones when we're at lunch."

Ray looked at me, then at Alex. "Wait . . . didn't *you* invite her?"

Chelsea stacked all the phones up into a neat little pile and then started cutting and recutting them like a deck of cards.

"So," she said. "It's really simple. We'll go through by class order. So, Reshma. What college is getting your early app?"

Five heads swiveled toward me.

"Well?" Tina said.

"Oh . . . I'm applying early to Stanford."

This whole thing was stupid, and I still wasn't entirely sure they weren't trying to trick me, but if Chelsea was really afraid to compete with me, then fine: I'd let her slink away.

Chelsea shrugged. "Fine. Harvard."

Jeremy knocked on the table. "Yes! Then I've got Yale."

Alex said, "I'm Princeton, of course." Both her parents and her grandfather had gone there.

"What about Aakash and Kian?" Jeremy said. They were fifth and sixth, respectively.

"They e-mailed me this morning," Chelsea said. "Both are applying to MIT. I tried explaining that one of them should choose Caltech or something, but they both started naming MIT professors they wanted to work with, so I don't know, whatever. They're set."

"All right, Tina," Jeremy said. "What about you?"

She let out a long breath before saying, "Dartmouth."

"Damn!" Ray said. "Then I guess I'll settle for Brown."

Tina flashed her condescending little smile. Ray had pulled back from the table, physically disengaging. Tina was actually the worst. Chelsea was reasonably smart, and Alex was stylish. Tina just had looks.

I whispered, "You know, this is pretty silly, Ray. You could just apply to Dartmouth anyway."

Alex glared at me.

Ray put out his hands and shrugged. "What can I do? We're pretty much the same person. I'm eighth and she's seventh. We live in the same neighborhood. We've taken pretty much the same classes. I play golf, she plays tennis. I'm in charge of the yearbook, she's president of the honor society. Oh, not to mention that she's Asian."

"What? Since when's that been a help?" Tina said.

Asians aren't a real minority. Colleges do their best to keep our numbers down. We get such good grades and SAT scores that if colleges only admitted based on merit (like MIT does), then every top college would look like MIT: 40+% Asian.

Although, whatever. Tina isn't a full Asian: her mom is white.

"God, this is so jejune," I said.

"What?" Alex said.

"Jejune. You know, immature?" What? Don't people say that?

"Let me stop you right here," Alex said. "Please don't ever say that word again."

"Whatever. Childish, then. Kids play games; adults go for it. Ray, it doesn't matter if they only take one of you, so long as *you* are the one that they take."

Ray put his half-eaten sandwich back into his bag. Jeremy glanced down at his watch. Chelsea's lips rose in that shy, reflexive smile. I looked across the table at Alex. I knew that if anyone would get this, she would. The rest of them were full of fear, but not her.

"No, don't ignore me," I said. "I'm serious. Beating Tina would be easy. All of your stuff is within school activities. Between now and application time, you need to find one outside award or honor—something not conferred by this school—that you can win. I have a list that I—"

"Look," Tina interjected, flicking a look at Ray. "If you want Dartmouth so badly, I'll go with Columbia instead."

The table froze. Ray looked at her, then me. "Really?"

Tina stabbed at her salad, but the bit of hard-boiled egg split and fell off her fork. "I mean . . . it's not . . ."

"No!" Alex said. "Those aren't the rules. Tina worked harder. She got higher grades. She gets an earlier pick. Suck it up and deal with it, Ray."

He was still looking at Tina, and she wasn't saying anything.

"That's it. We're done. Thanks for coming," Alex said. "Chelsea and I will go further down the list and tell everyone else where they're allowed to apply."

They settled back, trotted out their smiles, and started their little side-conversations: Ray and Jeremy talked about some movie they'd both seen; Alex and Tina exchanged gossip about Bell High kids who graduated last year.

I unwrapped my protein bar and tried to edge in on Alex and Tina, but Alex looked up and said, "Excuse me. I suppose we're *friends* now. But this is still a private conversation."

Friends. She was telling me she was agreeing to our deal. I angled away. I didn't mind her sharpness. Sometimes friends were blunt with each other.

Chelsea took out a little salad of her own. As she was dipping her fork in balsamic, she said, "I'm really glad that we reconnected," she said. "You see things in such an interesting way."

Her sunglasses were down, so I couldn't see whether she was serious or not.

"You always wanted to go to Stanford, didn't you?" I said.

Alex was talking to Tina, but I could feel her attention expanding and spilling over into our conversation.

"Oh, you know . . . I'll be happy to get in anywhere."

"Come on, that can't be true." I normally don't bother to argue with Chelsea, but this was too ridiculous. "Everyone has a top choice."

She shrugged. "It would be nice to stay close to home."

Which meant Stanford, of course, although she'd never say it. I nodded to myself, and then realized I'd been silent for a bit too long and scrambled for something to say.

"What was your poem about?" I said. "I tried to see, in class, but I couldn't read it."

A tall blond guy with a nose ring called out to her, then swooped over to our table, and she briefly embraced him. When she'd extricated herself, she said, "It was silly—the poem was about wanting something that I couldn't have."

It's been my experience that if you're willing to do what it takes, then there's nothing you can't have. But Chelsea doesn't think that way, of course. Her world is full of obstacles that she's too pristine and perfect to overcome.

"What happened to your novel?" I said. "Did you ever finish?"

"Oh, that wasn't a serious project," she said. "Anyway, I'm still tinkering with it."

"I'm writing a novel," I said. "I already have an agent waiting for my draft."

The bell went off. Thank God. I threw my wrapper onto the ground and grabbed my things. But Chelsea hugged me!

"That's great! You have to let me read it."

During our next class, she kept shooting smiles at me! She was faking it. She had to be faking it. That was the thing about her. Chelsea was never honest. At least with Alex, I knew where I stood.

That evening, I texted her:

Well, I guess we have a deal then.

(My text was thirty four characters, for those of you who are counting at home.)

An hour later, I texted again:

> An answer within three hours, remember? And of
> equal or greater length?

And at exactly two hours and fifty-nine minutes, she wrote:

> I hate you. You're fucking crazy.

WEDNESDAY, SEPTEMBER 12

After class today, Ms. Ratcliffe asked me to see her at the end of the day so she could give me the regraded poetry assignment.

I didn't think anything of it. Honestly, I haven't been thinking of school at all nowadays: I only have twenty days until the end of the month, and I've hardly done any regular American girl stuff.

I don't know. Maybe that was my mistake. I let myself get sloppy.

. . . .

The upper rim of her office was crowded with posters that had quotes from famous writers. With their yellow paper and bold black iconography, they shouted at me to be violent and original in my work and heap up one true sentence on top of another. I snorted. If Ratcliffe liked these guys, then their advice couldn't be that worthwhile.

Ms. Ratcliffe picked up her phone, dialed a number, and muttered, "She's here."

What was happening? My feet locked in around the legs of my chair, as if I was afraid of being pulled off the furniture and thrown out the window.

She slid my poem across the desk. "Is there anything you want to tell me about this?" she said.

"Did you regrade it?"

She tapped her fingers on the paper. With her close-cropped hair and her arm tattoo, she looked more like a San Francisco street kid than a teacher.

"The other day, I was in a Starbucks and I opened a copy of *Barista* magazine. They'd printed your third-place essay in the 'What Fair Trade Coffee Means to Me' contest."

I didn't say anything. She broke eye contact first.

"Do you actually care about fair trade coffee?"

"This poem doesn't have a new grade on it."

"I worry about you, Reshma. Why do you never allow yourself to be genuine? Are you still having trouble with your mother?"

My hand was shaking slightly. I'm far from unflappable. I'm flapped all the time. But I know how to plow forward despite the anxiety.

"I've been busy lately," I said. "I'm writing a novel."

The tension went out of her cheeks. "That's good. I'd like to see it sometime. What's it about? Or is it too early for you to be telling me?"

"It's going to be published," I said. "I already have interest from an agent."

Her eyes went wide. I bet that Ratcliffe once wanted to be a writer.

I pushed the knife in: "And I've confirmed that my plotline is guaranteed to succeed. I went to the Barnes and Noble and skimmed thirty best-selling books and figured out exactly what I need. All Indian American novels are about being trapped between our Indian and our American identities. And all young adult novels are about wanting to be popular and snare the handsome boy. Mashing them together is a can't-fail combination."

She glanced up at one of the literary quotes, then said: "Right . . . but what interests *you*?"

I shifted in my seat. "I just told you."

"No, you told me what sells."

"I told you about my novel. Was that not good enough for you? Isn't anything I do good enough?"

"It's not that it isn't good enough. It's that it's not yours."

I wanted to yell: *What does it matter if I use other books for inspiration? Isn't the point to produce a good book? An A+ book? If I know how to produce something that people will enjoy, then what does it matter how I did it?*

My face must've scared her, because she got up and stood near the window. The back of her blue cardigan had an eraser-sized brown splotch. Her office door creaked open and extruded the bullet-shaped head of Vice Principal Colson. He was wearing fingerless gloves, even though it was sixty-five degrees outside. His bald head is a sallow tea-stained color.

He tottered through the office like a gorilla with arthritis. "Right, ahem, then," he said. "Have you explained what's going to happen?"

I glared at him and said, "Nice to see you again."

"Ahem . . . err . . . umm . . ."

Last time we'd been in a room together, my lawyer had questioned Colson so vigorously that the vice principal was reduced to muttering incomprehensible monosyllables.

Ms. Ratcliffe put a hand on her bookshelf. When she pulled out the book, my heart began pounding. She put it on her desk, next to my poem, then opened the book to "Ode to a Lamp" by Rupert Hazill.

I kept my face completely still.

"You knew what you were doing," she said. "I ran your poem through three anti-plagiarism programs and turned up nothing. This book isn't digitized, so its text isn't on Amazon or Google. I only ran across it by chance, while hunting down a different poem that I was planning on using in class next week."

"Yeah, it's no problem when a teacher 'uses' a poem, is it?" I said.

Finally, the vice principal overcame his stuttering and started speaking very quietly. This was a major problem. They were very disappointed with me. Plagiarism was a serious offense. It imperiled the whole academic system. I was only cheating myself. And so on . . .

Since it was my first time, they would *only* fail me for this half-semester. My final semester grade—the only grade that would be reported to colleges—would be the average of the two half-semester grades. If I got an A in the second half, my average would almost certainly be a D or maybe even a C–. The only C or D on my whole transcript. It wouldn't kill me.

"This is a very light punishment for this level of plagiarism," Ms. Ratcliffe said.

I waited for that familiar coldness to come upon me—that feeling like a serpent coiling up in my gut. It's what allows me to lash out instead of retreating. But this time it didn't come, and I don't know why. Instead, my whole body was hot, and I felt like they'd carved a window into my torso and exposed my shriveled-up soul to the light for the very first time.

"I won't be valedictorian," I said.

"The . . . umm . . . final class ranking isn't determined until the end of this semester," Colson said. "You could still, umm . . . Your grade point average is very high."

"Arjuna was disappointed that you settled," I said. "He was ready for trial."

"We . . . err . . . uhhh . . ."

Ms. Ratcliffe leaned forward. "You could easily be suspended for this," she said. "And if we did suspend you, we'd have to report that to colleges. They take plagiarism very seriously. If you'd pulled this in college, you'd be fighting to avoid expulsion."

I tried to tell them that I wasn't a cheater. I said that maybe I'd checked out a copy of the poem and maybe I'd read it once, but that was it. I have a good memory, and a few lines from the book must've crept into my poem by accident. I told them, over and over, that it was an accident. That I didn't have any other disciplinary charges on my record. But they refused to believe me! No matter what I did or said, they kept repeating the absurd idea that they were going *easy* on me, and I knew that was a lie! I told them I knew of other people who'd gotten caught with little irregularities like this. Little mistakes. And in those cases the teacher usually just made them redo the assignment or, at worst, gave them a zero, but Ms. Ratcliffe's only reply was that she couldn't be held responsible for the way other teachers chose to conduct themselves.

Then she tried to tell me this would be a learning experience in the end. It'd spur me to finally live up to my potential. I'm tired of those words: *my potential*. Couldn't they see that I was past just having the *potential* to be a high achiever? I was already the best.

But not anymore.

. . . .

I came home, popped an Adderall, and opened my class rank spreadsheet. It lists the top thirty people in my class, along with all of their grades—I'm not above stealing a transcript if I have to—and their current weighted and unweighted GPAs. Then I crunched every likely scenario regarding their final semester GPAs.

I'm dead. There's no situation—barring everyone else falling prey to breakdowns, suicides, arrests, etc.—that gets me above the tenth rank. In the most optimistic scenario—I get a C– as my final grade, a 4.2 average in my other classes, and everyone else's average is about 3% lower than normal (to account for senior slump)—I end up as the eleventh ranked person in the grade!

Without the top slot, I'm nothing more than a decent student with a few extracurricular activities. I'm not even editor-in-chief of the newspaper: I only do layout. There are thirty-one thousand high schools in America. That means there are three hundred and ten thousand students who are graduating this year with a class rank in the top ten. And there are only sixteen hundred spots at Stanford.

My life is over. They've won.

THURSDAY, SEPTEMBER 13

Just got eight full hours of sleep for the first time since, I don't know, seventh grade.

When I woke up, I had a text message from Aakash and another insult from Alex, but I ignored them both. After all, there's no point in working on this novel anymore, is there?

THE END

Wait, here's the official ending.

From: Linda Montrose <lmontrose@bombr.co>

To: Reshma Kapoor <rtkap@bombr.co>

Subject: How's your work coming along?

Hope everything's going well! I had a few more thoughts about the novel: I was thinking it might be best, for the purposes of marketing, if we could pitch your novel as a proposal—all I'd need would be a few chapters and an outline—to editors *before* you graduate high school. Do you think you could get that to me?

—linda

. . . .

From: Reshma Kapoor <rtkap@bombr.co>

To: Linda Montrose <lmontrose@bombr.co>

Subject: Re: How's your work coming along?

Dear Ms. Montrose,

Personal circumstances have conspired to make it impossible for me to complete my novel. I've attached what I've written so far, in case you want a fuller explanation. I'm sorry the writing isn't as strong as usual. Normally, I pretty up my work a bit before I send it out, but this time I was forced to quit before I could reach that stage.

Sincerely,

Reshma Kapoor

SATURDAY, SEPTEMBER 15

I have plenty of free time now, so I thought I'd note some more weird stuff.

Lately, all my body wants to do is sleep: I'll be watching TV and then I'll suddenly be asleep; I'll wake up and feel energetic for fifteen minutes and then, bam, I'm asleep again.

That's why I was napping when Aakash rang my doorbell.

I'd totally forgotten about him. I mean, in my mind, giving up on the novel meant giving up on the dating thing, too, but Aakash, unfortunately, is not telepathic. Mummy called out, "Reshma, you have a visitor?"

I woke up instantly and began throwing off clothes and throwing on clothes and yelling incoherently to my mother, and then I stopped. What did it matter? I didn't really like Aakash. He'd just been the easiest material at hand.

I pulled my hair back and yelled, "Sure, Mummy, send him up."

He knocked on my door with the slightest possible pressure, but it still swiveled inward with a long creak. His hair was slick, and he smelled heavily of Old Spice. I rolled my eyes at his shiny black shirt with swirling patterns stitched into the front. It was such an Indian thing to wear. He looked around, taking in all the pink fairy princess stuff, and then his eyes dropped onto me—I was sitting on my bed—for a moment before leaping to the shelves on his left. I bet he likes to judge people by what books they have.

"Wow!" he said. "A lot of Voltaire. I didn't know you liked philosophy so much."

I shrugged. He was holding one of the books I use for inspiration when I'm trying to write an essay for a contest.

"I play around with it," I said. "Look, I should've texted you, but—"

"Do you like Rousseau? I read his *Confessions* over the summer. The book was crazy!"

"Yeah, I don't know," I said.

"How did you like it? I mean, I didn't know you were interested in the Enlightenment, we should really—"

"Look, there's no point pretending anymore. I don't know anything about Rousseau." I took a deep breath.

"Oh." He dropped the book. "You're looking beautiful today."

I pushed a strand of hair back behind my ear. Did his Bombr friends tell him to say that?

Mummy was rustling around somewhere within earshot. "Close the door," I said. "Just for a second."

Aakash's hand lingered on the knob for a moment after it clicked shut. "Hey, what happened to your class rank?"

I wiped my eye. "Does everyone already know?"

He sat on the edge of my bed. Only a foot of pink bedspread separated us. And then his arm bridged it. He murmured, "It's a rumor. You know Kian always has to be ridiculously early with everything, right? Well, he's already sent out his college apps and gotten his recommendation letters. But, when the vice principal filled out his class rank, Kian noticed he was fifth instead of sixth. Kian asked everyone else whether their rank had gone up and . . . well . . . we guessed it had to be you. . . ."

His arm lay dead and heavy across my back. "They're bastards," I said. "That's against the rules. Class rank can't officially change until new grades are added at the end of the semester."

"But the midyear evaluation would have your real class rank anyway. If it's different from the one on your recs, then the colleges will know you went down like six places in one semester."

"They're breaking the rules. If we break any minor little rule, we get punished. But they can do whatever they want."

His thumb was sketching little circles on my back. I guess it was meant to be comforting. He scooted over a little; now my shoulder was an inch from his. When his thumb crossed the axis of my bra strap, his whole hand twitched as if I'd electrocuted it.

"You'd have liked Rousseau," Aakash said. "He was a French philosopher who did whatever the hell he wanted. In *Confessions* he writes about how, whenever he fathered a baby with his longtime girlfriend, he'd force her to drop the kid off at the orphanage, where they probably died, since, as Rousseau himself used to tell everyone, kids in those days were way more likely to die if they weren't breast-fed by their mothers."

A chuckle wormed its way out of my throat. "And that's the factoid that made you think I'd like him?"

"Hey," Aakash said. "You're kind of a bitch. That's your thing. Everyone knows that."

I wanted to be offended, but my lips kept curling into a smile. "Really?" I said. "Everyone knows me?"

"You sued the school and won, like, a million dollars off them. Of course everyone knows you."

"It was only fifty thousand dollars."

I was resting my head on his shoulder.

"Do you . . . do you still want to go to this movie?" he said.

"What'll you do if I say no?"

"I would, umm . . . I'd need to craft a backup plan: I might make a decision tree and assign probabilities to each of the branches, then I'd . . ."

"Duck into the bathroom and ask some advice from your Bombr followers?"

His arm dropped to the bed.

"Come on," I crooned. "You had to know I'd find it . . ."

"You don't have an account. I thought you might be computer-illiterate."

"All right, let's go," I said.

"What?"

"Let's go. The show's in half an hour, right? I don't have anything else to do."

On the way out, my mom looked up from her chair and packed about as many questions into her glance as is possible. I said, "Just going to make out a bit in Aakash's car. We'll be back soon."

Mummy laughed, but Aakash missed a step and nearly tumbled down the staircase. I grabbed one of his flailing arms, and even after he'd recovered his footing I kept ahold of his hand.

I hate movies. They're a waste of time. I felt antsy during the whole thing. Aakash kept finding my hand and then letting go of it. I understand why people make out in the movies: it's a way to end this tension. I wouldn't have been unwilling to go along with that, if Aakash had started it. But I had a feeling that I'd somehow messed up his planned schedule for initiating physical contact with me.

After the movie, he nonchalantly suggested that we eat ice cream. Normally, I never eat sweets, but today, for some reason, I was ravenous. I ordered a large cup of rocky road with M&M'S. After I'd eaten all the M&M'S, I asked Aakash to go back to the counter and try to persuade them to put more in. I had assumed this would be against the rules—I guess because I'm too used to the perverse strictures of high school—but he handed the guy a dollar, and the M&M'S were dispensed liberally.

The store smelled like coolant and sugar. The hum from the refrigerators wiped out the noise from surrounding conversations and put us on our own little island.

Aakash told me about his scientific research. Over the summer, he'd interned at a cancer research lab at Stanford and, in his spare time, developed a method for marking lymph cells so that they showed up more clearly under MRIs if they were cancerous. In about 5% of cases, the test would lead to better treatment outcomes. But really, it wasn't a big deal, he said: his principal investigator had helped him a lot.

"You are full of shit," I said. "You basically said this thing is gonna save lives."

"Well, or at least make life a bit more comfortable for a few people."

"Don't be so modest."

He shifted from side to side. "I don't want to act like I'm a genius. Any grad student could've—"

"No, I'm serious. Don't. Be. So. Modest. People will believe whatever you tell them about yourself. No one knows anything about cancer research. If you act like it was no big deal, then people will assume you just answered e-mails and copyedited reports. If you tell them you were designing experiments and formulating hypotheses, they might hate you for your arrogance, but they'll also believe you."

"It's really no big deal. Every aspiring doctor has stuff like that on their resume."

"I don't."

"Yeah, but you're going to be a journalist, right?"

"I'm going to medical school, same as you. But I realized way back in eighth grade that I was never going to be a junior genius who could invent things and do research, so I'm going at it from another angle—I'll be the applicant with the provocatively weird, but still impressive, outside-the-box background. I'll work in a lab a little bit when I'm in college, but that won't be my focus."

"I don't get it," he said. "You love the paper. And you win all these essay contests. And you never talk about science or medicine or . . ."

The store was full of chattering couples. I even recognized a few kids from the hallways of Bell High. They sprawled in their seats and used fluid gestures when they talked. Or they leaned close and held hands across the table. Or both were on their phones, anchoring each other in companionable silence while they texted away at other people. Aakash was skeleton-thin and his slightly oily forehead glistened under the fluorescent light. Still, he had his upsides: if I'd been with any of those other guys, I wouldn't have had any idea what to say, but conversation with Aakash flowed easily.

"Come on," I said. "We both know how things work."

For people like us, there's only four acceptable fields: technology, finance, law, and medicine. But the first three are all too risky for me. Tech stuff offers the best chance of becoming *super* wealthy, but it's so all-or-nothing: if your company fails, you get no money. And even if you do produce something worthwhile, it's always possible for someone to swoop in at the last second and screw you over. Besides, the only people who succeed at that are the ones who really care about technology and software and all that nerdery. Finance also offers a chance of huge rewards, but the competition is too intense. Only a tiny fraction of associates end up making partner; everyone else has to find another profession. Law is the same, except that you also have to pay tons of money to go to law school, and there's a chance that the economy will tank while you're in there and you'll end up unemployed. That only leaves medicine. If you graduate from any med school, even a terrible Caribbean one, then you'll eventually (after your residency) end up making six figures. If you graduate from a decent med school, then four hundred thousand dollars a year is pretty common. And the best of the best can expect to make a million a year. But the main thing is that there's no *risk*. If you can get into med school—although it is, of course, extremely hard to get into even a bad med school—then you're set for life. No more worrying about the future. Just put in your time and collect your money.

During my explanation, Aakash kept moving forward and backward in his seat. Sometimes he'd be leaning close to me and other times it was almost like he was trying to escape. Finally, he said, "But that's your life. Do you want to spend every day doing stuff that bores you?"

I rolled my eyes. "How is that different from now? Do you enjoy homework? Studying for tests? Participating in bullshit extracurriculars? At least in ten years, they'll pay us before making us do stuff we don't want to do."

"I—umm—I kind of—"

He stuttered around the edges of that sentence for a few moments before I said, "You really do like it, don't you?"

Aakash wouldn't look at me.

"Well, you're lucky that you like the stuff that you're supposed to like," I said. "And lucky you're so smart that liking the material is enough for you to get good grades."

There were plenty of geeks and slackers in our class who were somewhat intelligent and liked the material well enough, but who weren't willing to put in the work to succeed. They thought that so long as they understood the material, it didn't matter what grade they got. And that's why they were never going to be as successful in life as they'd have liked to be.

"So . . . what happened to your GPA?" he said. "What did you do?"

I threw the little plastic spoon into the cup and got up.

Aakash drove a huge town car whose backseat was filled with white document boxes: their cardboard exteriors were neatly labeled, in fine black Sharpie, with the names of his experiments. My house is hard to find—it's on an anonymous, unlit cul-de-sac in Las Vacas—I let him miss the turn two times. It was nice to circle the neighborhood with him. He almost ran over an old woman who was walking her dog; if the golden retriever's eyes hadn't glittered in the headlights, I'm not sure he'd have swerved in time. He let out a quick "Shit!" and pulled over to the side until he had calmed down.

I was halfway hoping he'd ask me to go somewhere else, but, finally, he found the turn and stopped in front of my house. I put an elbow on my doorsill and angled toward him. "Well," I said. "I had a good time. . . ."

We looked at each other. Then he raised his hand and put it on my neck. He drew himself forward slowly. Then, at the last minute, he cocked his head, perhaps a little too far. Everything was so perfectly well-studied. I bet I'd watched the same "How to Kiss" YouTube videos as he had. I closed my eyes and opened my mouth slightly. He docked his lips against mine and applied slight pressure. I allowed the momentary insinuation of his tongue. It was wet. I felt nothing in my heart, but there were strange palpitations in my stomach.

As per the video, we both drew back after three seconds. He nodded at me. "I'll call you," he said.

"I'd like that," I said.

He pulled out his phone as he drove away.

My house's floodlights flicked on—they're motion-activated— and I went inside. I remembered, from my older sister's dates, that Mummy and Daddy would have a hundred questions, so I snuck upstairs to my room and lay on my bed for a few minutes, trying to sort myself out.

Aakash has worshipped me for years, and for years I've ignored him. So what's changed? How can I even consider going out with him again?

But let's be real. I'm not the person I was two weeks ago. When I was number one, I was too good for Aakash. But now that I'm number ten? Ehh. He's not unattractive. He has a certain amount of charm, too, I guess. And no one could accuse him of being stupid.

I've accepted that I won't get into Stanford or be valedictorian. I've become an ordinary person, and from now until the end of days

I'll be part of that huge faceless mass of humanity that lives and dies without amounting to much or being noticed by anyone. But Aakash is still a special person. And when I was out with him today, I felt . . . I don't know . . . he made me feel like I was a special person, too.

So yeah, I suppose he's the best I can hope for.

And I know that doesn't seem fair to Aakash. He's a good guy and he should date someone who's excited to be with him. But if he's been paying any attention at all, then he should already know I don't have a heart that can love him back. And if he's willing to take his chances, then who am I to stop him?

TUESDAY, SEPTEMBER 25

Today, I was walking through the cafeteria when Alex shouted, "Hey, Resh!" and called me over to the perfects' table.

I was startled—for years, Alex would never have deigned to talk to me in the cafeteria—but I realized that even though I'd given up on the novel, she was still bound by our deal. That was one bright spot. For the rest of the year, I'd have at least the semblance of a friend.

"No, no, Resh knows something about this," Alex said. "She might be able to help us."

The guy next to her stifled a laugh. I looked up. Alex was sitting right next to George!

"Sorry." I looked away from the two of them. "I . . . have some work to do."

"Are you sure?" Alex said. "Copying an assignment doesn't take that long, does it?"

I forced myself to laugh. For all I knew, this was exactly how Alex liked to tease her friends.

George said, "Hey, it's good to meet you."

She saw the glances between George and me and said, "Oh, do you not know each other? Resh, this is George with the unpronounceable last name. The other half of the school stuck me with him as senior class co-president." She looked at him. "George, this is Resh—she used to be our valedictorian until she . . . had some problems."

My skin was crawling. I'd kind of known that George was on the student council, but it was weird to see my worlds overlap. And his left hand was lying just inches from her right wrist. That was odd. They didn't belong together. Even their skin tones clashed.

"Hello there," I said. "What are you guys up to?"

"So . . ." said Alex. "Is it true that your parents know Susan Le?"

I was about to say no, but Alex was giving me a slight smile. I was finally getting somewhere with her, and I didn't want to screw it up. "I, umm . . . Why would you want to know?" My parents hated Susan Le. They switched off the television whenever her name came up on the news.

"We're trying to get Le to be our graduation speaker," George said. "And her speaker's bureau keeps saying her fee for a commencement address is a hundred thousand bucks. I don't think they understand that she actually graduated from this school. If your parents could get a message to her for us, it'd be . . ."

I shook my head. "No. No."

I thought of my parents sitting out there in the audience, listening to Susan Le deliver a speech about how to be a success in life. My shoulders and the back of my neck crackled with tension. No. The idea was repulsive. I needed to make Alex forget about this idea.

"I really don't think that's a good idea," I said. "I mean, is Le really a good role model? Her success is more due to luck than skill."

Alex spread the fingers of one hand and examined her nails. Then she looked up at me.

"Really, Reshma?" Alex said. "You think a billionaire isn't good enough to speak to our class? I mean, I'd beg to differ. The rest of the student council was very enthusiastic about the idea. Vice Principal Colson loved it, too. Le's really the voice of our times, right? It used to be that rich people all got that way by crushing their competition. Le is so different, don't you think? She made her money by making an innovative product that—"

"No! I don't think that's accurate."

George blinked and looked over his shoulder, as if he couldn't figure out who I was shouting at.

I tried to control my voice, but as I spoke, I kept getting louder and louder. "Le has nothing to teach us. She got lucky. Bombr was no different from a dozen other start-ups—worse, even, in a lot of ways—but because she happened to start hers at a rich, well-connected high school, hers expanded moderately faster than the rest. It had nothing to do with hard work or intelligence or creativity. Her speech would be arrogant, useless drivel. And that's not the kind of thing that Bell High should give a platform to."

People were staring. What'd happened to me? I wasn't like this. I didn't shout and scream in the cafeteria. I was usually silent and self-contained. I could feel myself splintering apart. There was no way I'd subject my parents to this. If Susan Le was our speaker, then I wouldn't even go to graduation. I'd stay home.

"I don't know." Alex's eyes were narrowed. "Maybe you'd have a point if Bombr was her only success, but she's had a hand in lots of businesses, hasn't she? What about your parents' company? That was more than luck, don't you think?"

"Just an aside," George said, "but I have no idea what you're talking about."

Alex let the silence extend for a moment too long, and then she looked at George. "Oh, Reshma's parents' company was about to go bankrupt, but Le saved them. She brought in new investors to buy out the original venture capitalists, then recapitalized it, put out a real product, and basically kept the buzz going until Apple swooped in and bought the whole company for a billion point one."

George gave me a blank expression. Was it possible that he hadn't known about all this history?

"So you can help us, right?" Alex said. "Maybe I could just drop by sometime and ask your parents about—"

I didn't have any witty comebacks. "Fine," I said. "If it means so much to you, then I'll talk to them."

"Really?" Alex said.

"Yeah, of course."

Alex ran one nail along the surface of the table, and I remembered how much she liked straightforwardness. Maybe this had all been a test?

"Good," she said. "Let me know how it goes."

I stood there with them for a few moments. George asked me something, but I couldn't hear it over the pounding of my heart. Alex looked up at me for a second.

"I didn't necessarily want Le, you know," Alex said. "Every year, it's always some tech person, and it gets boring, so I thought maybe this year we should invite a politician or activist. But the moment Le's name came up, everybody got so excited about it."

I nodded at her. Now it made sense. She was telling me that she would welcome some quiet way of disregarding Le. Well, I could do that. No problem. My parents were never going to hear about this conversation.

THURSDAY, SEPTEMBER 27

Yesterday was the annual Friends of Bell Fall Gala. It's a big to-do, with black ties and evening gowns and a catered meal and a silent auction. Bell doesn't really need the money, but my parents think they're somehow obligated to donate.

Anyway, they were seated next to Sadie and William Ozick—Jeremy's parents. The Ozicks hate me, of course, ever since my lawyers deposed them during the lawsuit, so Mrs. Ozick took great delight in asking my parents whether I felt okay about losing my class ranking. Apparently, the vice principal had told Jeremy that he'd moved up a rank.

At 11 P.M., my father shook me awake and shouted, "What happened!?"

I was so groggy that I thought we were in an earthquake. I was about to climb into the tub—all Californians know that's the safest place during a seismic event—when my dad caught up to me.

He pulled me downstairs and sat me at the kitchen table.

"This is what comes of dating around!" my father yelled. "How could you lose your ranking? We worked so hard!"

"It's okay," my mom murmured. "Whether she is valedictorian or salutatorian, colleges will still see her courses and understand what kind of candidate she is."

I clenched my teeth. I'd hoped to put this off until January.

"Actually, I'm not going to be salutatorian, either."

Daddy was speechless for a moment. "What?" he said. "You've let yourself slip all the way into third? Come now, *beta*, this is not good."

I gritted my teeth and dropped the bomb. I was getting a D in a class and I was probably not even going to end up in the top ten.

Silence.

Daddy massaged his hairless forehead. "This is not good at all," he kept saying. "Can you see that this is not good?"

Finally, Mummy said, "You'll be taking a drug test."

"What?"

"It's drugging. It has to be."

I thought of the Adderall: "No, no!"

"I know those classes of yours. You pass them for writing your name only. You must not be turning in any of your assignments."

"No! I never miss an assignment."

The whole story spilled out. The poem, the C–, the regrade, the charge of plagiarism. As I gibbered onward, my mother made chai tea and placed steaming cups in front of both Daddy and me, but I let the tea cool down to room temperature without touching it. We'd squished ourselves into the open mouths of the chairs that were shaped like martini glasses: I think it was the only time we'd ever tried to actually sit in them. Mine made a faint scratching noise against the hardwood as I spoke; I kept moving it farther and farther back.

"But you said that you did not intend the plagiarism," my dad said.

"Exactly! It was an accident."

Mummy folded up her hands and tucked them under the table, where they came loose and fidgeted under the glass.

Then Daddy said, "I'm calling Arjuna. We'll file suit in the morning."

"Wait, let us discuss this," Mummy said.

What? I didn't necessarily want to sue, but why was she against me? This was a school that had altered its entire grading policy just to dethrone me. A school where the vice principal had shown up personally to punish me for an irregularity in a single assignment. They obviously had it out for me.

"Come now," Mummy said. "We cannot sue twice in one year. The school, the newspapers, the town—they will all be against us. And even if we win, it will not be good for Reshma's reputation in the end. Please. At some point we must simply let your record stand for itself."

"Who says we can't sue twice?" my dad said. "We can sue twice. We can sue three or four or five times if we need to! The opinion of this town does not matter. All that matters is what is right."

My mom didn't answer. Instead she looked at me. And, after a moment, so did my dad.

I've only ever had one principle in life: *Never stop*.

I'd always thought that if I worked harder and pushed things further and was willing to endure more than any other person, then I'd win.

But, on the other hand, these last few days had been so nice. I was getting enough sleep. I wasn't anxious and stressed. And I was finally seeing someone!

"It is not too late for you, *beta*," my mom said. "You can still get into a decent college and achieve great things. But if you do this lawsuit, then they will go through all your past writings and papers. Are you not afraid of what will happen then?"

I gulped. I'm a good student and a good writer. And I am very, very careful with my sources. But when I thought about someone combing through every single thing I'd ever written, I felt a terrible fear take flight inside me. I mean, I couldn't stop thinking about Ms. Ratcliffe. If I hadn't pushed her to regrade my poem, none of this would've happened.

Part of me was saying, *No, it's crazy. If you take this grade, then your life is over. So if it's a choice between victory or death, then obviously you need to fight.* But another part was saying, *Well, that's a little over-dramatic, isn't it? I mean, one D isn't going to stop you from getting into some college somewhere.* Whereas if I fought the grade and something else turned up, well . . . who knew what would happen?

I shook my head. "I'm done."

Mummy stayed silent, while Daddy made a halfhearted effort to argue me into it. He kept saying that I shouldn't be afraid and that he was willing to do whatever I wanted. But after getting no encouragement from me and my mom, he finally went quiet, and asked permission to go back upstairs.

It's weird to have all this free time. Sleeping takes up a lot of it. But for the rest I'm at a loss. I downloaded some shows that I'd heard people talk about in the hallways. I tried to watch one that had a lot of good-looking twenty-five-year-olds pretending to be teens, but I could never forget it was just a bunch of actors reciting memorized lines on a soundstage.

I touched the spines of the books on my shelves. I'd read *Moby-Dick* in thirty-six sleepless hours, while I ran around frantically trying to arrange a charity toy drive. I'd gotten an A+ for my paper on the treatment of Islam in the novel. But had I enjoyed reading it? My only memory was of the twisty thrill of coming up with a thesis that the teacher would love, and then the anxiety, as I read through the book, that I wouldn't find enough evidence to support it. When I finally put it down, I wrote the paper in two hours, and I felt like I'd somehow *defeated* the book.

My door breathed open, and Mummy said, "How are you feeling?"

I slowly swiveled in my chair. "I really didn't cheat."

"I've made an appointment for you with Dr. Wasserman."

"I'll be fine."

She pursed her lips and then said, "When did you stop believing that hard work wasn't enough?"

"I told you, it was an accident."

"No," she said. "That is a lie."

"Please, I know that cheating is wrong. Do we really need to have this conversation?"

"It is poisonous to hold a position that you didn't earn. It is better to be tenth place honestly than first place dishonestly, because at least in the former case you know who you truly are."

"I gave up!" I said. "Isn't that what you wanted? I gave up. I'm not fighting anymore. So please. Please. Please. Please. Go away."

And then, mercifully, she did.

I guess nowadays this document is more my diary than it is a novel, but if I *were* still looking for a villain, then my mom couldn't have done a better job of turning herself into one.

THURSDAY, OCTOBER 4

My parents obviously have something to say to me, but for some reason they keep dancing around it. When my mom came home from work a few nights ago, she looked into my room and lingered in the doorway for a moment too long before going away. I thought maybe they wanted to lecture me a bit more about the cheating.

Last night, I tried nipping it in the bud: "Come on, Mummy, it really was a onetime mistake. You don't think I'm actually a cheater, do you?"

But she smiled at me sadly and put a hand on my shoulder for a long time before she finally went back to her work.

S ince my last visit, Dr. Wasserman's office had sprouted all these portable whiteboards; they were covered in black, red, and blue marker, with dozens of interlocking boxes and circles on one or a bunch of lines squiggling out in all directions on the other.

While I tried to talk to him, Wasserman's eyes kept glancing behind me, until I finally twisted around and looked. The whiteboard said:

— Woman Versus Self: struggle with perfectionism
— Woman Versus Society: fight to achieve high status by being admitted into a top college
— Woman Versus Woman: teacher is murdered? Or higher-ranked classmate?

— Internal Arc: overcoming her low self-esteem
— External Arc: is ordered by parents to go to psychologist, and must outwit his attempts to discover her crime

Wasserman hurried over and turned over the board to its blank side. "Those're nothing," he said. "Some notes."

"For your novel?"

He gripped the upper corner of the board. "I was trying to get a handle on your problem."

"I don't have any problems. Could you tell my mom that?"

"No, no. Not your psychological problems. I meant your story problems." Wasserman pulled at the fringes of his graying hair; they were sticking out in all kinds of crazy directions. "What would you say to including a murder in your novel? Is anyone causing difficulties for your protagonist? Maybe a teacher? Or one of her classmates?"

"Well, one of my teachers slammed me for plagiarism and the vice principal is failing me for the half-semester."

"Perfect!" he said. "Here's how it might work. First, the teacher tells your character that she's found the plagiarism. Then, before calling the principal, she gives your character a chance to confess. And, in that interim, your character murders her. I think it's very believable that such an intensely driven character would resort to murder to—"

"Are you insane? I would never murder someone."

"I thought you wanted to write a successful novel. People like to read about murder."

"Oh. I'm not writing that anymore."

Wasserman's chest sank and his shirt started to stick out a little. It was like his body didn't take up quite as much space anymore. Outside, a stream of cars and SUVs were honking at the lead car, which had lumbered out into the intersection for a left turn. We sat in silence for a minute. Then I started telling him about everything that'd gone on since my last visit.

When he heard about how my dad wanted to sue, he clapped his hands and said, "That's perfect!"

"Actually, it might make things much worse. . . ." And I tried to explain to him about how I wasn't sure I wanted that level of scrutiny on all my past work and how maybe something even more awful would happen to me, but he said:

"No! No! That is exactly what makes this perfect! Didn't I already tell you about the inciting event? In three-act story structure, there's usually an inciting event right in the middle of act one: it's an event so big and dramatic that it signals the beginning is over. And the character's reaction to that event is what drives the rest of the novel. You have your event: your character has fallen into disgrace. And you also have the perfect reaction! A lawsuit! It will increase the intensity of the conflict."

"I don't need any more intensity in my life."

"Right!" he said. "That's your internal conflict! As the external conflict—your fight against the school—proceeds, you become steadily more disillusioned with what you're doing. The reason this external conflict is good is because it involves precisely the same issues—perfectionism and status anxiety—that fuel your internal conflict."

I cracked my knuckles. "I think I'm done with all that."

Wasserman scratched his head. Finally, he said, "Have you heard of the Hero's Journey?"

"Are you going to bill my mom for this part of the hour?"

"The Hero's Journey is a pattern that is followed by most myths. It has many elements: the call to adventure, a wizard figure who gives supernatural aid, the crossing-over into another world, a meeting with a goddess, etc. And one of the main steps is the Refusal of the Call. It's when an ordinary person—a potential hero—is given a chance to go on an adventure, but, for a period of time, they refuse to leave their ordinary life. In most myths, it's a transitory step before the adventure begins. But, in some myths, the refusal becomes permanent. The myth becomes an anti-myth: a story of lost opportunities."

After that it was more plot diagrams and character sketches until the session was over. At first I was annoyed, but after a while it became almost interesting. And if I was still writing a novel,

Wasserman might actually have a good point. Sure, a lawsuit might make things worse, but it also might make things better. And being willing to risk those odds is exactly what separates a hero from a regular person.

FRIDAY, OCTOBER 12

From: Linda Montrose <lmontrose@bombr.co>

To: Reshma Kapoor <rtkap@bombr.co>

Subject: Wow!

Spent a *wonderful* hour reading the partial manuscript that you sent. I think that editors will really go crazy for this. Your protagonist has one of the most fascinating inner arcs I've read in a long time: her principles, though flawed, are unwavering—which makes us root for and admire her even when she's cruel or petty, but they're combined with an inner vulnerability, a tenderness, that resonates so deeply, even when she herself is unaware of it. Are you sure you can't be persuaded to resume work on the book?

—linda

P.S. I know that the "Reshma" in your book is an invented character, but if, by any chance, you need me to write a college recommendation for you, then I'd be happy to do so!

. . . .

From: Reshma Kapoor <rtkap@bombr.co>

To: Linda Montrose <lmontrose@bombr.co>

Subject: RE: Wow!

Dear Ms. Montrose,

I'm glad that you enjoyed it. Actually, I don't know . . . I suppose I could be persuaded to continue working on the novel.

Sincerely,

Reshma

. . . .

From: Linda Montrose <lmontrose@bombr.co>

To: Reshma Kapoor <rtkap@bombr.co>

Subject: RE: Wow!

Wonderful! When would be a good time to meet?

—linda

TUESDAY, OCTOBER 16

T oday, I was on my laptop in the living room, exchanging messages with Aakash, and when he teased me about how I'd have
to go to community college, I laughed out loud, which made my
mom look up from her laptop.

She smiled at me, and for a second it was like it used to be, back
before I took the SAT or filed that lawsuit or lost my valedictorian
slot. She actually seemed happy to see me, and when she asked me
what I was laughing about, I told her about Aakash's joke.

That's when her face became really grave. She folded her blanket
over on her lap, and I felt the room collapse inward on us.

"And have you thought at all about where you will apply early
for college? Is it too late for Berkeley? Or what about these liberal
arts colleges? Your aunt Swati has been telling me many good things
about Carleton College."

I gulped. I'd been thinking about this for a while. "Actually,
Mummy, I, umm . . . I already sent in my Stanford app."

"Acha." She nodded her head. "It is fine. You were always so good
at meeting these deadlines. But we will call them, ke nahi? And we
will explain that you've changed your mind. They will make no fuss
about withdrawing your application once I explain that things have
changed for you and—"

"Mummy, I sent out the application three days ago."

"What?" Her head twitched, like she was trying to knock a fly from her ear. "This makes no sense, *beta*. You can't get in."

I tried to explain to my mom that I still refused to sue the school—that still felt like too much—but after that e-mail from Ms. Montrose, I'd started thinking that, well, who knows? I still had an agent, didn't I? And maybe Stanford would see something in me that other people couldn't. And the rules were actually on my side, because I'd been looking things up and I'd realized that they aren't allowed to change my class rank until the final grades are in. So if I was to apply now, they'd be forced to mark me as number one.

My mom pulled one foot under the knee of the other leg. "But Mrs. Ozick said her son is being raised to number two for his Yale application. I do not think you are understanding the rules correctly."

I shook my head. "No, no, that's not right. I . . . I could challenge that."

"That is silliness. Even if you were to get in, what do you think will happen when the midyear report is mailed to Stanford next semester? They will withdraw your acceptance, and you will be left with nothing."

I was standing up now and pacing back and forth. I rubbed my palm against the outside of my blue sweatpants. Actually, no, it all made so much sense! My plan for getting into Stanford could still work! If I could just be calm and careful when I explained it to her, then I was sure my mom would back me up.

But what came out was, "You don't think I can get in? You don't think they'll want me? I'm valedictorian. I'm the layout editor at the paper. I've won writing awards. I have an agent."

"And those are all excellent things for which I am proud of you. And you know I have never pushed either you or Meena to go to the best college; always my primary concern has been that you should go where you will be happy. But with your SAT scores, it was always very unlikely that Stanford would—"

"I have a plan, Mummy! For years, I've told you that I have a plan for getting into Stanford! But no, you wouldn't believe me. You wouldn't trust me. Instead you've just been so . . . stupid."

The moment the word came out, I felt the world tip over onto its side. I might've thought that my mom was stupid, but I'd never ever insulted her to her face before. You know how you can say "Fuck fuck fuck" and curse up a storm all day, but there's an invisible mesh around your lips that keeps bad words from slipping out in front of your parents? Well, sometime in the last few weeks my mesh had disappeared.

"You're such a first-gen, Mummy," I said. "God, it's so embarrassing to hear you going on about test scores and grades. None of that *matters*. What matters is looking good and seeming smart. What matters is your resume and how well you interview. You never understood that. If I'd followed your advice, I'd be just another one of the thousands of faceless Indian girls who get good grades and want to be a doctor. But instead I made a plan, and I followed it: I took the valedictorian slot; I made sure to win those awards; and I even found an amazing hook. And even with all that, you've always been against me. You've always dragged me down. You've always insinuated that I wasn't good enough. Well, guess what? When I get into Stanford, you'll finally have to admit that I was right all along, and that I knew exactly what I was doing."

"Yes." My mom's eyes were steady and unblinking. "I know your plan. Your plan was to cheat."

I shook my head and then let the air hiss through my teeth.

"Daddy will call Colson and he'll make sure they don't change my ranking until they're supposed to. That's not cheating. That's just the rules."

"No," my mom said. "I cannot support that."

I stomped out to the hallway and grabbed the keys off the tray. "Don't bother your father," my mom said. "He's—"

But I cut her off by slamming the front door.

A blast of cold air hit me as I went down our walkway. I was in my slippers and my sweatpants. I twisted up my hair, trying to pull it back, but realized I didn't have a hair tie, so I let it hang lank and greasy around my shoulders. A bird hopped down out of the overhang above me and pecked around in the grass.

It was ten o'clock and the only person on our street was this one guy standing on the lawn at the edge of our front yard and staring at his phone. When the guy turned, his long hair whipped around in the wind. Oh, it was George. Of course he'd be out there. Just what I needed—another person to judge me.

"Hey," I said. "You waiting for someone?"

His hand shivered a little as he waved at me. "No, I'm about to walk to the Caltrain."

"Really? You going into the city?"

"No. Going home."

The bird was getting close to my foot, and I shooed it away. George lived in Fremont. Taking the Caltrain was insane: it'd mean looping up through San Francisco, then switching to the BART and going across the bay and down to Fremont.

"Isn't there a bus?"

"Look, I'm fine."

I shrugged. I never said he wasn't fine. I passed within arm's reach of him when I went down to my car, because I couldn't think of a way to go around him without being weird. When I started the car, he glanced up for a moment, and when he lowered his head again, the shadows pooled in his eyes and mouth.

"Oh, all right." I rolled down my window. "I'll at least drive you to the train station."

He didn't move. "Well, only if it's on your way."

"It's not. But come on, we're talking twenty minutes' walk versus like a three-minute drive."

After a second, he picked up his bag and opened the door to h~~ black Explorer.

I pulled out from the curb and heard a little bump when he rested his head on the glass.

George said, "Why are you using your turn signals? There's no one here."

"I always use them."

I tried to catch a glimpse of him in the rearview mirror, but the angles were wrong.

I took the turn at the stop sign, then pulled out into Alma Street and shifted over into the left lane.

"You always check your blind spot, too? You drive like a granny."

"You know, ninety-nine out of a hundred times, you can get away without doing it, but on the hundredth time, you die."

"It's weird how you're so cautious about some things, but not about other things."

"What are you talking about?"

"Like over the summer, with that lawsuit."

"That was my parents."

He laughed. "Come on. I was right there. I heard you arguing about it. Your mom didn't think it was a big deal for you to go down to fifth. You argued them into suing."

"I had to do it."

"I know. You need to win. It's not good or bad. It's your nature. I understand wanting to be better than other people."

Shocked, I looked over. I hadn't thought that he understood that about me. Then, as the car accelerated down Alma Street, I found myself telling him about the plagiarism and losing my class rank and the perfects and their stupid dividing-up-colleges game. At some point, we were at the train station, and I pulled over into the parking lot and I kept talking. And that's when I told him about my mom. About how angry it made me that she didn't believe in me. Other kids had private college counselors and compliant doctors who drugs and rich alumni parents who donated tons ⌐ Princeton. I hadn't had any of that, so instead I had to ⌐ smart: I'd studied the system, and I'd taken the right classes and gotten the best grades and even figured out how to write essays just sappy enough to pick up second or third place in a contest.

My parents didn't understand that studying hard wasn't enough. Studying hard turned you into another generic Indian girl: Someone you could ignore. Someone whose name you didn't need to know. Someone who'd go to Berkeley and become an engineer at some big company and live and die in complete obscurity. Someone who was maybe twentieth or twenty-first in the class, but didn't even get credit for being smart, because when people talked about her—which wasn't often—all they said was "Oh, she's not brilliant; she just works really hard."

And while I spoke, the anger compressed my insides and closed off my peripheral vision and choked off every thought other than: *I hate them. I hate them. I hate everyone.* I was so all-encompassingly angry that I twitched and gasped and couldn't even begin to describe who and what I needed to destroy.

And he was listening. I made him listen. There's a tone of voice—low and quick and perfectly enunciated—that demands to be taken seriously. I could feel that tone emanating from my belly. You can hate someone who speaks at you that way, but you can't laugh at her.

A cop car prowled past—we'd been in the parking lot for half an hour. I shifted into drive and circled the unlit streets, browsing the cul-de-sacs.

"Hey," he said. "All that stuff you said? That's how I feel, too— I've spent plenty of time hating you and your parents and your sister and your house and your cars and your vacations and your college funds and your futures and your whole lives."

"I know," I said, even though I hadn't known. How could I have known? To me, George was an annoyance who periodically emerged from our basement. But I had to say something, because a part of me felt so unsettled by the idea that to George I might be just another Chelsea.

"What should I do?" I said.

He looked around for a lever at the bottom of his seat and adjusted it back. "You should probably be in therapy."

"I am."

"Then hopefully you'll eventually get over this and become a healthy, functional human being?"

I broke out of Las Vacas and started driving down El Camino Real. The gas stations and inns were beacons that stood out against the unlit storefronts. I tried to remember where I'd meant to go. To my dad's offices, I guess. But to tell him what?

"What would you do?" I said.

"What would I do? Or what do I wish I would do?"

"The first one." Wishes are worthless.

"I don't know. Sometimes during a race, you get tripped by another runner, and it sucks, and you complain about it bitterly, but eventually you accept it."

I nodded my head. Yeah. That's what you're supposed to say.

"But if getting tripped up one time meant I could *never* get what I wanted, then you had better believe I'd push back."

"Really? So . . . you think I should sue?"

"Sure, why not? You don't have a case. You cheated and you—"

"It was an accident."

"You are so guilty. But that doesn't matter. You're rich. That's what matters."

I shook my head. No. I wasn't like that. I mean, my parents were comfortable, but they weren't *rich*. They still had to *work*. It was blue bloods like Alex who had enough money to just buy their way past—

He interrupted my train of thought. "Don't give me that. You've got money. You've got parents who support you. And you've got a kick-ass lawyer who terrifies them because he's already beaten them once. So if what you really want is to win, then go out and do it."

My fingertips went cold. I could argue with myself until the end of time, but I knew what I wanted. I wanted to be valedictorian. I wanted to speak at graduation. I wanted to get into Stanford. And I wanted to make my mom watch every moment of it, until she finally broke down and admitted that I'd been right all along.

I took a deep breath, pulled a tight turn—we were back in the parking lot of the Caltrain station—and stopped the car.

"You don't really hate me, do you?" I said.

My head was achy, and I felt the world shimmering a bit. I got out my purse and dug around inside it, not knowing exactly what I was looking for. Maybe some water, though I never carry water in there.

"Totally. I hate this whole fucking place." He shook his head. "I keep telling my mom that I'm fine going to the school near our apartment. But she won't shut up about how great this school is and all the amazing things it's allowed you and your sister to do."

"Then why've you helped me tonight?"

"Did I help? If you go ahead with this lawsuit, it kind of sounds like everyone, including your own mom, is going to end up hating you. Well, hating you more than they already do."

We laughed together. Mine was nervous and light, but his was slow and deep. When we stopped, I put a hand on the chest of his letterman jacket. My fingers brushed his varsity pins. I was in the driver's seat, same as Aakash had been with me. I felt slow and tense, the way I never did with Aakash. By now, he already would've kissed me. I unclipped my seat belt and leaned close to him, not sure what I was doing.

"Hey," he said. His breath streamed out over my face. It had a slight garlicky smell that, at that moment, felt exactly right.

"Yeah . . ."

"What're those pills you've been taking?"

"What?" I looked down. My hand was empty. I'd pulled a pill out of an inner pocket of my purse and gulped it down without thinking. "They're a medication."

He touched the hand that had held the pill. "You should be careful."

My whole face got hot, and I jerked my hand away. How dare he judge me?

After he popped open his door, I got out of the car and stood there, hovering weirdly, as he grabbed his backpack. When he left I wasn't sure if we were supposed to hug or what, but he mumbled his good-bye from a few feet away.

It was better this way. If I'd kissed him, the entire novel would've gotten way too complicated.

When he got to the platform, he turned and he waved, and I had a brief urge to go and wait with him, but instead I got back into my car and made my way to my dad's offices.

Arjuna wears a bolo tie and a pair of mud-stained cowboy boots and has thinning white hair that he combs over the top of his head. My dad knew him back when they were graduate students, some twenty years ago. They used to go camping together up in the hills. Arjuna would take along a fishing pole and dangle a lure—with no hook—in the water. He liked to feel the nibbles at the end of his line, but he didn't want to actually harm a fish, because he's a strict Brahmin. About ten years ago, he won a huge class-action lawsuit by some Asian kids who, they said, had been discriminated against by the resume screeners at a bunch of investment banks. Apparently, Asians had to have much better stats compared to white kids, in order to pass the screening process. The award was twenty million dollars. The ten thousand kids divided twelve mil among them, and Arjuna got the other eight mil.

At around noon, he marched into Bell High, trailing a reporter from the *Silicon Valley Examiner*. He camped out in the office, handing subpoenas to everyone on a long list. After an hour, the district's general counsel arrived, squawking about how Arjuna was trespassing. Then Arjuna made a short speech about how this school was "trespassing on justice" and how "their racism could not be allowed to pass unexamined."

During the intersession period, Arjuna and I went down to Ms. Ratcliffe's office together. As we passed through the courtyard, people ran out of the lunchroom to follow us. There was shouting and jumping and high excitement. I suppressed my smile. This was serious. I needed to look serious.

When Arjuna knocked on her door, Ms. Ratcliffe opened it and said, "Wait a minute." But he shoved the envelope at her.

After reading it, she twisted the paper in her hands and said, "So you want to talk to me? If you want to talk, we can talk right now. Let's talk."

Arjuna looked around to make sure the reporter was there, then he said, "I want you to right the wrong you've done! I want you to examine your privilege! Would you really subject one of your favorites—favorites who are largely white—to this same level of scrutiny and to this same life-altering punishment?"

I caught Ms. Ratcliffe's eye and held it for a long moment. She slammed the door. Arjuna pulled at the lapels of his coat, looked at his phone, and sailed away, leaving me behind in the midst of that crowd of strangers.

When I turned to walk to my next class, the crowd parted to make way for me

Aakash is so thin that running my hands over his ribs is like playing a xylophone.

I know: not a very sexy opening. I guess everything is going all right with him. I've gotten serious about the novel again, so I suppose it's good that I kept this relationship going.

It's easy. All I have to do is ask a few questions about his research and he talks for half an hour. Sometimes he asks me about my life, but I know better than to answer honestly.

And . . . well . . . he's always taking me places. Last week was a hike up through a promontory in Berkeley. And a few days ago, we went out for breakfast, before school, at a very trendy-looking diner in downtown Mountain View that makes a massive omelet that's meant for two people. That last one didn't feel quite . . . natural, so I did some Googling and found the MetaFilter discussion that Aakash was using to get these dates. Everything was on there. The very first item was a movie. Then midnight cosmic bowling. Then the hike. He'd gone down the list in order!

Before I even looked at his next text message, I knew it'd be asking me to karaoke at an all-ages club in San Jose.

I guess I should be offended? But I actually get a chilly enjoyment from Aakash's phoniness. He knows he's an awkward guy, which is why he doesn't rely on his instincts. Instead, he searches the Internet for the best advice he can find and then puts it into practice.

Actually, Aakash is the one who should be offended. Compared to him, I've done almost no legwork. And when I tried to look at his Bombr feed to see what he'd been saying about me, I got nothing. After I'd told him that I knew about it, he must've set it to protected status, so only his followers could see it.

To fix that, I created a fake Bombr account (@PrincessPattyKakes) and randomly followed a bunch of people and threw a whole mess of bombs so I'd look like a real person.

When I came back from my other schoolwork, Aakash had approved my follow request.

As I thought, he'd kept throwing bombs where he asked for advice. I particularly liked the panicked *"She found this account!"* of a few weeks ago.

People constantly sent him links to articles and videos about the mechanics of dating, conversation, kissing, even sex. I'd scheduled four hours for this research, but I way overshot that and spent most of the night following those links.

That's why I was prepared when he met me at the door yesterday for our date and boldly kissed me without saying a word. I knew exactly how much to lean into him and how much tongue to allow and how long we should last. When we parted, I was smiling like I'd never smiled before.

"I enjoy spending time with you," I said.

He smiled, too. Then he took my hand and held it between us for a moment, like the man did in the video. We were robots whose programming had come into alignment.

I let the resulting date play out according to his plan, though I, at times, wanted to hit fast forward. He took me up to the ridgeline, and, as we looked over the fog-choked Valley, I shivered, to allow him an opening to put his arm around me. After we started kissing, I pushed his hand when he tried to go under my shirt. I almost mouthed the words along with him when he pulled back and said, "I don't want to do anything you're not ready for."

We melted against each other. This time I let his hand do some exploring. After counting off five minutes on the dashboard clock, I pulled off his shirt and then shrugged off mine, and we followed that up with some relatively tame Internet-sanctioned making out.

G ot to the newspaper offices early and sat in one of the back offices so I could avoid Ms. Ratcliffe. But the office shares a wall with hers, so I heard her muffled words:

"No . . . I have her dead to rights. . . . You have to see these two poems. . . . Plagiarism is so obvious. . . . I'll be fine. . . . No, don't hire anyone. . . . The school is providing counsel. . . . No, I don't want you to spend the money. . . ."

Silence.

I got up, went around, and knocked on the door to Ratcliffe's office. When she opened the door, her face turned a deep red. She was still holding her cell.

"Look," I said. "This isn't a threat or anything, but you actually do need your own lawyer."

Her hand covered her face. The tattoo on her arm was some Chinese character. "I'm so sorry, Reshma. I was only trying to reassure my uncle—"

"I've read all the newspaper columns and heard all the jokes. It's fine that you think I'm a deluded brat. But Arjuna Rao doesn't take a case that he doesn't think he can win. The issue isn't whether you've got me 'dead to rights.' Everyone agrees that the borrowing—intentional or not—did occur. What's at issue here is racism. You know, freshman year, Alex got caught copying someone's Spanish homework before class. So where's the C– on her transcript?"

"That wasn't in my class," Ms. Ratcliffe said. "And, well, we expect more from you seniors."

"My legal team has done some research. We know that Asians don't cheat at a greater rate than white people. But, at Bell, Asians are more likely to be punished for cheating and, when punished, are more likely to receive a harsh punishment: failing a whole semester instead of only failing the assignment, for example."

Ms. Ratcliffe ran a hand over her buzzed hair. "Those are issues for your lawyer to deal with." She dropped her voice. "What I want to know is, how are your parents treating you? Despite what you think, I *am* your friend and you *can* come to me."

"These are the last words we'll ever exchange without a lawyer present," I said.

"Please," she said. "Don't you remember last June? You were struggling with that horrible dictionary"—my stomach spasmed—"and you came to my offices and you opened up to me. I thought we were finally getting somewhere!"

Fuck her. In some obscure way, everything she's done to me has been a punishment for shedding those tears in this office.

I said: "If you ignore my warning, then you're an arrogant bitch"—she gasped—"and you deserve what'll happen to you."

"I'm sorry Reshma, but that merits a detention."

Agh. Why was I doing this for her?

"Look," I said. "When my team starts winning this case, the school's administrators will want to limit their liability. And they'll do that by shifting blame. They'll say that they're not racist, but that a few awful, deplorable racist teachers managed, unfortunately, to slip under their radar. And that's why you need your own attorney."

She clicked her tongue. "Did your lawyer tell you to say that?"

"If you really knew how to 'question authority,' you'd have figured this out on your own."

I took the handle of the door away from her and gently pulled it closed.

WEDNESDAY, OCTOBER 24

The perfects shuffled around a little bit when I sat down at their table, but they didn't get up and spit in my face or turn away or do anything dramatic like that, because acting out isn't something that a perfect would do. Although if they had made moves in that direction, I'd have expected Alex to do something about it. No matter how pissed off she might or might not be about my new lawsuit, I *am* still blackmailing her.

I nodded at her as I sat down, and her head tilted a fraction of an inch in my direction. "How are you doing with your parents?" Alex said. "Have you asked them about Le yet?"

"They're, uhh, they're working on it." No, of course they weren't. Never. But I was pretty happy that Alex had said something to me that wasn't entirely sly and resentful.

Chelsea smiled at me and said, "Oh, hey! How's it going?"

"I guess I'm doing pretty well. . . ." I tried to see if I could spot even an inch of resentment in Chelsea's face, but her smile never dimmed.

Jeremy narrowed his eyes and Ray fiddled with his cuffs. When I looked around the cafeteria at the groups of friends sitting at their tables, they always seemed so fluid and natural, interspersing laughter and hugs and jokes, almost like it'd all been scripted for a television show. But I didn't feel like that. I felt weird and awkward.

"Umm, is anyone else looking forward to homecoming?" I said. Aakash hadn't actually asked me yet, but it seemed like the kind of thing that a perfect would talk about.

"Oh!" Chelsea said. "Do you need help finding a dress?"

"Yeah," Alex said. "I'm sure Chelsea will let you copy her look. Or why not just go over to her place and *steal* anything you want out of her closet?"

Chelsea turned and glared at her friend. The whole cafeteria had gone silent, like everyone could sense the drama going on up here on the dais. And as I looked around, I realized it wasn't my imagination. They *could* sense it. They were staring at us.

The cafeteria is a sea of liquid attention. Most people only notice the flowing currents subconsciously: in the glance; out of the corner of a scrawny freshman's eye; at the long, smooth leg from which Alex is dangling a flip-flop; in the slow scratch of chair legs on the linoleum as a table of drama geeks slowly orients themselves to look at Jeremy—oh, yeah, I think I remember that he was once in a play. . . .

Everyone in this room comes to school with a tiny bit of attention to give, and they bait their lines with it and dangle it out in that great sea and sit there on their tiptoes with throbbing hearts and wobbly eyes, and they pray that they'll reel back some attention for themselves. But usually people like Chelsea and Alex come along and gobble it up without thinking.

Wanting that attention is *not* just vanity. It's *not* just pride. That attention is money in the bank: it earns interest. Having attention means you don't need to shout to be heard. It means that you never fall into that bottom part of the application stack: the people who're glanced over but never seriously considered. It means that when you like someone, they at least consider the possibility of liking you back. Without attention, you need to work twice as hard to get anywhere.

And for as long as I sat at this table, I had it.

Meanwhile, Alex had gotten tired with the staring contest and had gone back to her phone, while Chelsea was chirping about a party that weekend.

"Wait?" I said. "A party?" I'd gone on a date, and I had a boyfriend and a friend—well, a sort of friend—but I still needed to go to a party in order to finish my novel.

"Yeah!" Chelsea said. "Saturday night. Most of us have sent out our early apps, and we're going to—"

She glanced at Alex, who shook her head.

When Chelsea spoke, she pitched her voice high, so the tables around us could hear: "You know what? You should come! Alex will text you the invite, won't she?"

Alex rolled her eyes.

"In fact, why don't you send it now?" Chelsea said.

Chelsea was smiling at me insanely. She is amazing. She never breaks character.

The silence went on for so long that Ray and Jeremy stopped talking and eyed Chelsea and Alex, as if they were wondering what was going on. Finally, Alex said, "Fine, I suppose it'll be at least somewhat entertaining."

. . . .

She sent me the party invite, sure, but she followed up by writing:

> Let me know how many you're bringing. Will it just be you or should I expect your lawyers, too?

I stared at the message for a long time, thinking of exactly how to answer. In just a few weeks, I'd made so much progress with Alex, but she still wouldn't let herself admit that she liked me. So I finally decided to lay everything out for her.

> Hey, Alex. You should know I'm not really that good at playing your low stakes games. Stuff like calling someone over and subtly insulting them and making them feel bad. Can't do it sorry. Wish I could but I can't. Maybe I'm just not quick-witted enough. But you should also know that nothing you say can really touch me.

I saw those three dots. She was composing a reply. And a weird sense of heaviness built up in my chest as I stared at the phone. It wasn't dread, exactly. It was anticipation. I needed to know: What was the worst she could do? The worst she could say?

> You know why Chelsea's been so nice to you, right? I told her about how you'd begged me to be your friend and now she's telling everyone to go easy on you because you're really just lonely. That's how pathetic you are.

That hurt, a little bit. I tried to tell myself that she didn't really mean it. That she was only being defensive.

> Your act is getting tiresome.

> Is it? Well guess what. If you want to be my "friend," then you need to know that I don't hold back. Although tbh when it comes to you I sometimes don't even know where to start. I mean I could call you a cheater and a liar and a sore loser and a vindictive friendless skank and that would all be true. But it wouldn't even come close to getting at the core of your awfulness. Which is that you're a robot. You don't care about anything. You don't have any interests. You really have nothing going on inside you.

I sat in my room and reread that last message for a while. Then I put my phone in my drawer and tried to do some homework. But I kept reopening it and going back to it and rereading it. I cried a little bit, yes. But they weren't tears of despair. I felt . . . something else. I don't know what it was. An aliveness. I'd never had a talk with anyone that was like the one I'd had with Alex. Finally, after hours of turning her message over and over in my mind, I got up in the middle of the night and wrote her back:

> You're right about me. Really I don't care about or need you. The only reason I want to be your friend is for my book. But the book can end however I want it to. So here's what will happen. I'll come to your party. We'll fight. You'll try to destroy me. We'll rage at each other over text message. And eventually you'll realize you respect me. Finally, you'll open up and confess you admire me b/c you feel trapped by having to be perfect all the time and you wish you were capable of going straight for the things you want. You'll say you respect me for ignoring your stupid rules and not playing your silly games, and you'll say you wished you had the courage to do the same.

Although I waited for hours, she never replied. Which wasn't a big deal. Now that I know how my friendship with her is going to go, I almost don't need her anymore.

I sent in the main part of my Stanford app a few weeks ago, but today I made sure that the teacher and the guidance counselor recommendations went out in good order. My teacher recs were from Ms. Lin and my Spanish teacher, Ms. Arroyo. Ms. Lin even let me see the recommendation that she was going to mail out.

Her rec included the phrases: *"most conscientious and diligent student I've ever had"* and *"if I could buy stock in my students, I would put my life savings into Miss Kapoor. She will achieve great things someday."*

I choked up a bit as I read that last part.

On the forms that asked her to rank me, she'd checked "one of the top students I've ever taught" for almost every field. After I put it down, I couldn't talk. My arms opened up. I wanted to throw them around that little gnome of a woman. Sometimes it's hard for me to remember that I really am a good student, and I really do deserve to get into Stanford.

She murmured, "Is that acceptable? Or should I change it?"

I nodded.

Before I left, she whispered: "Even exceptional people can make mistakes." My instinct was to reassure her that the plagiarism had all been unintentional, but I realized I didn't need to.

In our school, the guidance counselor recommendation is usually signed by the vice principal. That obviously posed some problems. I mean, I've sued the school twice, and one of the suits is currently in progress. Not to mention this plagiarism charge. Obviously, none of that could be in the recommendation. We used an injunction to force them to submit the rec to my legal team (to be reviewed for possible libel) and to make sure that Colson both gave me the number one class ranking and checked the box that said I shared my ranking with no one. We still haven't settled the plagiarism suit, but, for now, I am indisputably number one.

After checking my online status and making sure that everything had been entered into the Stanford database, I felt really weird. I'd entrusted my whole future to an online form. Dazed by the enormity of what I'd done, I got up and wandered downstairs.

My mom was sitting on the couch, as usual. But I don't even know what I would've said to her.

I went into the basement and knocked on George's door.

He shouted, "Someone's already in here!"

I opened the door and said, "It's not a bathroom. Two people can be in here at one time."

George was putting a bunch of textbooks into his backpack. "Oh, hey." He shrugged. "Sometimes your mom puts guests down here."

He had a knee pressed down on the suitcase and was trying to pull the zipper closed.

"I sent in my Stanford app."

Since driving him home that night, I'd avoided him. I hate people seeing me when I'm emotional.

He turned around and leaned against his bed. "You'll get in," he said.

I felt weirdly disappointed. I expected that pabulum from, like, a cousin: someone who didn't know me.

"No, it's hard," I said. "Even if I stay valedictorian, they might reject me."

"People like you are the ones who get into Stanford."

That might've been a compliment, but he also spun his finger around while he said it, as if he was also talking about the house and the cars and the maid and everything.

The room was pretty bare. Two twin beds that faced each other. All the walls were blank and white. Since we were in the basement, the only window was high up and was blocked by some bushes. It was basically a dorm room.

"Wow," I said. "This place is depressing."

"Thanks."

"I mean, I can't believe you've spent so many years down here."

He zipped his bag up, then cursed and tried to work the zipper down again. He jerked on it a few times.

"Is it stuck?" I said.

"What do you think?"

Then my hand was on top of his. "Let me try." I brushed aside his fingers; they were so long and thin.

He swung the bag around. "I'll carry it upstairs and work on it while I wait for my mom to pick me up."

Then he rushed out before I could say anything else. Doesn't matter. I was stupid to think that a person like George could understand what Stanford means to a person like me.

The article in the *Silicon Valley Examiner* wasn't too unfriendly. The headline was:

VALEDICTORIAN SUES SCHOOL OVER ALLEGED RACIAL BIAS

But the online comments were something else:

If she doesn't want to work for her grade, she should go back to India!

Another person wrote,

Sad to see that our "model minorities" have become as entitled, spoiled, slovenly, and whoreish as the typical American teen.

And at least those were on topic. Others were pure venom:

If that dothead bitch was my daughter, I'd bend her over my knee and whip her until she stopped whining.

God, did you see that picture? What a FATASS.

I go to school with her, and I can tell you that she's on hella drugs and is sleeping with like four guys. She doesn't do any work, runs her mouth constantly in class, complains all the time, whines to teachers to get her grades raised, and then sues them if they refuse.

Doesn't matter. I'm used to it. During the last lawsuit, I'd read the comments and cry every day. But I won in the end.

At school, I'm a ghost. I was never popular, but at least people respected me. Now students look through me when I pass them in the halls, and teachers don't call on me when I raise my hand. When I go to their offices and ask them questions, they look down at the floor and answer in short sentences. Ever since that day when I sat with the perfects, I haven't had the courage to go back. If it wasn't for Aakash, my days would pass in complete silence.

. . . .

But I've just gotten a text from Chelsea:

Hey. Haven't seen you lately. Hope you're still coming to the party tonight.

Looking at the text makes my hands twitch, but . . . well . . . I need to go to a party in order to round out my novel, right? Part of me wonders whether they're staging some elaborate plan for revenge. I don't even know what they'd do. Violence doesn't seem like their style, and by now I'm pretty immune to humiliation.

Today, Aakash was driving me home from a walk in the hills, and while he was talking about the e-mails he was exchanging with some MIT professor, I leaned my head against the window and worried about tonight's party. As we went over the Dumbarton Bridge, with the shining blue bay spread out underneath and around us, I looked at him and thought, I don't have to be alone.

So I said, "Hey, Aakash, can you put your arm around me?"

He blinked a few times, as if I'd disrupted his subroutines, but then he leaned over and rested an arm on the back of my seat and rubbed my shoulder.

"Thanks." I gulped. My voice was getting strange and croaky.

"What's wrong?"

"Hey, umm." I cleared my throat, trying to make myself talk. "Do you think you could, umm, go with me to this party that Alex is throwing at her place?"

"Uhh," he said.

The Dumbarton Bridge was windy, and I could feel our car wavering across the lanes as the cross-breeze slammed into it.

"It's tonight?" I said.

"I, umm, what time? I mean, sure."

His eyes were on the road, so he couldn't look at me, but his face had gotten long, with his mouth slightly open and his chin drooping. I reached over and touched his forehead. It was clammy and damp.

"You . . . you don't have to."

He gulped. "I'll do it if you really want me to. . . ."

"Hey." I shook my head. "It's okay. You don't have to go."

"No, no, I'll come. . . . It's just . . . I don't usually hang out with those people. I mean, I know they're your friends, but . . ."

"What? They're not my friends."

"Oh, I, umm . . . you just seem to . . ."

"No, they hate me. That's why I wanted you to come."

He bit his lip, and I could feel him sucking the saliva back down into his throat. The bridge ended and the road dipped down into the broad, flat, swampy part of the peninsula.

He slowed down for the light. "Then why do you even want to go?" he said.

"It's for the no—" I stopped. I'd never told him about the novel. "It's for the experience."

"Okay," he said. "I'll come. I mean, it'll be an experience for me too, I suppose."

I let my hand rest on his hair and then drift down so it was touching his neck. "I really like you," I said. "You're a good person. The best."

When the car came to a stop, he looked over at me with eyes that were so wide open and pleased that I impulsively popped my seat belt and shot over to kiss him on the lips and when he tried to break off the kiss after a few seconds, I pushed myself forward and our teeth ended up clicking together and our tongues got all jumbled up, too, but you know what? It was still pretty okay.

U gh. Woke up and vomited. Mummy thought it was from anxiety. She sat down cross-legged by my side and said: "Come now, *beta*. Won't it be best to stop this suit? Even if you still wish to apply to Stanford, they will be unhappy if they learn you are so litigious."

I heaved again, trying to keep her at arm's length so she wouldn't smell the alcohol on my breath. Went back to bed and entered a feverish half-life, sweating and turning around over and over again, until finally, half an hour ago, I started feeling better.

Alex lives in a mansion up in the hills. When Aakash and I arrived, she was sitting on her patio and watching the sunlight play off the bay. She had a bottle of Jack Daniel's and a bottle of green liquid and kept mixing whiskey sours. She sat in a wicker deck chair and waved the bottle with one hand—it was multiple bottles, at different times—and smoked a cigarette with the other hand—Alex smokes cigarettes!

I hovered around the edge of the patio for a few minutes, clinging tight to Aakash, but eventually Alex's head lolled in my direction, and I stood on the tips of my toes, waiting for her to scream and toss me out.

"Oh, I didn't think you'd actually come," she said.

"Hmm . . . did I maybe win your grudging respect?"

Alex snorted as if I was saying something absurd, but you'll notice she didn't reply with an immediate insult.

"Chelsea's not here yet," she said. "Texted to say she wouldn't be by until after midnight. Can you believe it?"

"That's too bad . . . ?"

"Which means I could throw you out. There are guys here who'd do it for me."

"Are there?" I looked around. A few guys were leaning against a balcony, talking about some computer science thing. One of them waved at me. I think he was in my chem class?

"Not those guys! Other guys!" Alex said. "I know a great deal of guys!"

Then I looked at the cup in her hand and realized she was already drunk, so when someone grabbed her around the waist and pulled her away from me, I backed off. I'd told the lion exactly what time I was going to come to its den, and in response the lion had gotten trashed and decided to take a night off from being a savage carnivore, I guess?

Maybe she had just remembered that I was blackmailing her. But that hadn't stopped her from telling me off in the past. So I don't know. Maybe she was actually starting to like me?

Which left me free to take note of the party. Parties are a waste of time—there's a reason I've avoided them until now—and all I wanted out of this one was to acquire enough material to believably fake my transformation into a fun-loving, hard-partying typical girl.

But the party was strange. It didn't quite look like what I imagined. I'd expected a hundred people packed into a sweaty living room, chugging desperately from red cups until everything exploded into an orgy of unselfconscious drunkenness. But it wasn't like that. Dance music emanated from the house's speaker system, but it was set very low. The patio door kept sliding open and closed, and I lost count of the number of guys in baggy cargo shorts who sauntered out, looked at the bay for a second, then turned, leaned on the railing, and nodded laconically at me while downing their beers.

Alex was initially very put-together in a tight pink sheath dress with black stockings, but then she lost her shoes. As the night went on, she kicked up her heels and tucked them over the arm of her chair, contorting herself into silly and unsexy positions in an effort to keep her unshod feet off the floor. The bay breeze mussed her hair so badly that she finally sighed and tied it into a ponytail.

And weird people showed up. Kian, the extremely nerdy Indian debate kid who would be bumped to number five if I lost my lawsuit, dropped by with a few of his friends, and when Aakash saw them he visibly melted with relief and went over to chat.

Then George walked in with this black girl on his arm. I caught his eye and tried to say hi, but George looked right past me and nodded at Alex.

George was seeing someone? Really? Did Auntie know? George's mom is really traditional and Christian, and I'm pretty sure she doesn't approve of dating.

At some point, I was feeling lonely, and I went to check on Aakash, and he'd entered deep into a conversation with Jeremy about, I don't know, chemistry things. Honestly, at times I think he was enjoying himself more than I was.

The party had a long buildup, as people slowly arrived and got drinks and asked each other about what they were going to do later in the night. There was so much laughter! Alex kept screwing up her face and doing a spot-on impression of Ms. Lin until finally even the word *covalence* was enough to crack everyone up.

There was a brief moment of light and heat around eleven, when everyone was standing and everyone was moving and the music turned up and drinks were chugged (but someone always poured just one more!) and cigarettes were stubbed out and calls were made . . . but then . . . it never went anywhere. Kian got involved in a long, heated debate with Alex about whether molly would actually destroy your brain (he was, surprisingly, on the "no" side), which ended— unless this is a drunken delusion—with them making out for a solid two or three minutes, until he vanished.

It was weird: at the beginning of the party, Aakash abandoned me, but just as it was heating up, he was following me around everywhere, constantly asking if I wanted to go home.

I began doing this teleportation thing, where I'd suddenly end up in some random part of the house without understanding how I'd gotten there. And I remember whenever I'd pour myself a drink, Aakash would ask to take a sip and then the drink would disappear!

Then it was midnight, and Alex was still out on the porch, wrapped up in a shaggy rug that she'd insisted on plucking off her living room floor even though the house held a hundred blankets, and talking in a low voice, an attention-getting voice, about how much fun she'd had today and how much she loved us all and how glad she was that we'd stayed and how this was the real party, wasn't it? Here out in the cool air, not running all around everywhere looking for the next thing but content to just be with one another. And for a brief moment she even looked at me, and I knew she was including me in that "one another."

I stayed on the porch and sipped a whiskey sour, and people came and stood next to me . . . and . . . you know . . . most of them knew who I was. I guess I hadn't understood how well-known I am. This huge soccer player kept saying, "Come on, Resh, you know my name. We were in precalc together!" And I kept guessing white-guy names ("Sean," "William," "Trevor"), but I never got it.

The lawsuit couldn't help but come up. Some people were surprisingly supportive. A weedy Taiwanese nerd—he's seventeenth in the class—whispered, "Your lawyer was right. They don't believe we can write a good paper. Whenever I turn in an English assignment, I can feel the teacher wondering if it's plagiarized."

A stoner said, "You're suing? Whatever. That's cool."

Even the perfects weren't as awful as they could be. Tina said, "Yeah, Chelsea explained it to me. You still should've stood up for yourself, though."

I kept hearing that Chelsea had explained something about me to all these people. But when I tried to ask them for more explanation—I guess I was mumbling—they would back away and change the subject.

"Hey," Aakash said. "You're really drunk. I think it's time to go home."

"No." I shook my head. "Alex! I've got to talk to you!"

And in my drunken haze, I felt like everything was so right and so perfect. Alex was my friend. I'd come to her party, and she'd finally accepted me. We were BFFs. Maybe even BFFLs. Or perhaps something beyond that. Was there something beyond that? I had to ask her right now!

I was so excited about trying to find Alex that I tripped over my own feet, and Aakash had to catch me.

"Come on," he hissed. "You're embarrassing yourself."

"Don't tell me how to party," I said. "Just go home. I'll be fine."

Then he was gone, and I didn't see him again for the rest of the night, but I didn't care because I didn't need him anymore. Didn't need anyone or any protection. I was the party and the party was me, and the only thing left to do was to confirm my BFFL-ship with Alex.

I raced around, asking everyone where she was, but she'd disappeared somewhere, and people kept pointing to other rooms that I either couldn't find or that maybe didn't exist, and then time suddenly jumped forward and it was 2 A.M. and the party had dwindled to a half dozen or so people on the patio. I'd drunk a lot, but after taking another Adderall, I was feeling pretty alert. And there she was! She flung open the sliding door and shouted something about dancing—the music was overpoweringly loud. But when she tried to dance, she kept falling over. And, finally, she stumbled onto the couch.

All my nerves were jangling. Now was the moment. I plopped myself down onto the couch next to her.

"I'm the best," I said. And I knew that was all I needed to say. I was the best, and that meant we needed to be friends. Alex looked up with wild eyes, and even though the night was cool, her hair was plastered to her forehead with sweat.

She grabbed my arm and leaned close to me with a secret smile, ready to whisper something, and that's when I noticed Chelsea sitting on the edge of one of the wicker chairs and smiling a shallow smile at us both.

"You see," Chelsea said. "I knew you'd fit in, Resh."

When Chelsea spoke, Alex's face closed down and emptied out.

"Oh, come off it!" Alex screamed. "You hate her! You *told* me you hate her!"

The whole party flickered and stood still. Chelsea's forehead wrinkled. Was this it? The fight where Alex finally opened up to me? I didn't know. It was kind of like that, but I actually felt more like a bystander than a participant.

"Alex, you should really drink some water," Chelsea said. "Actually, why don't I take you to bed?"

Alex's nails were digging into my arm, and she was looking around wildly at every face but mine. "I'm so tired of doing your dirty work, Chelsea."

When Chelsea smiled at me, her eyes trembled, and she said, "I'm really sorry about this. Normally, Alex is more—"

"Did you make me invite her here because you knew I'd get mad?" Alex said. "Is that it? Did you *want* me to insult her?" Alex's pupils were crazy and disjointed, like she was cross-eyed, but when I tried to pull away, her eyes snapped back into alignment. "Come on. We're almost done with school. Why can't we just—" Alex looked around wildly, as if she didn't recognize any of us.

Chelsea flowed up off the wicker chair and tried to pull Alex's hand off of my wrist. "Leave her alone, Alex. She's fine."

"No." Alex wouldn't let go of me. "You know what, Chelsea? Maybe I'll do exactly what you *say* you want. Maybe Reshma will be my new friend." She looked at me with a nasty smile on her face. "Oh, won't that be so delightful?" She looked back at Chelsea. "What are you still doing here? Why don't you fuck off? I'm trying to spend time with my new friend."

Oh my God. Was this really happening?

Eyebrows went up. Chelsea blinked really fast, and tried to say something else, but Alex shouted at her again, and finally Chelsea disappeared back into the house.

Alex was still next to me, holding on to my wrist. She looked at me with narrowed eyes, and I looked at her. I'd won. But there was a strange lull. We were left there for long moments, silently sitting next to each other.

"I . . . Thanks for . . ." I said.

"Too soon." Alex finally let go of my hand. Then her eyes lolled, and she slumped bonelessly against the couch.

"Are you . . . ?" As Alex's newest (and perhaps best?) friend, was I obligated to call the ambulance when she passed out?

But someone grabbed my phone out of my hand and said, "Oh God no! Don't get the cops involved!" And then they bundled Alex up and took her inside and that was the last I saw of her. I really hope she's not dead. I'm almost positive she's not dead. Probably someone would've sent me a text message if she'd ended up dead?

I drifted into the house after them. My heart was beating fast, and I couldn't tell if it was because of the alcohol or Alex's outburst.

George was standing just inside the door, in the kitchen, and his hair still looked amazingly coiffed, even though he'd been making out on the couch for the last hour.

"Oh, hi. What happened to your, umm, the girl you were, umm?" The world was spinning, which made it a bit hard to think. "Does Auntie know you're, umm, some girl? She won't like it if you girl with."

It was crazy: my mind was so lucid, but my words were coming out garbled.

"Cecily is passed out. And she's not really my girlfriend. . . ."

"Home you car?" I said, or something like that. Obviously, the night was getting a bit hazy around that point.

"Err, she was my ride. . . ."

We stared at each other for a bit, and I shook my head and turned to the side.

"Where's your, umm, that Indian guy?"

"Aakash." I shrugged. "Gone. Told him to go away."

We were about to break away from each other when Chelsea came down the stairs. Before she looked at me, she had a slight frown, but when we locked eyes, she attempted a smile. "Oh, there you are," she said. "I'm *really* sorry about that."

"Sorry what?" I said. "All friends every friend."

Her smile flickered, got wider and more abstract, and she looked past me.

"Hey, umm, my . . . there's a girl passed out on the couch," George said.

Chelsea shrugged and said she'd make sure nothing happened to Cecily. She was already going through the kitchen dumping out cups and throwing them away. When she came by with a bag of trash, she said not to worry, the party wasn't over necessarily, but she felt terrible if she didn't tidy up when she went over to someone's house.

I had a strong urge to ask her what the hell was wrong with her.

"Oh!" Chelsea said to George. "You haven't been drinking. Why don't you drive Reshma home?"

"I . . . sure." He looked at me with a totally immobile face and asked, "Where do you live?"

I laughed and laughed and tried to explain about how we lived in the same place, but Chelsea gave me a confused look, dug my phone out of my purse, and found directions for him.

I don't remember much of the ride back; George had to buckle me into my seat and brush my hair out of the path of the seat belt. At one point, he swerved across the lanes and my heart skidded, but when I yelled at him to stop, he slowed down and said a bunch of things to me in a low, serious voice. I think he was talking about that girl, Cecily.

But toward the end of the ride, the night air managed to sober me up a little bit.

I said, "Sorry about your room being depressing. About saying it, I mean."

"It doesn't matter."

"You wanna leave? I'll get you kicked out. You're not supposed to be in our school anyway. One two calls e-mails to Colson, then done and you're in school at home."

His hand closed around mine, crushing it. "Reshma!" he said. "Promise me you won't do that. They could arrest my parents for that, you know. And yours, too."

"Fucking you," I said. "You almost get it. So close to getting it! But you're too scared. Let me do it. I'll send you home. My gift to you."

The pressure got tighter and tighter. I could barely feel my hand. "Fine!" I said. "Keep suffering. I don't care."

Then he disappeared. I sat still for a long time, confused. We were in front of my house. I hadn't noticed the car stopping. Finally, I looked at my phone. I had seven text messages and two missed calls. All from Aakash. The first text said it was okay if I wanted to stay; he'd just wait around and I could call him when I wanted to leave. The next few were a bit irate. The ones afterward were panicked. It was after 3 A.M., and he was still there, searching for me.

TUESDAY, OCTOBER 30

Ms. Montrose is a darling. She's fifty years old but wears brightly colored dresses, adorned with big pink bows and wide belts, that look like adult-sized versions of a little girl's clothes. Her agency is on the twenty-second floor of a skyscraper in the Financial District. It's all bronze statues and oaken walls and frosted glass partitions and girls in pin-striped skirt-suits—Chelsea, five years from now—whose peach-colored fingernails never stop clacking away at their computers.

After showing me around the office, she took me down to the Italian restaurant on the first floor. The waiter conveyed us to a booth in the back and delivered two glasses of wine. Ms. Montrose smelled hers and swished it around in her glass. I pushed mine away. After last weekend, alcohol still nauseates me.

"Right," she said. "The 'Reshma' in your novel doesn't drink." Over the course of the dinner, she drank both glasses of wine, and, after we'd finished eating, ordered another one.

She started by saying, "I am absolutely in love with this book. . . ."

She went on and on about its rawness and honesty, and, somehow, our talk got around to my recent troubles.

"I read about the second lawsuit," she said. "They just won't stop going after you, will they?"

I ran my fork through the spaghetti. I'm not a big dinner person. Usually a handful of almonds is enough for me.

"Schools can be vindictive," I said.

She wiped her mouth with her napkin. "You know . . . you don't need to pull your punches in the novel. Even if we sold it tomorrow, it wouldn't come out for years."

I kept a blank face. "The book is fiction." Err, well, at least the names are fiction.

"Right," she said. "I thought about asking you to rewrite it as a memoir, but some of your inventions work fairly well. I loved the psychologist. What a clever way to thread in the metafictional element."

We laughed at the same moment. Sorry, Dr. Wasserman.

"All right, let me tell you how I plan to market your novel." She described a multipronged plan that involved capitalizing on my age and on the publicity surrounding my legal troubles. She'd already shown the sample around and elicited some interest from a few editors. Once the proposal was done, she hoped to bring it to auction and get a bidding war going for the publishing rights.

After she'd waxed expansive about all the editors she knew, I said, "But it's not even finished. What if it's no good?"

She put down her fork. "Honey, don't worry about that. The most important thing is the freshness of your voice. Once you send me a draft, I'll work with you to nail everything else into place."

She gave me a twitchy little smile, and for the first time I wondered if I might actually be some sort of literary genius.

After I got home, I texted Aakash to see if he wanted to break out and go celebrate my fantastic meeting, but he wrote back:

> Congrats. Sorry. I have a test in bio tomorrow.

That's all. I didn't even get an emoji!

The day after Alex's party he'd called me up and given me a

semi-parental lecture about how I needed to be careful when I drank. I'd apologized and asked him if he was mad that I'd ditched him, and he said, no, no, he was just worried about me, but I didn't believe him.

I wrote him back just now:

Hey, I really am sorry about leaving you at the party. How can I make it up to you?

It's okay.

Maybe you don't have to go to any more parties?

Really it's fine.

You sure? No more forcing you to go to parties. This offer is expiring in five . . .

Four . . .

Three . . .

Okay, come on. I'm not mad. Seriously.

Oh my God. You had fun. Despite everything you had fun.

Two . . .

One.

=]

Busted. Totally busted.

> Okay, fine maybe if you're nice to me from now on, I'll let you accompany me again.

> I really do have to study though. Sorry I can't celebrate w/ you.

I wrote something incredibly sappy and thought about deleting it. But you know what? Text messages are for saying the things you're afraid to say aloud.

> No don't feel bad. Your presence in my life is celebration enough.

> <3

· · · · · · · · ·

Later that night, Ms. Montrose e-mailed the recommendation to me so I could confirm it was what I needed. In it, she called me a *"burgeoning talent"* with a *"fully formed, mature prose style"* that'd someday make me *"the voice of my generation."*

After reading it, I couldn't sleep. I knew how my novel needed to end.

I, personally, am still going to be a doctor. Doctoring is secure. Even a bad doctor earns upward of two hundred thousand per year. Writing is too silly for me. There are no rules. One person tears apart everything you write while another person praises it to heaven. Doctoring isn't like that.

But still, at the end of my novel, "Reshma" will abandon medicine and decide to become a writer. That's an ending that the average white girl can relate to. Almost no one can become a doctor: you can't even begin to think about it unless you're one of the smartest people at your school. But anyone can dream about becoming a writer. Lots of girls want to be writers. I bet they tell themselves that doctoring is a dull grind and writing is so beautiful and free and empowering. My novel will flatter those second-raters.

Years ago, after I placed in my first essay contest, my mom tried to tell me that it'd be okay if what I really wanted to do was be a writer, but I got so insulted that she never brought it up again.

SATURDAY, NOVEMBER 10

Went to homecoming with Aakash. He planned everything perfectly, as usual. So much so that when the dance ended and we got into his car, I was sure that he'd be taking us to the after-party at Tina's house. But no, of course we ended up at the *other* after-party: the no-alcohol party hosted and chaperoned by the PTA in a rented hotel suite in downtown Las Vacas. He was, if anything, even more nervous at this party than he'd been at Alex's, and as I walked through, I saw why: it was full of Aakash's science-y friends. They normally didn't go out, but they'd made an exception for homecoming. Each of them had dug up a date somewhere and now were dutifully out after midnight, trying to milk a few more memories. And as Aakash wheeled me around the room, introducing me to this person or that person, I realized he was showing me off! Which I actually kind of loved, and I made an effort to be, I don't know—big.

You don't know this, dear reader, because you've never met me, but in conversation I'm not big. I'm not friendly. I don't shine. What I hadn't known, though, was that when you're in an expensive dress and you're next to a guy who's so happy to be there with you, then it's impossible not to become bright and happy and a little bit flirtatious.

And as we went from corner to corner, leaving a trail of slightly stunned nerd boys in our wake, I came upon the biggest surprise of the night: Chelsea!

She was there with a guy I'd never seen in my life: a tall white guy with dull brown hair and a mouthful of braces.

"Hey there," I said. "Didn't expect to see you here."

I came to a stop a few feet away, too far for a hug or even a hand-shake, but Aakash shocked me by giving Chelsea a big hug.

"So it worked out!" Aakash said. Then he shook the guy's hand. "Hey, Brandon, right? Chelsea told me about you!"

I looked from side to side, then all around the room. What in the world was happening?

"Are you going to Tina's place after this?" I said. I guess part of me was still hoping that the night would end up there.

Her date, Brandon, raised his eyebrows. "Tina?" he said. Even though he was six inches taller than Chelsea, he had a strange, servile aura around her. When he touched her, he did it so lightly, as if she was a photograph that he didn't want to smudge.

"It's nothing," Chelsea said to him. "Another party. But I don't want that kind of night."

Chelsea and Aakash chatted excitedly for a few moments, mostly about the dance itself, and then I maneuvered him away, to the other edge of the ballroom.

"What's with her and her date?" I said.

"Oh, Brandon," Aakash said. "She told me about him at that party you took me to. He's a friend of her family. Homeschooled. He's never been to a dance."

"So it's a pity thing?" I said.

Aakash got a little bit stiff. "I wouldn't characterize it that way."

"Yes, and that's why she's here instead of at Tina's," I said. "So they won't see him."

He had drawn farther away from me. "You're not being very charitable. Didn't you say yourself that she'd had a falling out with Alex? Maybe she just didn't want to be around them."

I laughed and ran a hand up and down Aakash's arms, like I was physically soothing his feathers back into place. "Oh my God, you and Chelsea really spent way too much time together at that party."

"We had to," he said. "While I waited for a cab."

I laughed and leaned over to kiss him. For a second I thought he might draw back, but then I made a pouting face at him and he smiled. We stood there, kissing, in the center of the room, until I caught a PTA mom glaring at us. Then we took a few more spins through the crowd, until Aakash began to yawn. I thought about offering him an Adderall but stopped myself just in time.

"You're wrong about Chelsea, you know," he said. "When you did this lawsuit, I thought . . . I don't know . . . I thought it might be too much, but at the party she explained to me that your parents were really the ones who'd pressured you to do it."

I stopped short and grabbed the elbow of his suit coat. "What?"

"Yeah." He yawned again. "That's why everyone was so nice to you at the party. No one blames you."

I glanced over my shoulder at her, standing there, gazing into the eyes of her date. She looked over at me and started to smile, but when she saw my expression, her face went pale. Chelsea. It's not that I hated her, precisely. It's just that right at that moment, I wanted bad things to happen to her. Okay, maybe I hated her. She'd not only slandered my family, but she'd come out of it looking good!

And the weirdest Chelsea interaction of the night was still to come. Our suite's bathroom was filled for too long—undoubtedly because someone had gotten or was getting drunk—so I went down to the lobby to use the bathroom there. Chelsea followed me into the elevator and said, "Hey, Resh. I just wanted you to know that . . . I . . ."

Her face was really red. "I don't know how to say this," she said. "But I'm . . . I decided to apply early to Stanford."

She patted her forehead, and I realized she was reaching for the sunglasses that would normally be there.

"And . . . ?" I said.

"I'm . . ." She shook her head. "I'm really sorry. It's just . . . now that I'm first . . . I thought that . . . if you want to apply to Harvard, there's still time to. . . ."

"Relax," I said.

Far from it. A little spark of elation had actually flared up inside me. Yes. Yes. Yes. Chelsea and I were finally going to be matched up head-to-head.

"I'm not mad," I said. "I always thought the dividing-up-colleges thing was silly."

Chelsea threw her arms around me. "That's fantastic. I'm so glad! Since we're the only two people applying from Bell's top twenty, I really actually bet we'll both get in!"

While she hugged me, I looked past her and stared at our reflection in the mirrored walls of the elevator. Her skin was smooth and unblemished, while my sleeveless dress was showing a spot on my shoulder. I reached around her and rubbed a little bit at the spot, but I couldn't brush it away. I wasn't sure if it was a mole or a pimple or insect bite that I'd never spotted before, but somehow it was a part of me.

THURSDAY, NOVEMBER 15

My life is hell.

Ten days ago, I called Linda and explained my plan for the "Reshma becomes a writer" ending.

"That could work," she said, "But how long is the book going to be?"

"It's forty thousand words right now, and I think I can wrap it up in less than two thousand more . . ."

I could hear her pursing her lips. "Hmm. Most young adult novels for older readers—age sixteen and above—should be at least fifty thousand words long. But, honestly, it'd be even better if we went up to sixty thousand. Is there any way to expand the story?"

"What?" I said. "I'm almost done. I am moments from the epiphany."

"Well, here's an idea. What if she doesn't get into Stanford? Maybe they defer her and say they'll consider her again during the regular-decision cycle? That'd give you more time to—"

"No. Then the epiphany would be irrelevant. The story works because it's about turning your back on a brilliant medical career. Without Stanford, she's just one more second-rate idiot who turns to the creative arts because she's not good enough for a real profession."

"Huh. Well, let me see how it works on the page. . . ."

Except now I'm stuck! I need some sort of twist or surprise. Or maybe a new ending entirely? But I keep writing pages and then throwing them away.

The truth is that I can't write it until it happens. And there's so much time between now and December 15.

Stanford has to take me, right? I'm the top-ranked student at a top-ranked high school. I have a literary agent. But what if they ignore Linda's recommendation? Then they'll only see another valedictorian with terrible SAT scores. One more over-groomed study machine who can regurgitate facts but can't think critically. At that point, maybe, I don't know, maybe they'll decide that they prefer Chelsea.

Or is it possible that they know about the lawsuits? What if my mom was right, and they decide they don't want to accept someone who might be litigious?

The *Examiner* article about the second lawsuit is the very first Google result for my name. But they usually get more than seven thousand early action applicants. They can't Google all of us, right?

But what if someone tells them? It would only take one phone call, one e-mail . . .

SUNDAY, NOVEMBER 18

Since her party, I've been texting Alex every weekend, asking if she wants to hang out, but she's always responded by saying she's busy with college applications. Which is understandable. But it's also a bit annoying that we still haven't brought the friendship plotline to its natural climax. So today I screwed up my courage and told her that I didn't think friends were allowed to blow each other off all the time.

And I must've finally gotten through to her, because she just texted back:

> You up for coffee in mtn view today? I've got something fun planned.

. . . .

After I sat down at Alex's table, she said, "Hey, sorry I couldn't talk earlier. Had applications to send out."

"Oh," I said. "Mine went out weeks ago."

Suddenly, I wondered why I'd one-upped her like that. I was always competing. Trying to show people up, even about tiny little things. Which was fine when I was talking to someone like Chelsea. But was that really how friends acted?

"Of course you did." Alex took a sip of her latte. "Makes sense. Although I guess you must think you're a shoo-in at Stanford. I mean, unless they find out about your lawsuit."

"I don't know," I said. "I think for me it was just anxiety. I've, uhh—" I paused for a moment. I'd never really . . . I'd never actually confided in someone before. And trying to do it made me feel squiggly and unsettled. "I've been a bit worried about that."

"Huh." Alex frowned. "Yeah. That worry is pretty legitimate."

"You're not going to try to reassure me?"

"We live, like, five miles from Stanford. C'mon. Of course they heard about your lawsuit. Even if no one in the entire admissions department reads the local papers, all it would take is one anonymous e-mail from someone at Bell who has something to gain from you being rejected."

I thought about Chelsea, applying to Stanford after all.

"So what should I do?"

"Write to them." Alex tapped her nail three times on the table. "Explain yourself. Be honest. If you're the first to tell them, then you can spin the whole thing in your favor. It's a long shot, but they might respect you for being up-front about it."

"That's . . . interesting."

She shook her head. The line for the counter was snaking along the side of the café, and people were now standing between our table and the window. "That's so typical of you," she said. "Always trying to get away with something, even when it makes zero sense."

My heart was tender, and each of her words made it jump. But I was also enjoying this. I'd spent so many years hiding who I was. And I'd mostly fooled everyone. Either they were like my parents and thought I was honest and golden, or they were like my teachers and thought I was slimy and stupid. Only Alex understood that I was something else entirely.

"Just be honest?" I said. "That's so naïve. Colleges don't want you to be honest. They want you to be effective."

Alex glanced at her watch.

"Come on, you know that," I said. "You and the rest of the perfects. You're all about appearances. Let's pretend we don't care about school. Let's pretend we don't study. Let's pretend that getting straight A's is sooooo effortless."

Alex waved me off. "That's Chelsea's thing. I study. Of course I do."

"Maybe alone. At home. But not at school," I said. "Not at lunch or in the hallways, like everyone else."

"I study when and where I need to. I dress in what's comfortable. And I do and say exactly what I think."

I shrugged, but Alex seemed genuinely incensed.

"You're even dishonest in little ways," she said. "Like when I asked you to help me talk to Susan Le, you could've just said no. But instead you told me what I wanted to hear."

Really? That again?

"When you asked me, we weren't really friends."

"Oh, and now we are?"

I shrugged and glanced around the table as if to say, *Huh, look at us sitting here. Seems pretty friendlike, doesn't it?*

"I could've used your help," Alex said. "I tried to work around the speaker's bureau by getting directly in touch with Susan Le's assistant. And he told me to get in touch with her lawyer. And her lawyer sent me to her publicist. And her publicist sent me back to the speaker's bureau! And I'm pretty sure not one of them have bothered to forward my request to Le."

"Aren't you overlooking the obvious?" I said. "Maybe she doesn't want to do it."

Nowadays, everyone at the school was really proud of Le, but I'd noticed that she hardly ever mentioned Bell in her speeches and interviews.

"Maybe," Alex said. "But, like, most grads would kill for the chance to come back to their old school and trumpet how successful they are."

"Le doesn't need to trumpet," I said. "Maybe she cares more about sticking it to the school than she does about being applauded by it."

Alex made a terrible scratching noise by running her nail across the rim of the table. Then she picked up her phone and tapped at it for a few seconds. She looked at me, and I raised my eyebrows. What the hell was going on? She pushed a button, and the phone made a tiny *zoop* noise.

"I was only joking around when we were at the party, you know," Alex said. "Chelsea and I are still best friends."

I shook my head. "No. I don't think so. Not anymore. Maybe not ever."

Alex smirked. "You know the biggest joke? I just e-mailed Stanford about you. And it wasn't an anonymous e-mail at all. I don't care if they know who I am. No one's going to think less of me for warning the world about you."

My heart dropped into my stomach, and I could feel my face and shoulders getting hot. After she'd blown up at Chelsea at the party, some part of me had thought that maybe Alex was done fighting back against me.

"I don't believe you," I said.

She took a sip of her coffee and looked me up and down as if she was trying to think of something else to say.

"You wouldn't do that to me," I said. "Not to help Chelsea. You don't even like her."

When Alex tapped her nail against the side of the paper cup, it made a thin, hollow sound.

"You know what?" she said. "It's not about Chelsea anymore. The truth is that I can't afford to have a blackmailer on the loose. I mean, who's to say you'll stop after you get into Stanford? Maybe next year you'll want money. Or for my dad to give you a job? Where would it end? So I thought, What can I do to neutralize her? And then I got it. No one trusts you. You are a liar and a cheater. And everyone knows you like to use the law to force people into line. And that's when I realized, Hey, you know what? If I provide even a tiny reason for people to think you're making up your allegations against me, then I'll be fine. And now I've provided it. If you go to the police or to the school, I'll point to my e-mail to Stanford and say you faked up the drug-dealer charge in order to get back at me."

She kept looking at me. "Well," Alex said. "Now at least you know for sure that Stanford knows."

I couldn't believe it. Everything was over. Stanford would turn me down.

"You gave me the chance to follow your advice," I said. "Oh my God, that's why you called me here. You wanted to feel good about yourself. Reassure yourself that I deserved what you were doing. That's it. That's the only difference between us. You're just as devious as me. But you *also* need to feel like a good person."

"Whatever," Alex said. "Stanford is gone. And so's your hold over me. What now? Do you still want to be my friend?"

She could've said the last with a sardonic smile, but she didn't. Her face was still. We sat there for a few seconds and I tried to understand what had happened. Then she tapped on the side of her cup a few more times and said she had to go.

I looked up just as she went through the door.

"Yes," I said. The word twisted my stomach. It made me feel so small and pathetic, but . . . yes, I *did* still want to be her friend. I whispered the word again, but by then she was long gone.

've always thought my teachers were bastards, but now I have proof. Over the last two weeks, we've deposed almost every teacher I've ever had. Arjuna didn't want to give me the transcripts, but I forced him to.

My AP American history teacher, Mr. Kooning, said, "I sometimes had to avoid calling on Ms. Kapoor. She always participated in class—ninety-five percent of the time, her hand would be the first to rise in response to any question—but her comments were often quite general and rarely provided any particular insight."

Mr. Cordoba, my AP calculus teacher, said, "Ms. Kapoor was a great student. However, I got very tired of her behavior. When she got a problem wrong, she would come to my office and insist that I personally demonstrate the solution to her. Then she would try to convince me that I hadn't provided them with the analytical tools in class to solve that type of problem."

Ms. Smithson said, "It's not my policy to ever give an A plus. But she would not accept that. After getting an A on her final paper, she made me go over it and explain, in detail, why it wasn't an A-plus paper. In the end, I gave in and changed the grade."

That's what teachers are like. They don't want you to learn, they want you to pretend like you already know everything. But I don't have Chelsea's sprezzatura. I need to try. It takes me hours upon hours every night, grinding at every problem in the book—even the ones that don't get assigned—and reading every word three times, taking note after note, taking notes about my notes, beating the subject matter into my head. Do they think that's how I wanted to spend my teen years?

No. They don't think. They don't care. They wish I would sit quietly in class and pull down a string of B+'s. Then they'd remember me so pleasantly and wish me a thousand good wishes when I got into UC Santa Barbara.

Last night, Mummy found me with my head on my laptop, sobbing. She thought it was about the lawsuit, but it wasn't. It's . . . none of my teachers or classmates think I'm really the best. But if I win in the end, then I'll prove them wrong. I have to beat them. I can feel the need burning up my chest. All I want is to stand up front at graduation and incinerate them all with my greatness.

But I can't even finish this stupid novel.

Dr. Wasserman doesn't have a receptionist anymore. When I walked into the empty anteroom, he poked his head out of his office and said, "Come in."

Whiteboards were stacked up ten deep along the walls. In order to reach my chair, I had to move one out of the way. The only thing on it was bunch of wavy lines coming together and breaking apart, but Dr. Wasserman watched my hands like a dog watching a steak. He didn't relax until I'd rested the whiteboard against a file cabinet.

"Are you still feeling a bit manic?"

"You never diagnosed me with anything like that."

"Hmm, I think I remember writing about a mania in my notes."

I looked at the whiteboards. "You're a hack," I said. "No, a hack would be exactly what I need. You're . . . you're nothing! I followed your advice. I introduced the lawsuit as an external arc and now I'm nowhere! None of it fits together. I'm done with my interior arc. In ten days, my personal journey will end. But I still need at least another hundred pages or my agent says it's not even salable! And this external arc is worthless. It's all legal stuff. I barely need to do anything to move it forward. It's taken up maybe ten pages out of the last hundred-fifty."

I threw my head into my hands. My hair was long and uneven. The magic haircut had run its course, but I almost couldn't bear to go back to my regular stylist. Even the ruins of Pompeii are more beautiful than if they bulldozed everything and built some shiny new McMansions, right?

"Last year, Tranh got into Stanford and he was only fourth in the class," I said. "I mean, he'd played at Carnegie Hall, but still. I have an agent."

"That's the second time you've mentioned your agent," he said. "Who is she, if you don't mind me . . . ?"

"Linda Montrose. Connor and Pavlovich."

He sucked air through his teeth. "She's good. She represents Marley Trudow and Camille Thorstein and Saul Alleman and—"

"I don't know who any of those people are."

"As a plot twist, not getting into Stanford is too predictable. It's the first thing anyone would think to try—what we'd call 'the first option.' With a novel, you always want to aim for that third option."

"So I'll get in?"

His fingertip hooked the corner of his lip. "I don't know. . . . That's the second option, which is usually just the opposite of the first option. That's fine, but still a bit too expected. That third option is the thing that surprises the reader, but also, in hindsight, feels like it was inevitable."

"Okay. Like what?"

"You could murder someone?"

I got up, smoothed out my skirt and walked to one of the whiteboards. He sprang upright when I wiped my hand across the mass of tiny, cribbed writing on the board.

"Don't worry about it. That stuff was probably all part of the *first* option," I said.

I erased the rest of the board, and wrote:

- Get into Stanford
- Don't Get into Stanford
- Murder Someone

"What else?" I asked.

"I think murdering someone is solid," he said. "You have so many options. Your parents. Your boyfriend. Your new friend Alex. This girl Chelsea. Your teacher. The principal. Even the lawyer. Actually, the lawyer sounds like a very good candidate. I would think about—"

"No. Something else."

He pursed his lips. "Honestly, murder is too perfect. I'd be committing literary malpractice if I gave you any other options."

I clenched my fists and groaned. "Well, what if I get into a car crash?"

"That's too surprising. This story isn't about recklessness and mortality."

Well, at least that got him talking. He still refused to suggest any more options, but he was willing to give comments as I diagrammed my polylemma on the board:

- Stanford defers my application until the spring.

"Too dull," he said. "Doesn't increase the intensity of the action."

- Aakash breaks up with me.

"No one would believe it," I said. "We've just been too perfect together."

- My parents announce their impending divorce.

"You'd need to go back and revise everything, in order to make the father into a more vivid character. And you'd have to foreshadow it by inserting some marital tension and such."

— My family loses all our money and becomes poor.

"Fits the theme of accomplishment and status anxiety and perfectionism, but there's nothing there for *you* to do. That would just be a story about enduring a catastrophe."

— Chelsea sabotages me somehow.

"No! No! This story already struggles with her. She feels more like a hero than a villain. In addition to being perfect, she's also underprivileged? She works okay as a foil—someone who is different from you in a way that illustrates your own qualities—but if you start giving her an internal arc where she agonizes over whether to lose out on her dreams or to violate her moral code, then she'll take over the whole story."

— Arjuna refuses to go forward with the lawsuit.

"That's the stuff. But you can go deeper."

— My mom steps in and terminates the lawsuit.

"Right. That's wonderful. A perfect grounds for murder, I might add!"

— My mom steps in and terminates the lawsuit because she's realized that she's hurting me by teaching me to avoid the consequences of my actions.

"She's doing it for your own good. There it is. That's the knife, twisting deeper."

— My mom steps in and terminates the lawsuit because she's realized that she's hurting me by teaching me to avoid the consequences of my actions and, as a result, the school alters my class rank and notes the disciplinary action in its mid-year report and I don't get into Stanford?

"Hmm," he said. "The consequences don't feel right. Is Stanford really the only thing at stake here?"

— My mom steps in and terminates the lawsuit because she's realized that she's hurting me by teaching me to avoid the consequences of my actions and . . . I try to kill myself.

"Whoa!" He got up from his seat. "Reshma. This is very serious."

I composed myself before turning around. "In the novel," I said. "In. The. Novel."

"Look, let me call some specialists who can intervene and—"

He was dialing someone on his phone. I took out my iPhone and snapped a pic of the whiteboard.

He said, "It's Leo—"

I shouted, "Dr. Wasserman told me to kill my mother!"

His phone dropped.

I waved the picture. "You can't have it both ways. Either it's a novel or it's real. Either the murder is a real murder or the suicide is a novel suicide. And let me tell you"—I twirled my finger around the room—"when they see this place, it's not me they'll cart off to the hospital."

He ended his call. We sat down. I talked to him in a quiet voice. We ran over my hour, but he didn't complain. I don't think he has any other patients. Finally, I patted him on the hand and got up.

He said, "You . . . you're not going to do anything rash, are you?"

"You are never going to see me again. This is a waste of time."

A tear fell from one of his eyes. When I left, his head was in his hands.

FRIDAY, DECEMBER 7

Of course I wasn't actually going to let Mummy shut down the lawsuit. But before I could write it, I needed to talk to her about it. I don't get it. In her life, my mom has always tried to be the best. But when it comes to my future, she's always trying to get me to stand down or back off.

Finally, I cornered Mummy on the couch and said, "You don't really like this lawsuit, do you?"

She looked up. Then she closed her computer. "No," she said. "Not particularly."

"Why?"

"You cheated."

I gritted my teeth. "But I already explained to you that—"

"Enough. I know. I understand what you've said. But I don't believe it was an accident. I heard you complain and complain about that poem assignment. So instead of doing it, you decided to cheat."

My mouth hung open. She'd reached down through my throat, hooked my intestines, and pulled out my guts.

"Why let me go ahead with the lawsuit, if you think I'm so useless?"

"You made a mistake, it's true. And it's my right to criticize you for that mistake. But, in return for that right, we have to support you. I won't ever let you say that we didn't give you everything you needed to achieve your dreams."

After that, I hugged her for a long time and told her that I loved her.

I crept up to my room with tears in my eyes and sat down to write a scene where she yanks the lawsuit away from me. But I couldn't. Maybe that'd be a good story. But it wouldn't be fair and it wouldn't be honest.

I'm honest, dammit.

So here I am, staring at the screen. I have three papers due in the next week. The week after that are my final exams. And, in between, Stanford said it would notify by the fifteenth. I need this story to be finished.

I haven't been able to sleep. I get tired, and I lie on my bed and hover right on the edge of sleep for hours. Sometimes I close my eyes and the barest wisp of nothingness descends on me and then, when I open them, I know that I'm not getting any more, and that, yes, that little bare hint of sleep that you wouldn't even think was enough to support even the most senile old person is gonna have to be what I use to get through the day, and not an easy day, either—one where I nap in class and pay no attention to anything and stumble around like the stoners—but a hard day where I take tests and quizzes and participate in class and try to learn the material because if I don't learn what they teach in class, then I have to come home and teach it to myself out of books and sometimes I'm so tired when I come home that all I want to do is cry because the letters are swimming around and I read the same sentence over and over and over and over and over and over and over and over and then twenty minutes have passed and I can't even tell you the name of the book that's in front of my eyes. And it won't end. It won't. I don't see any ending for any of it.

SATURDAY, DECEMBER 8

've written 15,429 words since my last entry. And exactly zero of them were usable. You should've seen the endings that I spun. Honestly, it started getting weird. A prince swept in through my window. He was riding a unicorn, and he told me that I was the queen of a distant land that needed my help. I got really into it. I wrote three thousand words before I finally read what was spilling out from under my fingertips.

Parents are gone on a wine-tasting tour for the weekend. I'm going to power through and finish this. I haven't slept since Thursday.

MONDAY, DECEMBER 10

Yesterday evening, I was sitting at my computer, typing my way through another fifteen thousand words of false endings—I now have a file called "Useless Trash" on my computer that contains over thirty thousand words of endings for this book. No joke, my wrists ache. This is all that I did for almost sixty straight hours.

I finally got so desperate that I took Wasserman's suggestion. I murdered so many people. I murdered them in the school and at my house and in my car and in Wasserman's office and on Alex's patio and in the hair salon and at the library and at the park and in outer space. I murdered them with poison, guns, pickaxes, shovels, toxic waste, garrote, lead pipes, nuclear bombs, missiles, and genetically modified influenza. I murdered murdered murdered.

And then, finally, I started murdering myself. Hard to do in a first-person, journal-style book. But possible. Very possible. So I wrote notes. A dozen very plaintive suicide notes. And it was dark outside and the rain was coming down and I can swear that I even heard thunder and saw flashes of lightning, even though George tells me that the sky was clear last night.

I was seeing all kinds of things. My computer bulged outward and shriveled down. When I stared at the walls, they separated and moved sideways, forming these infinite concentric circles that I could stare at for ages. When I closed my eyes, my entire vision was filled up with a fiery ring that got larger and larger and larger. Eventually, I became afraid to lower my eyelids. Even though my eyes dried out and got all crackly whenever I moved them, I still refused to blink.

But that meant I couldn't escape from all the other things I was seeing: my chair was floating a few inches off the ground and the table was spinning in slow circles. And still, I kept typing typing typing.

But, after a while, I noticed that all I was typing was *"murder murder"*

I really did try to stop. But when my fingers paused for even a second, the drumbeat continued in my head. If I didn't let my fingers say *murder* then my head would say it:

"Murder murder murder murder murder murder murder murder murder murder murder murder murder murder murder murder murder murder murder"

And I felt like if I typed faster, then my heart would beat faster and I needed to type faster because if my heart and my typing got out of sync, then I'd vibrate so fast that I'd explode.

The edge of my vision was red. My fingers were numb; I had to look closely at them to make sure I was really hitting the keys. Then my feet went numb, too. When I tried to twitch my toe, it moved, but I couldn't feel it move: I realized I was wearing a stranger's feet!

"Murder murder murder murder murder murder murder murder murder murder murder murder murder murder murder murder murder murder"

I didn't *want* to murder anyone, but the word filled me up.

"Murdermurdermurdermurdermurdermurdermurdermurdermurder murdermurdermurdermurdermurdermurdermurdermurd"

I think dropping the spaces is what saved my life. Because, after a while, the word blurred together and faded and became:

"Murdmurdmurdmurdmurdmurdmurdmurdmurdmurdmurdmurd murdmurdmurdmurd"

And *murd* is not a word. *Murd* is nothing. I closed my eyes and looked straight into that burning ring. My hands wouldn't stop moving. I didn't have the strength to make them stop. But I gathered the will to open my mouth and shout, "Hello! Is anyone here? Help! Help! Mummy! Daddy! Help me!"

I had no idea if anyone was around. I hadn't been downstairs in hours. But I kept shouting for help and typing.

"Murmurmurmurmurmurmurmurmurmurmurmurmurmurmur murmurmurmurmurmurmurmurmurmurmur"

But eventually my shouts degenerated into sobs. No one was coming. Soon enough my heart would explode and I'd die. I honestly thought those were my last hours on earth. When I closed my eyes, the ring expanded to fill my whole vision and a booming voice said, "YOUR JOURNEY IS DONE. WHY DO YOU RESIST?"

I wasn't even thinking about what was happening to me or why. All I wanted was for my life to end.

Then I heard someone say, "What's going on? You were shouting."

I couldn't turn. I wasn't even certain the voice was real. But I said, "Help me, please. Call the ambulance. I'm dying."

Footsteps. Then George was next to me. My fingers were still jabbing the keys.

"Mumumumumumumumumumumumumumumumumumumumumumu mumumumumumumumumumumu"

"Reshma!" He interposed his head between my face and the computer screen. His unshaven beard had come in patchily on his normally smooth face, leaving most of his chin bare. "Look at me. What is happening?"

"I don't know." My unblinking eyes were latched onto his. "I don't . . . I need a doctor. . . ." The keys clacked underneath his face.

He put two hands on my shoulders and physically pulled the chair away from the computer. The last word on that screen was an *"mmmmmmmmmmmmmmmmmmmmmmmmmmmmmmmmmmmmmmmmmmmm mmmmmmmmmmmmmmmmmmmmmmmmm"* from where a fingernail caught on the edge of a key.

As I struggled to hold on, something fell from my desk. George's hand swooped down and came up with my Adderall bottle.

"This is almost empty," he said. "How many did you take?"

My fingers twitched, as if they were still typing. But that was only physical. The word was finally out of my mind. My eyes were heavy, and all I wanted was to crawl into bed, but I knew that'd do nothing. Every heartbeat felt like it would send blood gushing out my nose.

"I need to go to the hospital," I said.

"I'm calling nine-one-one," he said.

"No! No! I can drive."

I stood up. Walking on numb feet felt like being whisked around on a magic carpet.

"God, what happened to you?" I could hear the tears in his voice. He snatched my keys from the desk. "Come on," he said.

He put a hand on my waist and I shook him off. "Not crippled," I said. "Only dying. I can walk."

I jabbered nonstop nonsense as he coaxed me down to the car. I kept wanting to touch everything. I remember that I ran my hands through his slightly oily hair like a monkey searching for nits.

He drove like a maniac down the Lawrence Expressway. When I got into my car this morning, the seat and the mirrors were still in the same place, so I guess he didn't even stop to adjust the settings. He kept saying, "You're not dying. You're *not*. Hang in there."

He screeched into the front drive of Stanford Hospital and dragged me into the emergency room. Everything was melting: the whole hospital was a vaguely yellow puddle at my feet.

When we got to the front desk, my head was bobbing back and forth and I was murmuring, "Sorrysorrysorrysorrysorrysorrysorry." I knew that if I shook my head in exactly the right way, I could rocket the blood back into place and everything would be all right.

George talked in a too-loud voice to the admitting nurse. "You've got to get her in right away," he said. "She . . . I think she overdosed on study drugs."

The nurse was a Hispanic woman with two black moles next to her right eye. She glanced over me. I was still wearing my purple polka-dot pajamas. I'd been wearing them for three days straight.

A baby was crying in the corner. An old man was clutching his side. A young girl got wheeled in on a gurney. A nurse took my arm and put a finger to my neck and shined a light into my eye and put the blood pressure cuff on me and then I was sitting in a corner on one of those padded seats and George was next to me and I was rocking back and forth and back and forth and back and forth and he said, "This is good. I'm sure if it were serious, they'd see you right away if . . ."

I felt like my whole body was splitting open and my viscera were flying out in every direction. I wasn't thinking in whole sentences. I wanted this to stop stop stop stop. Then my hands flew out and went into his hair. As I clambered over him, his breathing got shallow and he said, "Easy . . ."

My fingers massaged his scalp and drifted through his curls. That went on for ages and ages. My fingers were shiny with the grease from his unwashed hair.

Then I was sitting on a bed in an examination room. A nurse was looking down at me and getting annoyed because I couldn't understand any of her questions.

George answered:

"No, I don't know where she got them. I think they might be her prescription, but I couldn't find any bottles."

Liar! He was lying. He'd been holding a bottle earlier. Lie lie lie!

"I don't know."

"Pretty happy, I guess."

"No."

"Absolutely not. She's eighteen years old."

"No. You don't have the right to tell them. She's eighteen."

"You can call him in if you want, but there's no crime. The pills are all gone."

Then she left. My fingers and toes weren't numb anymore; now they were tingling. I wanted to lie down and die.

"What's happening to me?" I said.

George threw himself into the chair next to the bed. "You took too many of those pills, obviously," he said. "But your heartbeat and blood pressure aren't at dangerous levels. Aside from monitoring you to make sure you don't have a stroke or heart attack, I don't think they're gonna do anything except wait for the drugs to wear off."

My back hit the butcher paper with a crinkly smack, and I said, "Dammit."

"You could have died."

"Can't they give me a sedative?" I said. "There's time to get at least one night of sleep before school tomorrow." My eyes were twitching constantly. The hallucinations were diminishing, though. Or, at least, when everything throbbed and mutated, I understood that it wasn't real.

"They said it could be dangerous to add more drugs to the mix."

I turned my head. The floor was made up mostly of white tiles. There were some black ones, though. A lot of black ones, actually.

"I have an econ test. I've barely studied."

He rubbed the inside of my wrist. I wanted him to stop—I could feel all of my blood throbbing beneath his fingers—but I couldn't speak: I was focused on counting every single black floor tile. We didn't say anything for an hour. The nurse came in and checked my pulse and then went out.

Finally, George said, "Why would you do this? You were winning."

Five hundred and twenty-nine black tiles. Unless I'd miscounted. Better to start again.

"Shouldn't I at least call your boyfriend or . . . ?" he said. "Someone needs to be here with you."

Black thoughts kept leaking in from the gutters that surrounded the black tiles: Aakash couldn't handle seeing this. He'd leave me. No one could ever love the real me.

"It was an accident," I said. "I was trying to stay awake."

"Don't give me that. You know what this stuff does. You've taken it for years."

The clock ticked above us. Outside, the fluorescent light flickered. The hospital had turned into a palace of sighs.

The words came out very softly. "I'm not good enough."

"What?"

"I work harder than anyone. And there's nothing I won't do. But I'm still not a success. I'm not good enough."

The rubbing of my wrist had become insistent. "Resh," he said. "You're smart. You're pretty. You're wealthy. What else do you want?"

"That's my problem," I said. "I'm . . . I'm broken. You've felt it. Everyone I meet can sense it. I don't care about anyone or anything. All I want is to be better than everyone else. I don't know how I became this way, and I don't know how to change."

"There's more to you than that," George said. "You see things that other people don't."

My stomach wriggled. I extricated my wrist from his grip.

"All I can see now is how I should've been good, kept my head down, and tried to get into Berkeley."

"Berkeley isn't so bad. I got in."

I lifted my head. "What? Have they notified?"

"I mean, I signed a letter of intent. It's done. I'm gonna run for them."

"But . . . your grades . . ." For years, I'd heard George's mom yell at him about his grades. He had a 1.93 GPA—way too low for the NCAA.

He waved his hand. "That's taken care of. Coach told me to take these online classes from Las Vacas College. Yesterday, I signed up for five of them."

I rolled my eyes. God, George had no savvy at all. "Grades on college classes don't affect your high school GPA."

"I dunno. Coach said it'd be fine."

"They'll probably make you do a year of community college. I bet these classes'll count for that."

"If you say so."

"So, Berkeley . . . Maybe we'll see each other there next year."

He shrugged. "Will we? Right now we're in the same house, and we still do our best to avoid each other."

"I don't like to disturb you."

"Remember in fifth grade we had to write a book report on *The Hobbit* and I found out, at ten P.M., that I was missing my book? I asked if I could borrow yours. You'd already finished your report, but you wouldn't give me the book."

"No. I don't remember that at all."

"After that, whenever you left a toy lying around, I'd sneak out and steal it and bury it in the yard."

My eyes opened real wide. "What! That was real?"

"Yeah. You kept telling your mom that someone was breaking in. But she said it was your fault for being messy. Eventually, you became super neat, and I had to stop."

"I knew I wasn't crazy."

"You never thought for even a second that it might be me?"

I stared at the chart of a human chest on the wall. One of those red spindly things was a heart.

"I'm sorry," I said. "We should've been better to you."

My heart was still slamming around in my chest. I wanted desperately to sleep, but knew I'd never be able to.

He wound the curtain into a tight cord. When he let go, it whipped around and around.

"Don't worry about it," he said. "And give yourself a break. I know that good things will happen for you."

I hated that he wouldn't look directly at me. Before, he might not've liked me, but at least he respected me.

"You must be tired," I said. "I'll call an Uber—" Wait. My Uber account was linked to my parents' card. I couldn't imagine what they'd do if they found out about this. "I mean, I'll reimburse you for whatever you spend on a cab."

"You gonna be okay?"

I looked at him helplessly, with eyes big and wide, and said, "Yeah, of course."

The ceiling was still shifting around and weird, hollow voices were still beating in my ears. But as long as I wasn't alone, my filipendulous sanity remained unbroken.

"No, I think I'll stay," he said. "I'm not tired yet."

He was lying. His eyes had a fixed, dull look, the way I bet a sleeper's eyes would look if you pried their eyelids open. I just felt so weak and humiliated. I'd never needed someone else to step in and take care of me before.

Okay fine, I told myself. This had happened, but now I was better, and I was ready to take responsibility for myself again.

"Go home," I said. "Go to sleep. I'll be fine."

He murmured, "Is okay. You shouldn't be alone."

"Get out! I don't want you here!"

He was startled upright. I clicked the button next to the bed and called the nurse and said, "Is he even allowed to be here? Aren't visiting hours over?"

"Come on, what're you doing?" he said. "I don't mind staying."

I turned my head away from him.

After a huge ruckus, the nurse escorted him out, and I was alone.

I lay there for four hours, while that weird tension slowly squeezed my whole body. My thoughts went around in an endless loop of self-hatred. The world would be better off without me. I swore that first thing, once I got out of here, I'd kill myself.

But I couldn't even move! The voices were floating in the thin half-darkness created by the light on the bedside table. Ghostly figures swam down around my head and whispered that my days were numbered and that hell was going to come and take me soon.

Finally, sunlight bled past the edges of my dead eyes and a very wide-awake nurse came in, read my chart, and said that I could go. When I staggered out, George was asleep in the waiting room. I woke him up, and he drove me home. In the car, he didn't betray a hint of annoyance over the way I'd hijacked his weekend. Instead, he was all concerned smiles and solicitous questions.

I wanted to feel grateful to him, but I had no emotions left: I was a candle that'd burned all the way down.

When we got home, my parents still weren't there. They'd left a message on my voice mail: they were gonna stay up in Napa for another few days.

So here I am, back in my room, writing. And in a few minutes, I'll go to school. What else is there to do? I have a test today.

Monday was hell. Halfway through the day, I popped a leftover Adderall. I knew I was flirting with death, but the alternative was to collapse right there in school. Then I went and laid out the paper. Ms. Ratcliffe put a hand on my shoulder and said, "Reshma, what's wrong?" But I shook her off and shot her a *go fuck yourself* stare. That night, I slept for four hours—my first real sleep in three days.

Finally, on Tuesday, my awful condition downgraded from "I almost died last night" to "I just pulled an all-nighter," and I flushed all my remaining pills down the toilet.

That night, I went home at 4 P.M. and fell back onto my bed and woke up at 8 A.M.

Today, I feel . . . surprisingly good.

Stanford notifies in a few days. But who cares? I almost died. It's so hard to wrap my head around. My life almost ended.

So, like, a half an hour ago, a rumor went around school that if you called Stanford's admissions office, they'd tell you their decision. When I heard, I excused myself from class and went to the bathroom and dialed the number. A woman with a tired, harried voice came on. She'd probably been rejecting people all day. I told her my name and then she paused for a second. "Reshma Kapoor . . ." she said. "I'm pleased to say that you've been given an offer of admission."

(Yes, you heard me, dear reader, dear Ms. Montrose, dear whoever. I actually got into Stanford.)

I thanked the admissions woman and ended the call and went out into the courtyard.

Everything was a different color: blue was yellow and red was green. I glided through the crowds of kids. They were already gone and out of my life. My future was expanding in all directions. In fact, at that moment, I was already charting out how my future would go. The next thing to do would be to find some way to skip the horrendous premed classes that colleges make you take in your first year. So as I was walking around in circles I went online and quickly researched those Las Vacas College classes that George had been talking about, just in case.

I guess I was in shock, because it was only then that I realized I could have everything I'd ever wanted. I could be a doctor. I could win a Rhodes Scholarship. I could be elected president. I could do anything. I'd won. I'd won. I'd won.

And I know that when you win by cheating and maneuvering and scheming, it's supposed to taste like ashes in your mouth, but it didn't. It tasted . . . it tasted like relief. It tasted like, thank God, my life can finally begin.

The first person I called was my dad. He was so shocked that he lapsed into Gujarati and rattled off a string of excited words. Then he finally came back to himself and said, "I am so proud of you! Let's have a victory dinner, *ke nahi*? Tonight! Invite all your friends!"

Aakash was next. He was happy for me, but he did say one weird thing. "And what about Chelsea? Did she get in?"

"What?" I said. "Since when do you care about Chelsea?"

"Oh, you know, I was just wondering."

"Yeah," I said. "I don't know about her."

But the truth is that I *did* know. Or at least I suspected. And during our afternoon English class—the one where Chelsea always sat next to me—I kept turning around and trying to catch a glimpse of her face, because I wanted to see what failure looked like.

As class was breaking up, I couldn't hold back. I said, "I got into Stanford."

"Oh!" she said. And then she smiled, and before I knew it, her arms were around me. She held on for three seconds, and when she'd pulled back, her sunglasses had dropped down over her eyes.

"What about you?" I said.

"Oh, I haven't called," she said. "I thought I'd just wait for the letter."

"What?" I said. "I don't believe you."

She laughed. "Oh, Reshma. I suppose I'm just not as brave as you."

My teeth ground together, and I tried to think of something that would pry open her shell and expose the shame that I *knew* was lurking underneath, but before I could speak, she yelled across the room, asking Trina about some newspaper story that was overdue, and after that I couldn't get in another word.

During the gap between classes, I thought of calling my mom, but I didn't, because I wasn't going to pretend like she'd had anything to do with this. If it'd been up to her, I'd be headed for a lifetime of obscurity.

You know what? This means that I beat her. Right? Didn't I beat her? I completely beat her! And unless my memory is really hazy, wasn't she the villain of this book? So if I beat her, then . . . this novel is over.

Which I guess means this is the last paragraph? Hmm, can't a novel just end wherever it wants? Like, right between one word and

Wait, in the interest of reaching fifty thousand words (I'm so close!), I have a few more epilogue-type addenda to yesterday's "ending."

Today, at lunch, everyone was so excited about the early decision results that our barriers broke down, and all the top students just milled around at the edge of the cafeteria.

Jeremy was in at Yale, and Alex was in at Princeton. Her mom had opened the envelope, and Alex hadn't even had to tell people about getting in. Somehow the word got out on its own, and Alex spent the lunch period leaning against a table and shooting me ironic smiles every time some random person came up to congratulate her. I couldn't believe the number of people at the school who knew her name.

Aakash wandered over, too. He put his hand on my waist and gave me a quick kiss. My whole body went tense; we'd never kissed at school before. But no one turned and jeered. It was normal. My behavior was completely normal.

He looked at everyone, meeting their eyes for maybe the first time ever, and said, "Hey. I got into MIT."

My eyes went up and my heart leapt. "Wow."

Then he was flooded with congratulations. Each time he said,

"Thank you," his head dipped lower, and I could tell he was getting a bit overwhelmed. It'd started out feeling natural, but now his touch felt dead and strange on my waist, and when I moved away, his hand dropped down and stayed at his side.

The other schools hadn't notified yet. However, two dozen other people had gotten rejected by Stanford: delusional idiots—none of them were in the top twenty—who thought they were *so* special that they'd be accepted despite not even being the best students at this school. However, a few others—the kids of Stanford faculty or heirs to millions of dollars—had gotten in, too.

But I only cared about one person. As we all volunteered our news, I kept glancing at Chelsea, but she didn't say anything. My body expanded and expanded and expanded.

Finally, she murmured, "I didn't get in. They deferred my application."

Immediately, everyone fell to clucking at her and smoothing her feathers back into place. Alex seemed genuinely distraught: she shook her head and told Chelsea not to take it to heart. Those guys just didn't get it. They had no idea what they were missing. Which I thought was a little insensitive, considering they'd chosen me instead. And anyway, why was Alex trying so hard? I thought she and Chelsea weren't friends anymore.

I looked at Aakash. He'd cared so much about whether Chelsea got in, but he didn't say anything to her.

The commiseration went on for so long that eventually I felt awkward about not joining in, so I said, "I'm so sorry. They might still accept you in April, though."

Tina's head snapped around. She glared at me and said, "Why are you even here?"

"No, no . . ." Chelsea gave me a thin smile. "Congratulations, Reshma. You deserve it."

Alex said, "Come on, Chelsea. Still? She stole your spot."

"Hey," I said. "You know, maybe you should just calm down,

Alex. Because, really, I didn't do anything. If Chelsea had just applied to Harvard like she'd originally intended, she'd have gotten in. In a way, she's kind of a victim of her own hubris."

Tina and Ray and Jeremy stared at me like they couldn't believe what I'd just said. Aakash pulled on my hand and murmured, "Reshma, what's wrong with you?"

What? What was the big deal? Everyone knew I was right. And I could see Alex wasn't offended at all. This was exactly the sort of talk that she liked.

Chelsea stood weakly, looking pale and trying to muster a smile.

"I guess that's sort of true," Chelsea said.

"It's okay," I told her. "I can help you send out more applications. Maybe even do some brainstorming on how to make them stronger."

Chelsea nodded at me, and the two of us shared a moment. Now that I'd won, I saw she wasn't some unearthly perfect. She was just another girl. No better or worse than me.

"Are you serious, Resh?" Alex gave me a hard look.

"What?" I said. "I know how to apply for things. Maybe Chelsea overlooked something that I can spot."

"You're really going to join the charade?" Alex looked from one of us to the other. Then she shook her head. "Oh my God, I can't believe I was ever friends with either of you."

When Alex stormed off, I asked around to make sure I'd heard her correctly. And yes, the wording was strange, but she'd definitely implied that she and I are—or had until recently been—friends.

· · · · · · · · ·

There were shattered beer bottles scattered around the edge of the parking lot, and one pool of greenish glass from where a car had been broken into, I guess. When I knocked on the door of Alex's car, she narrowed her eyes at me for a few seconds, like she didn't recognize me. Then she leaned over. Opposite me, the passenger door opened with a puff of smoke.

I crossed over, but then I wrinkled my nose. If I went in there, I'd smell like marijuana all day. Still, this is what a friend would do, right?

She took another puff from the hand-rolled cigarette—a joint?—but waited to exhale until I'd closed the door.

"All right," she said. "How many pills?"

I shuddered. A weird mass blocked up my throat and my heart began to thud. There was a part of me that wanted to empty my purse and go home with as many pills as I could carry.

"Umm, I'm off that now," I said.

"Come on, you've still got finals."

"Are you . . . are you okay?"

Ahead and below us, the light at El Camino turned red, and cars spurted off the Embarcadero expressway, going left and right, and then diffused through side streets like a pulse of arterial blood.

"You seem upset," I said "Maybe you shouldn't be smoking right now?"

"Are you kidding me?" Alex said. "You're doing an antidrug PSA? You?"

"So, what was that all about? Out in the cafeteria? I don't know if you're aware of this, but you made a bit of a scene."

She snorted. And then the snort turned into a cough. "*Scene* seems like too strong of a word."

"No, I think *scene* is the word with exactly the right amount of emotional weight. What is up with you?"

"I don't know," Alex said. "Just emotional. Things are ending. You know. That sort of thing. High school is over. Et cetera."

"That was awful," I said. "No wonder you hate lying. You're so bad at it."

She narrowed her eyes, and I could tell she was getting annoyed. "I don't know. I guess I haven't really talked to Chelsea since my party. I mean, we've texted a few times, but we haven't done anything together outside of school. And then to see her making an effort to get along with you? I . . . It's disconcerting, you know, to think I'm not friends with her anymore. Someone I spent like every single day with. For years. And now she's gone."

"I never wanted you to stop being friends with her," I said. "Only for you to, you know, be friends with me in addition to her. And perhaps to slightly prefer me over her, although that wasn't a requirement."

She looked up at the ceiling and muttered something. "You are so self-absorbed. You're just awful. Oh God, you are *so* awful."

I would've been offended, except she'd started smiling.

"Look, you guys didn't really understand each other that well," I said. "It's okay. It's nothing to be mad about. You'll make new friends."

"Yeah, but I've known Chelsea for . . ." Alex trailed off. Then she shrugged. "I guess. I mean, of course. You're right."

"Speaking of new friends, you haven't congratulated me," I said. "Even after you e-mailed Stanford, I got in anyway."

The joint had been trailing twin lines of smoke. Alex stubbed it out in the ashtray on her lap. Then she licked the tip of her index finger and her thumb and carefully extinguished the last ember of flame.

"You shouldn't have done that," I continued. "If I were a different kind of person, that would have made us enemies."

She chewed the inside of her lip, then said, "Yeah. I guess I'm a bit surprised you're even here. I thought if I took away Stanford, then you'd be out of my hair."

I was about to categorically deny her and say, *Oh God no, I'm not that kind of person. I'm steadfast and true.* But I stopped myself. Because I'd realized why I'd come up here. This was it: the closing of our friendship arc.

"Well, it's a good thing I have a novel to write, because if I didn't, then you would have no friends. Zero friends. And then where would you be right now?"

"Umm, alone in my car," she said. "Which is exactly where I *wanted* to be."

She rolled her eyes and stowed the joint in a tiny silver case that she kept in her purse. Then she put both hands onto the steering wheel and opened her eyes really wide.

"All I want to know from you is one thing," I said.

"All right, fine!" she said. "We're friends. I'm glad we're friends."

"Umm, my question was going to be: Is the marijuana smell going to stick in my hair?"

When she looked at me, her eyes were red and her expression slack. We sat there for a long time. I tried to roll down the window, but Alex rolled it back up. Finally, she said, "Yeah, I guess. Probably."

"And your usual solution to that is . . ."

"I don't know," she said. "I've never smoked during the school day before. But I figured, I got into college, so . . ." She looked down at the steering wheel for a really long time. I was about to tap her on the shoulder when she shook herself back to life and said, "I think I'm going to stay here for a while."

When I left her, she was still staring at her steering wheel, although both her thumbs were splayed out, just inches away from the horn. I was standing at the intersection when I heard the horn go off. Three short beeps, followed by one long blare that rang out for twenty straight seconds. Pedestrians craned their necks, whirling around and around, trying to figure out where it was coming from. Cars rolled down their windows. One car took off, screeching. And then the horn was silent.

I ended up going back to school. A few people sniffed at me when I passed them, but no one said anything.

One more epilogue-ish chapter:

The thing I like about Indians is that when we're around each other, we have zero sense of decorum. Like, you can ask people about how much money they make, how many stores they have, whether they're underwater on their mortgage, how well their company is doing, why they're not married yet, and all kinds of other things, and it's more or less appropriate.

But even by those standards, my dad's plan for my celebration dinner is pretty tacky. He's booked the private room in the back of a fancy Indian-fusion restaurant, Jantar Mantar, where they mix Indian food with East Asian food and give you tiny portions that are arranged artfully on the plate amidst drizzles of sauce, and he wants to invite a bunch of people: some distant relatives who are studying at Berkeley and Stanford; a first cousin of my mom who runs a pharmacy in Orinda; and a whole bunch of his college friends—which means George will be there, along with his mother and father. And all for the purpose of bragging about how great I am.

I tried to tell him this was completely weird, because it's not like I'm the only person who got into college. At the very least, George got into Berkeley, too. But my dad just said, "Aha! Then it will be a party for him as well!" And he rushed off to call George's dad and tell him.

So, I don't know, I guess that's a bit better. But still, it makes me feel queasy. I don't . . . I don't want all these Indian people crowding around me, congratulating me. I just want to put my head down and finish out high school and go to college and then never think about any of this ever again.

Oh, and when I asked Aakash to come to the dinner, he got all sweaty and weird and said, "No, umm, I don't think I'd feel comfortable."

"Come on," I said. "I need you there. It's just a dinner. You don't need to be nervous."

"I, umm, I can't," he said. "I, actually, it's not that I'm nervous, I just have an experiment to run that day."

I knew he was lying, and I didn't really understand why. "I thought we agreed that you could enjoy these things."

"Umm . . ." He took a long time to answer. "Yes. Things with other high school people. But not with your family. That just . . . It seems really awkward."

"Okay. Stay home," I said. "I guess I owe you one anyway. But you *are* coming to Alex's New Year's Eve party with me, right?"

He nodded his head very quickly, as if he'd say or do anything if I'd just go away.

SUNDAY, DECEMBER 16

The party at Jantar Mantar went all right. Just lots of old Indian people congratulating me and then whispering about me in corners. The only real drama came before it started. My dad had gone ahead to set up the restaurant, and I was left behind, waiting for my mom to get ready.

As we were sitting in the foyer together, getting our coats, I realized that this was the first time we'd really been alone together since I'd gotten into Stanford. Maybe she realized it, too, because she kept her back to me as she wrapped her shawl around her shoulders.

But as we were walking down the front path, I couldn't resist chipping a word off of the block of ice that'd formed inside me. "Well?" I said.

She went around to the front of the car and got in, and I sat there, grabbing the handle every few seconds, until it finally popped open.

"I got into Stanford," I said.

The car started, and cold air blew out of the fans. She looked over her shoulder. We waited until a bicyclist in blue spandex cruised past.

"You thought I wasn't good enough."

"I never thought that."

"No, you did. You didn't even think I should apply."

"Your SAT scores were not on par. I didn't want you to be disappointed."

"You wanted me to set my sights lower," I said. "You wanted me to settle for less than the best."

We pulled out, and she accelerated through the falling leaves.

"Don't you have something to say to me?" I said. This was it. The dénouement. The part where I triumphed, and my mom finally admitted I was right.

But even though the restaurant was ten minutes away, we drove in complete silence. She refused to give me that one single moment of recognition. My mom was just like the rest: the teachers, Vice Principal Colson, the perfects. None of them ever thought I was good enough. But I'd proved them wrong, hadn't I?

I mentally composed and deleted half a hundred cutting remarks. But what was the point? I'd already gotten the last word.

MONDAY, DECEMBER 17

y lawyer, Arjuna, called to congratulate me. After saying he was sorry he hadn't been able to come to the party, he said, "I'm glad that the university ignored these legal issues."

"I think they forgot to Google me."

"Actually, a few weeks ago, I contacted the relevant admissions counselor so I could explain how you'd been mistreated. Even before I called, she knew about the case. And although I tried to put the case into context for her, she remained somewhat hesitant about you, so I was forced to call the provost."

"You talked to the head of the school?"

"No, that would be the president. I spoke to the provost. It was a friendly chat. We've known each other for many years, ever since I chaired the commission to raise funds for a new law school dormitory. After talking to him, everything was simple. He immediately understood that it was very important to the entire Indian American donor community that you be evaluated fairly."

"Really? And he can intervene in admissions?"

"Well, it would have very much hurt our case if you failed to be admitted even after we had your number one spot restored to you."

After a few pleasantries, I got off the phone.

Jesus. Arjuna got me into Stanford just so he could win the case. I hadn't even . . . I couldn't think. My mind was so empty. Everything, all my scheming for good grades and a hook and a high class rank, had been unnecessary. All I'd really needed was Arjuna on my side. I thought of my mother sitting in the car with me two days ago and saying nothing. Had she known? Did everyone know?

I turned around in my chair. Beyond the window, I saw leaves and darkness. Nothing more.

TUESDAY, DECEMBER 18

At Wasserman's office, the receptionist's desk was gone, leaving a bare patch on the carpet. The whiteboards were stacked five deep all around the edges of the front room. But the back room only had one whiteboard, and Wasserman was in the process of erasing it. When he saw me, the eraser dropped from his grip. He rushed over to shake my hand, pumping it up and down, and frantically saying how glad he was to see me.

When I sat down, I said, "It's time. There's something wrong with me. I got what I want, but I just . . . I don't feel right. Fill me with some of that real therapy."

He nodded his head. "The mania is over. You're in the depressive part of the cycle."

"No, that wasn't a mania—I might've been addicted to prescription amphetamines." I sketched out the events of the last month.

"Just ending abruptly? No, no, no! That's a terrible ending! There's no revelation. No surprise."

"You haven't read it," I said. "It actually worked pretty damn well."

"You made extremely poor use of this hospital visit. Your protagonist's delusional breakdown should have come much later, right before the culmination of the lawsuit arc. Then, she could have used the self-knowledge she gained from the breakdown to make a stirring statement to the court, thus neatly merging the internal and external plotlines."

"No," I said. "The novel is over. I finished it. Now we're here to talk about me and my fragile mental health."

Wasserman put his head in his hands. "God, if I'd had your opportunities . . ."

I waited, but he didn't speak. For the first time, I saw the rip in the lining of his tweed jacket and the grayish pallor of his skin.

"Well," I said. "Actually . . . there might be a sequel."

His head tilted upward, and his eyes stared out from behind the lattice of his fingers. "Go on."

"It'd start the day after the other book ends," I said. "And . . . it's about finding some way to keep Stanford from withdrawing her acceptance. . . ." I filled him in about what Arjuna had said, and about the status of my lawsuit and the fights I'd been having with my mom.

"Hmm," he said. "I see now."

"So what do I do? How do I feel better?"

He shrugged. "You don't."

"What?"

"Well, at least not yet," he said. "This is the part where you walk in darkness for a little while and question your values and your sense of self."

"And then?"

"Something happens. You mentioned the lawsuit? Maybe you lose it. Yes, I think you lose it."

"And, what?"

"You mur—"

"Don't even say it."

"Well fine, then," he said. "You . . . you grow as a person and learn to recognize that your cheating was wrong and that it came from a deeply wounded place inside of you."

"Are you kidding?"

He looked around. "Mmm no," he said. "It's pretty much what people expect. Either that, or for you to be given some horrible comeuppance."

"That's absurd," I said. "I won! I planned hard, and I worked hard. And I . . . I did everything. And I won. Why can't people respect that? Are you really telling me that my readers want it to be so neat and simple? That what they want is for me to be transformed into some pathetic whining sorrow-filled regretful . . ." I trailed off into a slurry of exasperated noises.

"Perhaps we should discuss this lawyer figure, then?" he said. "Isn't he the one who ultimately got your character into Stanford? I think you need to sit down and look at your own book. After all, this isn't my story. You wrote it. And what you wrote is the story of a spoiled girl who uses external influence, rather than personal merit, to get into college. And that, I am afraid, is not the sort of character who deserves a happy ending."

I ground my teeth together and tried to think of something to say.

What does Wasserman know anyway? He's not a writer. I'm a bigger writer than him. He doesn't even have an agent.

FRIDAY, DECEMBER 21

I texted Alex to see if she wanted to hang out, and now that Alex and I were friends for real—and not because I was, you know, blackmailing her—she responded by inviting me over. Her house was really different in the morning. Before the sun burned the fog off the hills, everything down below us was wreathed in gray. And even though it was cold, Alex insisted on sitting out on the soggy, leaf-strewn deck in a pair of wrought-iron chairs.

"Can't smoke inside while my parents are here," she said, while she toyed with the cigar in her hand.

"They're here?"

She waved her hand. "Oh, yeah, somewhere."

"And they're okay with the fact that you're out here—"

"Please, you're getting to be as bad as Chelsea," she said.

While she fiddled around with the cigar, I watched the sun etch a hole in the sky.

"Hey," I said. "Do you think you would have gotten into Princeton if you weren't a legacy?"

She tapped the cigar against her palm. "I don't know. Who cares? Do we still need to talk about this stuff?"

"But doesn't it bother you? The thought that you might not really have deserved to—"

Bits of tobacco sprayed out as Alex dropped the cigar onto her lap. "Seriously, Reshma," she said. "If you want to know why people don't like you, it's because there are some basic human concepts that seem to baffle you. Like, let me ask you this, do you understand that getting into a nice college doesn't change who you are as a person?"

"Yes." I frowned. I knew there was only one right answer, but I felt there was more to be said. "I mean, I know everybody is intrinsically valuable and everything. But Stanford students are . . . They're so intelligent and so accomplished, and whenever you hear about someone who—"

"No." Alex picked the cigar up and swept the loose tobacco off her lap. "You're really not getting it, and it's kind of freaking me out. Please tell me you understand that college admission decisions are made by people—human people—based on words that you shot at them through a computer, and that those people have zero ability to reach back through the computer and down into your soul and in any way add or subtract from your intelligence or character or determination or whatever else it is that, in your opinion, makes someone into a valuable person. *Stanford student* is just a label on a jar. You can rip that label off, or maybe forget to put it on, but the contents of the jar stay the same."

Alex was the one who wasn't getting it. Obviously, getting into college didn't change who you were. But . . . what if you knew your contents were high-quality—the best possible contents—but no one else did? What if they treated you like you were a plain old jar whose contents could be dumped out or thrown away or used up? Wouldn't you do anything you could to get the right label? And . . . what if you'd done everything? What if you'd worked really hard? Maybe . . . maybe not in the approved way of working hard. But, you know, still pretty hard regardless. And what if you'd been brilliant and analyzed the labeling system and insinuated yourself into just the right place at just the right time so you got the label you *knew* you deserved? And what if you then discovered that the labeling wasn't like that at all? That it was pointless and arbitrary all along? And that your brilliance and your maneuvering had been completely beside the point?

"Don't just shrug," Alex said. "Tell me you know that."

She drew out a match that was almost as long as her finger and used it to light the cigar, creating great clouds of sweet-smelling smoke in the process.

"You really don't care that you might not have gotten into Princeton if it wasn't for your name."

"No, Resh." Alex coughed out some smoke. "Yes, I was happy when I got into Princeton. But that wasn't because I thought a Princeton acceptance had somehow proved that I'm smart and capable. No. I know I'm smart, and I know I'm capable. What made me happy was that a Princeton degree will make it easier for me to effect the changes that I want to see in this world."

"Changes? What changes?"

"Isn't it obvious?" Alex said. "I mean, I've always been part of the student government. And I'm a debater. I mean, I don't talk about it, because that would be gauche, and I'm not one of those self-righteous activist types, but . . ."

"Oh my God. Are you political? Is that what we're talking about? You care about political change?"

"And you're saying you don't? I mean, look at our racist prison system. It's a national disgrace. And what about global warming? Do you know the likelihood that all of this is going to be underwater in—"

"Come on, please. We cannot be having this conversation," I said, but Alex kept talking, and finally I let her words flow out unimpeded into the valley. She had years upon years of ranting saved up, so we were there for a pretty long time.

SUNDAY, DECEMBER 30

My lawsuit has been getting more and more publicity. The other day, I even got a call from someone at *The Huffington Post* who was thinking about doing a story. For a while, I thought they wanted me to write another column, since it was someone from the Opinions page, but when they started asking me questions, I figured out that it was research for an editorial of their own, so I redirected them to Arjuna's office.

After I learned that I'd only gotten into Stanford because of Arjuna's influence, I considered dropping the lawsuit, but I decided against it. Stanford reserves the right to revoke an acceptance if there's a change in academic performance and dropping ten or more class ranks certainly qualifies. Moreover, Arjuna took this case as a way to make a point, and if I give up the suit, then I might make him angry. Without the lawsuit to protect my grades and without him to step in and intervene with the provost, I'd be totally defenseless.

Tomorrow I'm going to Alex's New Year's Eve party. Normally, my family stays up and watches the ball drop on TV. Then we write our resolutions on 3x5 index cards and burn them in the fireplace. Mummy's resolution is always the same: to lose weight. My resolution is always random scribbles. Making a resolution would mean that I hadn't already been doing everything I could possibly do to achieve my goals.

But this year, Meena won't be around, since she's visiting her boyfriend's family in Wisconsin, so there's no real need to make a thing of it, and when I asked my mom if I could go out to a friend's house on New Year's Eve, she looked relieved that she wouldn't have to spend a whole evening with me.

Even though he'd promised to come, Aakash tried to wiggle out of the party at the last minute, but I finally said, "You know what, Aakash? I actually really like you. You're one of the best things that happened to me in this last year. And I know it's stupid and superstitious, but I want you with me when the New Year starts."

He got red and started sweating, and we made out on my bed for a while, and he finally said he'd go to the party. I think I would've let him sleep with me then, if he'd tried, but he didn't. I really ought to check out his Bombr sometime to figure out the timeline on that. You know, I guess that by this point I could've easily dispensed with Aakash and either written the breakup or happily-ever-after or what have you, but you know what? I like him. He's a good guy. And romantic, too, in his own way.

TUESDAY, JANUARY 1

When I got into Aakash's car last night, he didn't lean over for a kiss. All he said was "Hey."

I asked him whether he was content with MIT or if he'd send out more apps and his only reply was, "No."

The car scurried up the winding, unlit roads of the hill where Alex made her home. Her parents were off skiing in Utah, and they'd left her alone with an unlocked liquor cabinet. In her text to me, she'd written:

> Now that I'm into Princeton I can do _anything_
> I want.

What did that mean? Had she been restraining herself?

I learned the answer when she opened the door. Her normally perfectly tamed blond hair was puffed out in every direction and all the tension was gone from her face.

"Oh my God! Resh! You came! I'm so happy to see you!" Her tight hug forced the breath out of my body. Then her hands started browsing up and down my back. Was this about to become a lesbian thing?

(Wow, wouldn't that be a twist!)

Then she said, "My God, what is this dress made of? It's, like, the softest thing I've ever felt!"

I untangled myself from her hug and gently pushed her back into the house.

Inside, a hip hop beat was bouncing from the speakers and people were swaying on the patio. George was in the kitchen with that girl, Cecily. He looked over at me, and I dropped my eyes. Since the hospital, he'd tried, a few times, to ask how I was doing, but I'd done my best to avoid him.

When I looked up, he'd put his arm around Cecily.

A group of senior girls walked in and tossed their coats into a corner. I knew one of them and I expected her to be surprised when she saw me, but she just said, "What's up?" Had I actually become someone who people *expect* to see at parties?

Aakash and I stood there, awkwardly clutching cups of beer. He touched the cup to his lips but didn't drink. Finally, he said, "How long do you want to stay here?"

"I don't know. At least until midnight."

He gave me a sour look and turned back to his beer.

What the hell was up with him? Obviously, we were going to stay until midnight. This was a New Year's Eve party!

I took out my phone, shielded it from view, and logged into the fake Bombr account that I used to monitor the protected account that Aakash thought I couldn't see. There it was, his latest bomb:

@Korylambis

Yeah, I thought I was okay with what she'd done, but she's been so smug since getting into college.

I shook my head. No. There was no way he could be talking about me. Then I scrolled down until I saw a bomb from earlier today:

What? So much for Aakash being a good guy. I clicked out of the screen and stowed my phone. Did Aakash really think he could drop me as casually as that? His back was to me. I thought about flinging a beer at him. How dare he? To put that on the Internet? To humiliate me in front of God knows how many people who went to our school? I wanted to scream at him, but I didn't. Instead, my body went completely cold. Aakash was my enemy now, and I knew exactly what to do with my enemies.

. . . .

Despite the cool air, everyone was sweating and disheveled. In a corner of the kitchen, Ray and Tina rhapsodized over a green apple.

"This is the best apple that I've ever tasted," Tina said. "Do you think it's, like, genetically modified?"

"Oh my God, let me have another bite." Ray took it and flicked it with his tongue. "Where can we get more of these apples? Do you think Alex's parents would give up their apple connection?"

"I dunno." Tina plucked the apple from his hand and ran her lips over its wounded flesh. "Maybe it's, like, a vintage, twenty-year-old, three-thousand-dollar apple?"

It was strange, I didn't respect them or their opinions at all, but I still experienced a desire to join their inane conversation.

"Can I try it?" I said.

They looked at me with eerie smiles. Their pupils were so wide that their eyes were more black than white.

Aakash pulled on my upper arm. "They're high," he said.

"I know," I said. "I can see more than you think I can."

He stared at me uncomprehendingly.

You know what hurt the most? I was the one who had made the effort. I didn't have to be with him. He'd worshipped me for years. No one would've faulted me for thinking I was too good for him. But instead I reached out to him. Not just that. I allowed myself to like him. Allowed myself to feel feelings for him. Allowed myself to think that he was a good person, and that we were right together.

The apple fell out of Tina's hand and rolled under the dishwasher. They giggled at each other and started humming along with the music. Tina bent down and ran her fingers through the grooves in the tile countertops.

"Those two are being so silly," Chelsea said. "I've been watching them for the last hour. You should've seen them try to peel a banana."

"Chelsea," Aakash said, "I don't think I mentioned it at school, but can I say how sorry I am that you didn't get into Stanford? They made a serious mistake. You, at least, deserved to get in."

What? He was actually angry about the cheating? I got it now. All the jokes about me going to community college. He was okay with things as long as he thought I'd been punished. But now that I was winning, he was angry.

How could I have ever allowed that idiot's tongue into my mouth?

Chelsea's eyebrows went up.

"No, it was my mistake," Chelsea said. "I should have gone ahead and applied to Harvard like I originally intended."

Aakash wouldn't look at me.

"My boyfriend doesn't agree," I said. "He thinks you're better than me."

"I never said that," he countered. "But . . . you *did* cheat."

"It's not that simple," Chelsea said. "Reshma has said all along it was just a mistake. Or an accident."

Wait a second. Was Chelsea going to try to defend me? I don't know why, but her ingratiating smile brought out something hard and cruel inside me. I needed to find out what Chelsea really thought of me.

"Aakash thinks that I don't deserve to go to Stanford," I said.

There was a newly formed tightness around Chelsea's eyes. "I don't know about that," she said. "Maybe . . . I mean . . . you could've . . . no . . ."

She took a deep breath.

I ran my tongue along the underside of my teeth. Dear God. I was going to see Chelsea crack! Where was Alex?!

"I know how hard you worked." My voice was sly and high-pitched. "Don't you maybe deserve it a bit more than I do?"

Her smile rotated slightly. The tensions working within her were written out neatly on her face.

Aakash gripped my arm. "You're being a bitch. Come on. We should leave."

"No, Aakash, if you think she's so great, then let her talk." I turned to her. "Come on, Chelsea. Don't be polite for my sake. This isn't about ego or awards or honors. It's about what we can give to the world. Stanford can give someone a world-class education and an amazing set of mentors and a ton of wonderful research and job opportunities. But aren't those things only useful to a self-directed person? A person who's willing to explore with an open mind? Which of us would've made better use of all those opportunities?"

Chelsea's teeth were ever-so-slightly grinding against each other. I drew in a breath and then let it out, and put on my widest smirk. This was going to be perfect.

"I . . . I think . . ." she said.

And then, her face became different. I mean, she didn't change expressions or anything. Or, if she did, it was only a millimeter of alteration: the slightest relaxation of a few muscles. But some inner light flooded in.

"I wouldn't agree with that at all," she said. "The world needs people who push the limits. Even back in ninth grade, you saw the absurdity of our school and, ever since then, you've done your best to circumvent the system. Yeah, I'm disappointed I didn't get in, and yeah, I think I could've done good things there, but let's face it: you're pretty capable, too, and I think you'll be a great success."

Aakash said, "Don't humor her delus—"

Her gaze flipped over to him, and he was forced back a few paces. His hip hit the counter and a red cup would've spilled if he hadn't caught it in time.

Chelsea shook her head. "No, she deserves everything she's gotten."

Aakash watched her until she disappeared into the hall. He looked a little bit in love with her. I shook my head. I didn't know whether to be disgusted or impressed: Chelsea kept finding new ways to be perfect. She couldn't possibly be like that in private, could she? But who knows, maybe the act never ever stops.

. . . .

Eventually, Aakash settled into a nerd klatch on the patio, and I hung out on the living room couch with Alex.

She was really communing with that couch. Every so often, she'd stop talking and push almost her whole body down into its crevices. I think she wanted to strip naked and roll around on it.

But she kept saying, "You're wooooooooonderful, Resh! I love you sooooo much! I'm soooo glad we became friends! This makes me want to bring back BFFs. Are BFFs still a thing? It should totally still be a thing. I want to be your roommate while we struggle together in our shitty big-city jobs. I can introduce you to your future husband and have *Sex and the City*–type brunches with you and be one of your bridesmaids and . . ."

However, the glow of friendship dimmed a bit when she said,

"Oh my God, isn't Chelsea great? You have no idea how nice she is! I love her!"

As midnight approached, the druggies might've calmed down a little bit, but it was hard to tell, because everyone else had gotten *much* drunker. George came and sat down on the edge of my chair.

"Ironic," he said. "Today, you're the only one who's *not* on drugs."

I shot him a death glare, but he touched my shoulder and smiled a little bit. "So, umm, where's your boyfriend?"

"Outside," I said. "I'm trying to think of the most devastating way to break up with him."

George slid down off the arm of the couch and sat down next to me. We were both flushed and a bit sweaty, and I'd acquired Alex's wild-eyed look.

"Oh," he said. "I guess it had to happen eventually."

"What? I thought we were fine. I *liked* him."

George's breath smelled like whiskey. It was weird to be so close to him, but it was nice to be around a guy who wasn't a two-faced liar.

"Yeah," George said. "No offense to Aakash, but, umm, he seemed like a bit of a goober."

That stung, and my instinct was to defend Aakash and talk about how nice he could be underneath, but then I was, like, wait, what? George was completely right.

"Like that's news to me?" I said. "I never even liked him, but I was on a deadline to find a boyfriend. I was just using him for the novel."

"Oh yes." He snapped his fingers. "The infamous book that almost displaced me from my room. Your novel seems pretty hard on the guys in your life."

My stomach felt wriggly and uncomfortable about George's implication that he was one of the guys in my life, but I decided to let it go.

George continued, "I mean, novels are fiction, right? If you absolutely needed to include a boyfriend, then why didn't you just make him up?"

"I don't know," I said. "I couldn't visualize the kind of guy who'd like me."

"Isn't that the beauty of making stuff up?" George said. "You don't write the guy who wants to get with you. You write the guy who *you* want to get with. Now come on, who's your dream guy?"

Chelsea was standing in a corner, face turned upward, as Jeremy jabbered to her about his astrophysics research. She nodded appreciatively. Did she ever worry that people might not like her?

"I'm all alone," I said. "I hate these people. Why am I here?"

"Hey," he said. "You don't hate me, though, right?"

"But you're here with, uhh, what's-her-face?"

I don't know why I pretended to not know Cecily's name.

"Oh yeah. Cecily and I hang out sometimes."

"And besides, you're secretly one of them, aren't you?"

"Them?"

"Yeah, class president. Going to Berkeley like your mummy always wanted."

"To you, it's always 'them' and never 'us.'"

He rested his chin on my shoulder for a minute. Suddenly, the room lit up with eyes glancing over at us. No one had ever looked at me this way when Aakash touched me. George was wrong. Aakash had very much been part of "us." Well, at least until he decided he was too good for me.

I curled one of George's long strands of hair around my knuckle. It made me feel weirdly powerful. George was actually pretty hot. I'd never let myself think about it. What would it be like to date one of them? I glanced down at my phone and smiled.

Then I threw my head back and shouted: "Twenty seconds left . . ."

Drinks clattered. The music shut off. Someone said, "Wait . . . wait . . ."

Aakash came rushing in from outside. He was scanning the crowd, looking for me, desperate to kiss someone at midnight. I guess even though he didn't like me anymore, he still didn't want to be left out. I caught his eye for a second and screamed, "Ten! Nine! Eight! Seven!"

He raced toward me.

The shout caught on. I went silent, but the countdown bellowed around us. I kept my eyes locked on George, like a snake charmer, and drew closer to him. At "one," my lips touched his. There was nothing studied or controlled about this kiss. His hand passed up my thigh. Our legs got tangled up in each other. He sucked on my lower lip and then lightly bit it. My whole body was hot and then cold. I was breathing in his exhalations. We were locked together for a good ten seconds.

Then someone shouted, "Jesus, it's still ten minutes to midnight!"

My laughter broke off the kiss. George looked a bit confused. But I couldn't stop laughing. It pulsed up my throat and flowed out of me.

And, wow, Alex was making out with Kian in the recliner.

Aakash was standing over the couch. His face was bright red.

I smiled at him. "Was that painless enough?" I said.

His reply caught in his throat.

George grimaced, then moved me around by the shoulders, shifted my weight, and hopped off the couch. Aakash stood there, baffled, for a few more seconds until he disappeared, too.

When the New Year *actually* came, George was in the kitchen, exchanging kisses with Cecily.

A CORRECTION, RETRACTION, AND APOLOGY

From the editors of *The Huffington Post*

Several weeks ago, we were alerted to a well-publicized charge of plagiarism against a previous op-ed columnist, and we were motivated to begin a post-facto scrutiny of this person's contribution to our site.

After careful investigation, we have concluded that Reshma Kapoor's August 29th column, "Double Standards for Asian Students," contained unattributed text and ideas from a number of off-line sources.

. . . .

I knew about the article before I got out of bed, because the phone calls and text messages and Bombr messages and e-mails kept coming in. Most were from unknown numbers, and almost all had an angry, jagged tone. Finally, I turned off my phone and pulled the covers over my head and stayed there. Ever since I was little, I've had this weird intuition that nothing bad can really happen to me as long as I stay in bed. And what with the constant drowsiness now that I wasn't on the Adderall, I felt like I could sleep forever.

Voices rose and fell and drifted out of range, while dread filled the empty space beneath my stomach.

Around sunset, hunger finally forced me to get up.

When I appeared on the steps, three heads rose up in the dimly lit living room. My mom and dad and Arjuna were sitting around the kitchen table. They looked at me, and my mom's eyes narrowed. She said, "Oh," as if I was a detail that they'd forgotten.

I crept into the kitchen and poured myself a glass of orange juice. With one hand on the stone counter to support myself, I drank down the glass. Behind me, the refrigerator door beeped; I'd left it open for too long.

"It was . . . it was an accident," I said. "I must've just remembered those passages. You know I have a good memory. . . ."

My mom shook her head and gave me a look, as if it wasn't even possible to put her disappointment into words.

"I know, *beta*," my dad said. "I told them it is not your fault."

"The facts don't matter," Arjuna said. "Legally speaking, this has no bearing on your case. In fact, even had you *intended* to commit the original plagiarism, it would've had no bearing on our argument, which was, in any case, built on constitutional grounds and . . . It's of no use. Public opinion is not with you. It's become substantially less likely that we'll win the case. We'll need to drop it."

I blinked my eyes. "What? But you said the law's still with us."

"Go back to your room," my mom said. "I'll call you soon."

"No," I said. "You can't drop the case. Not if we can win. That's crazy."

Arjuna put up his hands. "My opinion as both your lawyer and your friend is the same. The school came to us today with a settlement offer: no fault admitted on either side and no recovery of court costs. It will be as if this had never happened. And you should take it."

My dad gave his vague, absent smile, and ran his hand over his head. "Thank you, Arjuna-Bhai, we will discuss this and—"

"No. I'm eighteen. This is my case, and you're my lawyer. And I'm saying we refuse their offer."

"Very well," Arjuna said. "But I can no longer represent you. If you find another lawyer, please let me know and I will transfer your files."

"Fine," I said. "I don't need fair-weather friends."

"Reshma!" my mom said. "Apologize to—no. Don't say anything. Just leave. Adults are speaking now."

"Mummy. Daddy," I said. "Arjuna is old. He is already famous. He only wants to take cases he can win. Somewhere in this country, there's a lawyer who's looking to make a name for themself. He or she will take this case and will win it."

Arjuna had already begun to pack up his suitcase. He smoothed out his white suit and adjusted the strings of his bolo tie. My dad got up, and he hovered nervously by the table, smiling at Arjuna and then at me.

"I'll find the lawyer myself if I have to," I said. "Do you think I can't do it? Really?"

Neither of them said anything. I felt like I was going crazy there, screaming into my kitchen. These were my parents. But they'd become ghosts who puttered around in a half lit room and tried to ignore the voice of truth. As Arjuna drifted toward the door, my mom pulled out her laptop.

"I'm not like you," I said. "I know how to fight."

I was expecting her to explode, but my mom looked up at me with tired, sunken eyes as if she wondered why I still existed.

"Susan Le stole from you, and you let her get away with it," I said. "But I would've fought, and I would've won."

"*Beta*, how many times must we argue?" my mom said. "Everything was done legally."

"I wouldn't have cared about that," I said. "She knew what she was doing. She knew the algorithm was valuable, and that the next generation of smart cars would need it. She convinced you to sign away your rights. And then she made hundreds of millions. That's stealing. And you let her do it."

My mom looked up at me with an openmouthed expression. "Are you still punishing us? I admit that I was stupid. Your father did not want to sign, but I thought the market was going in a different direction and that soon our company would be worthless. I gambled poorly and—"

"No, Mummy." I shook my head. "Stop blaming yourself! That's their rules. They're the ones who say things like, 'Oh, you should've known better.' They're the ones who say some ways of cheating are legal, and some are illegal. But I don't care about blame. No, you made a mistake. So what? People make mistakes. They trust the wrong people. Does that mean they should lose everything? What I'm telling you is that I don't care what the law says. I would've fought her. And I would've beaten her. And you know why? Because I would've done *anything*. And I know you think, Oh, she doesn't know what she's saying. She doesn't know the kind of power that Le has. But I do know. And I would've figured something out. I would've hired private investigators to follow her. I would've broken into her house. I would've gotten thugs to beat her up. I would've framed her for murder. I don't care! I would've done anything before I let her get away with robbing our family! Do you understand? I would've done anything. Anything!"

Her mouth opened and then it closed. My dad had disappeared somewhere. I waited there for a long time, staring down at her. Then she opened her laptop and started typing. I wanted to stand there until she cracked, but I finally decided it wasn't worth my time.

I had calls to make.

MONDAY, JANUARY 14

In between researching lawyers, I've been calling news producers, trying to get them interested in my story. I know that if I'm going to get a lawyer to represent me for free, then I need to be a bankable, nationally known property.

It's interesting. They all want me to be contrite. That's the angle. They want to rehabilitate me. And that's okay. I'll play that game. But only so far. Because if I was really contrite, then I'd have to give up the lawsuit, wouldn't I? And I won't do that. Honestly, I still haven't figured out what I'm going to say about the cheating.

What do you think of me, dear reader? I haven't really addressed the cheating up to now, have I? I've just played it off as an accident: a onetime thing. Honestly, I haven't known how to explain myself. I know that the outside world hates cheating. Even Alex, when I brought it up with her, started spouting that nonsense about how cheaters are really only cheating themselves.

So here's what I'll say: I didn't cheat that often. Just a few times, here and there. And I only did it when my work really needed to be perfect. Most of the time, cheating would be pointless. The standards are so low that all you need in order to get an A+ is to turn in a paper that makes a coherent point. But if you want to publish an essay in a magazine? Or placate a teacher who's got some silly idea about reforming you? Well, that takes something extra.

People say, "Oh, cheating means that deserving people lose their spots, in favor of the less deserving," or "When cheating is rampant, then all that grades measure is who is best at cheating," or "Would you want to be operated on by a doctor who'd cheated their way through medical school?"

And I let them say all those things. I don't argue with them, because what would be the point? They'll believe whatever makes them feel good about themselves. But let's look at the facts:

When Susan Le stole my parents' money, everyone knew what she'd done. She got appointed to their board of directors. She made secret overtures to another company about licensing the technology to them. And then she quietly bought out my parents for pennies before the deal went through. But no one called it cheating. No, they made a movie about her. They gave her awards. They put her on magazine covers and called her a savvy businesswoman.

And when the parents of the perfects pressured Vice Principal Colson to change the way that grades were weighted, so they could get bumped up a few places in class rank, no one called it cheating. They were just good students who'd taken the hardest classes and deserved to be rewarded.

And when Arjuna got me into school with a word, or Alex's money got her into Princeton, that wasn't cheating, either. No one talked about the "deserving" kids who might've lost their place because of Alex. It was just how things are done.

And yet when I take a few words from a now-dead author and use them to create an essay that people can genuinely enjoy and empathize with, then somehow I'm the cheater.

From: Linda Montrose <lmontrose@bombr.co>
To: Reshma Kapoor <rtkap@bombr.co>
Subject: TV Appearance

Reshma,

Got a call from a producer on *The Marshall Henderson Show.* I don't normally handle television appearances—that's the job of our publicity division. I'm forwarding you to an agent in our LA office.

—linda

. . . .

From: Amy Zazo <azazo@conpavliterary.com>
To: Reshma Kapoor <rtkap@bombr.co>
Subject: WELCOME!!!

Hey there!

I'm so happy to discover that you're our client! Just the other day, I was reading some of your public statements, and I thought: "That girl is so articulate. We really ought to see if she's represented."

We're still considering how to manage your story, but I think the Marshall Henderson appearance is a great way to start! The show'll be taped in LA on Saturday, February 2nd. Their advance department will be in touch to schedule your plane tickets and hotel room.

xoxo

Amy

FRIDAY, JANUARY 25

'm going on TV soon, where I'll undoubtedly be jeered and humiliated. But I can't waste another opportunity. I have to use this to advance my story.

Ugh. I thought I was done with this novel. I had a party in my own head when I finished it. But here I am, writing. Mostly, I'm afraid that if I e-mail Linda Montrose and tell her that I can't finish this thing, she'll write back: *Oh, that's all right! Good luck with all your future endeavors!* and say to herself, *Thank God I dodged that bullet.*

I need her more than ever. She's an essential part of my case that I'm not just some soulless study machine. And at least Amy in the publicity department seems to like me: she's been e-mailing me some tips for my upcoming appearance.

But I'm stumped.

Yesterday, I was awake, staring at this screen, until well after midnight. And I got so tired and frustrated that I found myself going through my drawers, not really knowing what I was looking for, until I finally turned it up: a single Adderall that must've slipped out from a pocket at some point. The pill was orange and vaguely rectangular: a 40 mg pill. If I took it, I'd be full of energy for at least the next twelve hours.

I heard footsteps. My parents had their own bathroom, so why would anyone be in the upstairs hall at 3 A.M.?

"Fine!" I shouted. "You can come in!"

The door squeaked open.

"I'm sorry," George said. "It's . . . you're up pretty late. I got worried."

He looked around. I was in the only chair, so he sat quietly on the edge of my bed.

"It's the novel," I said. "It's always the novel. There are too many things to juggle."

I explained to him that I needed to:

- Ratchet up the tension in the story: make things better, faster-paced, more emotional
- Choose the third option, instead of the first, most obvious, option
- Find some way to incorporate me questioning myself

"So all you need is something big and unexpected that makes you question your course?" he said.

"Yep, that's all. And I need it in the next ten days."

I glanced down into the drawer. The orange tablet stared up at me. George made a sound that never turned into a word. I closed the drawer and turned back to my computer, but he didn't leave. When I looked over at him, I saw he'd pulled a calculus textbook off my shelf and was glancing through it.

"Are you in calc?" I said.

"Oh, it's these LVC classes. By the way, coach said you're wrong. I won't have to go to community college."

"Good," I said. "Congratulations."

I stared at him with narrowed eyes, trying to make him leave, but he seemed totally oblivious. My hand was on the drawer.

Finally, he looked up and said, "Hey, this calculus is kicking my ass. You have any of those study pills left?"

"You know I don't."

"Actually, I thought I glimpsed one at the bottom of your drawer when I walked in."

"I flushed them all."

"You mind if I check?"

He went right for that drawer and acted all surprised when he found the pill. As he pocketed it, he brazenly said, "You don't mind if I take this, right?"

And then he walked out.

At least now I know that George isn't too good to take something when he needs it.

SUNDAY, JANUARY 27

know he wasn't right for me, but, in some ways, that makes it even worse that Aakash rejected me. I wasn't even good enough for the guy I'd settled for. Sometimes I can't help scanning his Bombr feed for mentions of me. In the beginning there were a flurry of them, but now they've gotten less and less frequent.

January 10

Had a good result in the lab, but don't know anyone who'd really understand it. Kind of miss having someone to talk to.

@Yablokov

January 14

Yeah, we broke up. No, no, your advice was good, but I just didn't love her.

@Keith292

January 17

I don't know. It's really no big deal. It all feels like it happened a long time ago.

I can't say that I don't miss him. It was nice to know that someone was thinking about me.

SATURDAY, FEBRUARY 2

S ince the studio had no windows and all the lights were on, there was no way to tell if the sun had gone down yet.

The audience was exhausted, disheveled, and wired on too much cheap coffee; they'd been waiting since 4 A.M. They were tourists: men in shorts and women with fanny packs clipped around their waists, and they had close-cropped hair and wide noses and leathery, sunburnt faces. They spoke with a low, huffing sound, like cows snorting through their cud. And they booed when I entered.

The host, Marshall Henderson, is a hulking former football quarterback with a soft, high-pitched voice who makes a living dispensing tough-love advice to people with ridiculous problems. My couch was so plush that I got wedged into the back of the seat, while he sat on a chair that, under his huge frame, looked like children's furniture. He rubbed his jowls and started the hatchet job:

"On the Internet, they've gone through all of your essays, and, my gosh, it looks like you were lifting stuff right and left, weren't you?"

I forced a smile.

Marshall leaned forward and pried into my hesitation. "Come on now. Cheating is nothing new. But when a cheater sues to get her school to ignore the cheating . . . well, that's asking for trouble, isn't it?"

The audience screamed and booed. But . . . one voice, at the edge of the crowd, shouted, "You tell them! Don't be afraid!"

I'd decided that I'd be honest and sincere; hopefully that would drum up a little sympathy. So far I'd had a few lawyers reach out to me, but not many. And the ones I'd heard from hadn't seemed very good.

"You're right," I said. "Initiating the lawsuit was simple arrogance. I'd gone so long without being caught that I was sure no one would turn up the other essays."

Marshall raised his eyebrows. "But you're continuing the lawsuit. The trial's starting later this month, isn't it?"

"Well, the lawsuit isn't exactly about cheating. It's about discrimination. Students cheat. It's unethical, but not uncommon. But why was my paper the only one that was examined? And why did they exact such a severe punishment for a first offense? Sad to say, but my lawyers believe it's because school officials are quick to assume that Asians are cheaters."

Marshall parted his tobacco-stained lips and gave me a xanthodontous smile. "So you're playing the race card, are ya?"

"I was approached by several civil rights groups who thought a suit could highlight important issues. But I wish I'd said no. I can't sleep at night for worrying about all this."

The audience was booing me again. Marshall nodded; this was usual for his show. A man in the front stood up and shouted, "You oughta be ashamed!"

I was amazed: even though it was an act, my cheeks ran wet with real tears!

"I deserve that. I'm a disgrace. Honestly, my family puts up with me because they have to, but . . . I think they'd be better off without me. Everyone would."

Marshall leaned across with his trademark handkerchief: a red Jack Daniel's bandanna.

Then he looked at his audience: "Come on, guys. Open your

hearts. This is only a kid. The real question is: Who's responsible? How did she get that way?"

What was he getting at? All the faces were angry. How was I being set up?

Marshall blathered on about how, during his on-field days, they'd get some rookies who were so wound up on adrenaline—*and other things*, I mentally added—that their moral compasses had stopped pointing at true north.

After Marshall monologued about God and Jesus for a bit, he asked for comments from the audience.

A man who was entirely bald but for a thin fringe of white hair above his ears said, "You're so entitled nowadays. You think you deserve the world. But not everyone can have what they want."

I said something contrite, while thinking: *Maybe you can't get what you want. But I can. You just wait.*

The next man who came up to the microphone said, "The thing no one's talking about is affirmative action. I know plenty of kids who didn't get into any schools, because, look, if you go to the schools, you'll see it: everyone's Asian! They only want to admit Asians!"

I tried being conciliatory, but the man started bellowing. Security guards ran up and pushed the man back. They tore the microphone out of his hand and wrestled him into his first-row seat. Whenever I looked his way, his eyes would narrow slightly and his leg muscles would bunch up under his shorts.

"Seems to me there's a hidden element here," Marshall said. "Who is providing moral guidance to these children?"

The audience roared.

I said, "Uhh, we do go to temple somet—"

Marshall's voice overpowered me. "Reshma, we have someone who wants to talk to you."

The lights dimmed and the band played ominous music. A figure walked through the dark space beyond the curtains at one end of the stage.

It was Ms. Ratcliffe.

Shit.

She shook hands with Marshall and then sat next to me. I scooted down on the couch, but I was trapped between her and Marshall. He briefly introduced her and said that, with the blessings of the school administration, she'd called the show because she was having so much trouble getting through to me.

"During the three years I've known her, Reshma has grown up in reverse," Ms. Ratcliffe said. "She's transformed from an intelligent, thoughtful freshman into a robotic, amoral senior. I—"

"Would you say she's got a demagnetized moral compass?" Marshall said.

"I don't precisely know what's wrong. Reshma, why won't you talk to me?"

Marshall nodded his head. "It's hard to find safe harbor when you have a faulty moral compass."

The audience broke out in a riotous cheer, except for the lone voice, which shouted: "That makes no sense! What is the 'safe harbor' in this analogy?"

Ms. Ratcliffe shifted in her seat and looked directly at me. "I know that cultural expectations differ from country to country. In my travels, I've seen that some cultures don't place as much value on original creative expression. But, it's—"

"In America, that doesn't fly," Marshall said. "You gotta use that moral compass to hack out your own trail."

"Exactly." Ms. Ratcliffe took my hand.

A weird sensation oozed up my arm. I brushed at her hand. "Let go," I said.

Her other hand captured mine. "Please. Talk to us. You've been under a lot of pressure, haven't you? Come on, Reshma, you're an adult now. You can follow your own heart."

For once, the audience was quiet.

"You know," Ms. Ratcliffe said. "I remember one of your

tenth-grade teachers telling me a story: You'd gotten an A minus on a quiz, but you'd misused a few words. A few days later, you came in after class and handed her a thick stack of paper. You'd constructed a hundred original sentences for each word, and you spent twenty minutes begging her to use them as extra credit for the quiz."

I smiled. "And she did."

"Come on, Reshma," she said. "What kind of fifteen-year-old does that? Your teacher told me that when she called your parents to complain about the high-pressure tactics, all your mother wanted to know was whether the words in the extra sentences had been used correctly."

The audience was utterly still. The man who'd shouted about affirmative action was wiping his glistening eyes. Suddenly, the crowd was on my side. I was amazed. Ms. Ratcliffe had whitewashed my black heart with just a few sentences.

This was it. The big and unexpected thing. By slandering my parents, Ratcliffe had won over the crowd. All I had to do was say nothing.

She leaned close to me and a pendulous tear fell down her cheek. "And what about the dictionary?" she said.

A tremor ran through my heart and a light sound escaped my lips. The silence cloaked us. All the muscles in my face were pulling against each other at right angles.

"Please," I whispered. "That story doesn't belong on television."

Ratcliffe bit her lower lip. "In the summer before her junior year, Reshma took the SAT for the first time. Her family was unhappy with her outcome. They made her take an intensive SAT class for the whole fall semester, even though she'd already taken one over the summer. Then she retook the test in January."

Ratcliffe squeezed my hands. I tried to tug them away, but she wouldn't let go.

She continued, "Her score improved, but not by enough, and both times her verbal score was significantly lower than her math score. Which is why her family bought two identical dictionaries."

Sour saliva flooded the back of my throat and I swallowed repeatedly, trying to keep it down.

"Reshma carried one of these dictionaries in her backpack for six months and read it cover to cover. Then she read it again. She made flash cards: thousands upon thousands of flash cards.

"Sometime in March, her mother started taking out her copy of the dictionary, flipping to a random page, and reading out a word. On the few occasions that Reshma was able to reel off the definition, she closed the book and ended the quiz. But if Reshma didn't get it right, then her mother would drill her—going through word after word after word. This would sometimes go on until two or three in the morning."

A woman in the audience cried out. "Lord, no! Poor baby!"

"And when Reshma finally retook the test, her score went *down* by twenty points. She was so distraught that she came sobbing into my office and confided this whole story to me. And you know what? The original score—the one that started all of this—was a seventeen-ten! Higher than seventy-five percent of test-takers."

An audience member broke the silence: "No wonder."

Ms. Ratcliffe pulled on my captive hand. "We know this isn't your fault. Work with us and we'll work with you. No matter what your mother wants, the suit can't continue without your cooperation."

They were all with me. And didn't I deserve it? Hadn't I suffered? This was all owed to me. This was it. This was the thing. The moment. If I let her embrace me, then I'd win. It was perfect. People distrusted Indian parents even more than they distrusted Indian kids. I'd win back their sympathy, and then I'd worm my way around to making them see my point of view on the lawsuit. Hadn't I screamed to my mom that I'd do anything to win? I hadn't known, at the time, that *anything* meant selling her out in front of an audience of millions of people. But so what? Wasn't I prepared to do it? Wasn't I?

Ms. Ratcliffe looked up at me with tear-clogged eyes. Her face was close as a lover's.

I spat on it.

Silence.

She recoiled backward and dropped my hands so she could wipe at the line of spittle that crossed the trails of tears.

The audience erupted with noise.

I slowly turned my head and looked straight at the camera.

"I learned that dictionary cover to cover. Would your kid do that? No. And you know what? Neither would most Indian kids. My mom didn't force me learn it. In fact, she thought it was crazy and self-destructive. She begged me to stop, and even made me see a therapist. But when I told her that I needed her to help me with this, she put aside her own work, and she made the time."

Ratcliffe was wiping frantically at her face. Everyone was yelling. Marshall waved his hands, saying, "Please! Please!"

What was wrong with me? All I'd needed to do was agree with Ratcliffe, and instead I'd made everything so much worse.

I stood up. So did the man in the front who'd shouted about affirmative action. "For those people, that's a deadly insult! That woman's being marked for death!" Then he plowed through the cordon of security guards and rushed toward me. But another person jumped up from an aisle seat in the back. He leapt from the top row to the ground and sprinted, with limbs pistoning and long black hair flowing behind.

I got one close-up glimpse of the onrushing man's face, big and snarling, and then he went down under George's tackle.

Security officers grabbed George and the man. Bodies were everywhere, and the din of the crowd died down, as people struggled to avoid trampling each other.

As he and George were led away, the man raised up a titanic shout: "Go back to where you came from!"

From the couch, Ratcliffe beseeched me with an outstretched hand, but I ignored her.

I strode out of the emergency exit and into the warm Los

Angeles day. I was on a placid back lot: two guys in jeans and tight T-shirts were sipping coffees by the door and exchanging gossip about some new movie.

George was leaning against a concrete bollard. He visored his eyes with his fingers; he'd no sooner focused on me than I was standing next to him. He placed a hand, featherlight, on my back.

"You looked crazy up there," he said. "You only blinked, like, maybe two times in the last three minutes."

"You came all this way. . . ."

He shrugged. "I thought I could manufacture that third option," he said. He exerted a slight pressure with his fingers, pulling me closer.

"Umm, you want to go home?" I said.

He nodded. "The bus'll come right to the gates. There's one in fifteen minutes."

"Oh. I have a return flight."

His hand dropped off me like the last bit of eggshell off a newborn chick. "You better get going."

"You want me to wait with you?"

"Well . . ." He looked around. "Actually, yeah."

So we walked over to the bus stop and waited. His hand brushed against mine for a second. My fingers reached for his, but he didn't take them. He said he'd had the weekend free, and he'd thought I could use his presence: it'd be an unexpected element that I could work into the novel.

I looked up at him. "Oh yeah?"

Then he cleared his throat and tried a few times to say something that eventually turned out to be: "I knew you were going to freak out again."

"I'm not the one who assaulted someone."

"Spitting on someone is definitely assault."

"No, it's not. If I'd wanted to assault her, she'd be assaulted."

He laughed. And when the bus took him away, I sat there and

watched after it. No one had run out of the studio to bring me back. A car was supposed to return me to my hotel, but it never came. And even though I told myself that I'd go home and keep calling lawyers and fighting this thing out, I think I knew at that moment that it was over. I'd been given my chance. I could've done it, and it would've been so easy. Just turn away from the camera, make some sobbing sounds, and collapse into Ratcliffe's arms. So simple. But I didn't. And now everyone hated me more than ever.

SUNDAY, FEBRUARY 3

When I got home, my mom didn't give me a word of thanks for how I'd defended her. In fact, she didn't give me any words at all. Maybe she thinks gratitude is unnecessary, since all I did was tell the truth. She's not media-savvy, so I'm not sure she even understands what I gave up for her sake.

A few calls came in from lawyers. Most of them hemmed and hawed, and when they learned I had no money they retracted their offers to represent me. One even admitted he'd have been willing to represent me on contingency, but now that I'd gone on TV and alienated the entire country, it seemed pretty unlikely that I'd win this case.

In the end, only one lawyer was receptive: Everett Kilming is a tall lanky man with skeletal fingers who has spent years at a famous criminal defense firm, even though he doesn't seem, according to my due diligence, to have ever won a case.

I waffled back and forth about retaining him, but in the end I decided there was no point. Before I went on TV, the case was decent. Now, though, I'd need a pretty good lawyer in order to have a shot. And instead all I have is Mr. Kilming.

Maybe it's for the best. If I'd really wanted to win, then I'd have gone along with Ms. Ratcliffe when she slandered my mother. I still wonder, sometimes, why I didn't do it.

THURSDAY, FEBRUARY 14

Abit disappointed that Aakash and I didn't stay together long enough for me to get a real Valentine's Day. Instead, I spent it lounging on Alex's patio while she smoked a blunt. Her mother leaned out, rolled her eyes, and said, "At least close the door," then did a double take when she saw me. She'd obviously watched my interview.

Alex held a tiny box of Cheez-Its: "This is all I can eat," she said. "Don't let me go and get another box."

She sank into a circular wicker chair and used the blunt to weave a thread of smoke around us. After a while, she asked me about my lawsuit. When I told her that my old lawyer had withdrawn and I hadn't really been able to find a new one, she scoffed at me. "Good," she said. "The suit was ridiculous. You're so much better than that sort of thing, Resh."

Four months ago, Alex would've taunted me about the lawsuit. Now it was just another quirk. Something she didn't agree with, maybe, but not a reason to hate me. I couldn't believe how far we'd come.

"So you ended it with Aakash?" Alex said.

"Yeah," I said. "We haven't spoken since the party."

"Tchyeah, no wonder. Everyone saw you pull that little stunt with George. Is no Indian guy safe from you?"

"I was only trying to torment Aakash. George is not a real option."

"What? Why not? He seemed into it."

George was . . . I mean, it was fine to tease him out as a romantic interest for the sake of my novel, but the reality was simple: George had seen me, pale and sweaty and running up and down the stairs trying to calm down. He'd seen me typing furiously and screaming murder. He'd seen me in the hospital. And no one who'd seen those things would ever want to be with me.

"Just, no."

But she wouldn't stop speculating.

"We're practically cousins," I said. "I mean, not really. But our families are that close. He just doesn't see me like that and, umm, he sort of lives with us . . ."

Alex's eyes went very wide. "Are you kidding?"

I grimaced.

"George? My copresident? The George that I thought I had introduced you to? That George?" She repeated the phrase "That George? My George?" for so long that I wondered if she'd somehow done permanent damage to her marijuana-laden brain, and then said, "Oh my God. Oh my God. Oh my God. This is the most amazing news I've ever heard in my life."

"So you see . . . it's . . . it's pretty impossible, right?"

Her eyebrows went up and she broke into a huge smile. "You've loved him this whole time! And you concocted this 'I'm writing a book' nonsense as a way of turning yourself into someone who could be with him. Which is why you weren't mad at me when I outed you to Stanford. That was never the point. You . . . you're not a robot. You're . . . you're just an awkward, lovesick . . . I . . . this is amazing." She was looking straight up, not even talking to me anymore. "I am so happy right now."

"That's a bit of a stretch," I said. And I really think it is. I'm almost 99% positive that my true aim, all along, has been to get into

Stanford. I mean, you've read the whole thing, right? Doesn't it seem that way to you?

Alex raised an eyebrow and adopted a very arch tone. "Hmm . . ." She stared off into the distance for so long that her blunt fell from between her limp fingers.

"Hey, Alex," I said, tugging her on her arm.

Then she gave an exasperated sigh, stood up, and beat out the burning embers with her twelve-hundred-dollar handbag.

This morning, I was forwarded an e-mail that had a link to a squib on an online gossip site:

THE SPITTER IS DATING HER "BROTHER"

Sources say our favorite rageaholic ex-valedictorian has been seen swapping spit with a member of the track team. Another perfect high school love story? Not quite. We're told that her new squeeze is actually registered—by the school district—as her brother! Yes, folks, the lovebirds live under the same roof and, according to official documentation, the spitter's parents are also the legal guardians of her new squeeze.

Fortunately, this isn't a case of incest. The truth is that, for years, the Kapoors have allowed a friend's kid to use their address to gain access to their school district without paying the hefty surcharge—Las Vacas is one of the most expensive towns in the United States—required to live in it. Apparently, fraud is a way of life for the spitter's family.

. . . .

I called Alex.

"What the hell is this?" I said.

"It's a tiny computer you're holding in your hand," she said. "And it also makes phone calls."

"You told some reporter that something was going on between George and me? What's wrong with you?"

There was a pause. "Wait, that's not exactly what happened."

"You betrayed me." Tears were coming to my eyes.

"Let me explain. Yes, I told a few people that you and George were living together and maybe I encouraged them to spread the word, but I'm trying to help you here, I mean, come on—this is part of my *plan* to get you guys together."

"My life is not a game. It's not a joke. It's not—"

Sobs choked off my voice. I threw the phone into my closet without ending the call and lay on my bed for God knows how long, sobbing extravagantly into my pillow. I don't know, maybe I over-reacted. It's just . . . you can't cry for something like your phony trumped-up lawsuit being dropped or your plagiarism being discovered or your boyfriend dumping you because you're a cheater. No. The only way to bear those things is if you *don't* cry about them. But when you work all year to make a friend, and then realize she doesn't think of you as anything more than an item of gossip? That feels like something you're allowed to cry over.

Eventually, I realized someone was knocking on my door. Sure that it was my parents, I told them to go away, but the knocking kept coming, and I finally heard George's voice saying, "Hey, can I come in?"

But when I opened the door, he just stood in front of me, looming in my doorway. My arms and back felt hot, and I was starting to sweat. I was sure he was there to yell at me. And not just for this, but for all the craziness and stress I'd put him through this year. George didn't deserve this. He deserved to graduate high school in peace.

"I'm . . . I'm sorry," I said.

"It's okay," he said. "I think it might be okay. It's a stupid gossip site. And it doesn't mention me by name. I bet no one in the school's administration will put it together."

"But it *does* happen sometimes, I mean . . ." I felt so guilty. I never should've mentioned him to anyone.

"Actually," he said, "I'm more worried about the part that says we're hooking up."

A thrill went through me. I'd been trying not to think about that. My whole body was rigid. Our toes were just a few inches apart, but his were on one side of the threshold and mine were on the other.

"Yeah," he said. "I hate the kind of guys who spread false rumors, you know, that they've been with this or that girl. That's not me."

"Oh." My mind was blank. He was wearing a Bell High T-shirt, and I was focusing at a black spot—maybe it was ink?—near his left shoulder.

"Which makes me think," he said, "that perhaps we ought to kiss."

"What?"

"Ever since New Year's I've been wanting to kiss you again," he said. "Can I?"

I wiped my eyes. "R-really?"

He put one foot inside my bedroom and then leaned down a few inches. His hair smelled like soap. I tugged on his varsity jacket.

I'd expected a replay of our last kiss: mouths coming together instinctively, knowing exactly what to do. But I guess it's different when you're not fuelled by rage. Our lips met awkwardly. I tried to push my tongue into his mouth, but he resisted a little bit, so our lips just sort of lay there, pressed against each other. This weird awkwardness bubbled up in my stomach. What was supposed to happen now? It was enough to make me wish for the precise, machinelike movements of Aakash's tongue.

My face got hot, and my hand shook. I put it on his waist, just to settle it, and he put a hand on my back, pulling me closer, and I thought, Wow, this is a person. This is a real person who wants to be with me.

My hand started stroking his waist, working its way under his shirt, until I was probing at a thin valley of skin right around his hip-bone, and I couldn't get over the sheer personyness of George. It sounds stupid to say, I suppose, but in that moment he felt very real to me.

I broke away from him. "Wait," I said. "You know I'm only doing this as research for my novel, right?"

"Hmm, I don't know if I buy that," he said. "Does your book really *need* a love interest?"

"There's always a love interest! I mean, that's a really basic part of pretty much every YA novel."

"What is this, a Disney movie? I don't see you as the star of an 'and then she got the guy' sort of story."

He smiled. His two front teeth were caved in a bit and angled backward. I suddenly realized that his parents had probably never been able to afford a visit to the orthodontist.

"Well, tough," I said. "Because I'm under a lot of deadline pressure here, and there's no way I'm doing this if it's gonna be purely extracurricular."

"Fine. Have it your way. But do you think you could give me long hair? Coach makes me keep it short, but I've always felt like I could really rock that Prince Charming look."

"Are you kidding? That'd look absurd."

"Hey, you're talented. I know you can make it sound good. Now get to work."

I laughed, and then let his lips fall onto mine.

SUNDAY, FEBRUARY 24

I don't think we've been apart since my last entry. It's nothing like Aakash. That was so sedate and well-ordered. This is awkward and intoxicating and new.

Yesterday, I crept out to see George compete at a track meet and sat in the stands next to the girlfriend of another runner, and she kept trying to remember who I was. I said, "Uhh, I was the valedictorian. I was in the news." And she was totally uncomprehending. Eventually, she got excited because they thought I was the chick who'd stabbed a teacher, and I had to tell her no, that was one of the chess kids, way back in September.

During his race, I wasn't sure what to do. Everybody was standing up and cheering and the girl next to me pulled on my arm, dragging me upright, and said, "He's gaining, and gaining!"

I couldn't see what was happening: George already looked like he was running as fast as a person possibly could. I could see every muscle in his legs as they sprang forward. But then something happened—he was like a machine that'd been wound up—and everything started moving faster. He sprang past the guys from Menlo-Atherton and then he was way ahead. My throat was hoarse and I was jumping up and down like a crazy person, arm in arm with this girl I didn't know, and it felt like we were at the Olympics even though there were maybe only a few dozen people in the stands.

At the end, George suddenly collapsed on himself and limped off to the side, shaking and winded. He bent over, hugging his knees and huffing, and he seemed so totally self-contained. I wanted to cheer even louder, to force him to hear me, but when he got up, I saw his eyes scanning through the bleachers looking at each person, and for some reason I got shy at the last moment and sat down before he saw me.

But that night he called me up and asked if I wanted to come to a party, and when I asked him what the party was for, he said, "Oh, it's just a party."

"A victory party?" I asked

He didn't say anything, but I could hear him smiling over the phone.

Halfway through the party, we retreated to an upstairs room, and, as much as I enjoyed kissing him and feeling his body press against mine, I spent the whole night in a state of high anxiety over whether he was ever going to let his hands creep down my hip. If he'd tried for it, then I would have had sex with him. I mean, I kind of *had* to let him, right? When I started this book, I made a list of five things that I needed to do in order to write it, and that's the only one that's left.

But, even though we lay there for hours, George never made the move.

With Aakash, I'd *known* how it would go. We were on a very orderly progression. Each date he'd try to get a little further with me. Sometimes I'd shut him down, and sometimes I'd let him keep going. By extrapolating outward from our rate of progress, a person could've run a regression and calculated, to within maybe a week or two, exactly when Aakash and I would've had sex.

George, though, is on a much weirder timeline.

Today, we drove to Ocean Beach and sat on the hood of my car until the sun had boiled away the fog, and it was only blue skies all the way to the horizon line. At some point, George mentioned that he was anxious about the workload at Berkeley, so I explained exactly how to find the easy classes and the easy majors. I windmilled my hands, spinning out a plan for his life, until he laughed and grabbed at them, and I had a weird vertigolike moment where I wondered whether he expected to do it right there on my car. I mean, he was an athlete. That's how they do it, right?

But he leaned forward, never breaking eye contact, and gave me a long kiss, and then asked me to wait a minute so he could get his phone—he wanted to take a few notes on what I was telling him.

Every day, we wait for consequences. Some Silicon Valley police departments have arrested the parents of kids who've used fake addresses to attend their towns' schools, but so far there's been nothing. Maybe Bell has decided, for once in its institutional life, to show some compassion.

E arlier today, I printed out all two hundred and fifty double-spaced pages of this book and gave them to George, with the admonition, "Aside from my psychologist, no one else has read this far into it."

We were downstairs, in his room. I sat on one of the twin beds and he sat on the other one. George wet his index finger with the tip of his tongue so he could flip the pages faster. The sun sank down and puddled through the slice of window at eye level, and still he was turning pages.

I got up and got out of the house. I pulled my sweater tighter around my shoulders and walked through our neighborhood. I decided that I was only going to follow the left-side curb. I'd follow it wherever it took me. So I traced the contours of each cul-de-sac, following the edge of the semicircle, before finally finding myself back on the main street. I did this again and again and again until I ended up at the exit out onto El Camino, where I crossed, and followed the curb to my house.

When I got back to the basement, I asked what he thought, but he said, "Come on, I'm still reading."

Finally, he turned the last page. Then he clipped them back together and returned them to their folder.

"I wonder how it'll end," he said.

"Did you like it?"

"I like you."

"What does that mean?"

"It's a great story. That girl's voice gave me chills. That part about being so desperate to incinerate everyone with your greatness. . . . I mean, you try living in someone else's basement."

My stomach wrenched sideways. "So, now you know everything about me. . . ."

He flipped his hair out of his eyes. "This girl is a great creation. But she isn't *you*."

"But that's still my voice. Those're my thoughts!"

He shook his head. "Nah. They're a few of your thoughts. You're telling a story about a girl who's forced to deal with the fact that she's not really special. And it's a good story. But it's not your story. You're still in the process of becoming an amazing person. And someday you're going to make and do and think some pretty revolutionary stuff."

A tear wavered at the edge of my eye. I scrambled toward him. My heart expanded and expanded until it was enveloping us both.

The twin bed was really narrow, so I ended up wedged between him and the wall, but I didn't mind: it made me feel safe.

He grimaced, pried up my head, and inserted a pillow between me and the wall.

"Better," he said. "Now I'm not worried about giving you a concussion when you start flailing around in the throes of passion."

"Hah." I blinked, and then rubbed my eyes. "You wish."

He started to kiss away my tears, but I pushed him back and stared into his eyes. My left hand, the one that was lying on top of him, was clutching his T-shirt. "It's time," I said. "This is the last thing that I need to do."

I reached for his belt and yanked on the buckle. His hand drifted down, until it lay on top of mine, but I put it on my bare thigh, just below the hem of my skirt, and then went back to work on his belt. It took me a few moments, but I finally pulled out the free end, and—

He was laughing.

"God," he said. "You're so goal-oriented."

"Let's just do this," I said.

One of his hands took mine, and his thumb rubbed the top of my palm. Then he leaned forward and whispered, "We will, but it's not like it's a race," as his other hand drifted upward, along the contour of my hip. When his fingertip worked its way under the seam of my underwear, my leg started to twitch. Although we weren't even really doing anything yet, the feeling was already a little too intense—none of the books or articles or videos had told me to expect anything like this—and I almost wanted him to stop, but then his hand paused, and he said, "Hey, just tell me if anything doesn't really feel like it's working for you."

I looked into his eyes and then touched my lips to his.

I can't say that everything went as smoothly as that—God, I don't even want to talk about the part where I fell off the bed—but it was fun enough.

(Yes, dear safe-sex enthusiasts, we used protection. It was my first time, not George's.)

Well, there we go. That's the big transformation, right? Isn't this the point where this book stops being the diary of a buttoned-down Indian overachiever and starts being the confessions of a wanton American slacker?

But I don't know. I don't feel very transformed. I just feel like myself.

THURSDAY, FEBRUARY 28

Alex has texted me a few times, trying to tell me she didn't understand the legal precariousness of George's situation, but I don't think I can forgive her. I told her something in confidence, and, without thinking about the consequences, she repeated it to the entire world. And you know what? That's not something she would've done if she actually cared about my feelings.

The truth is that our friendship was something I forced into existence. First, I blackmailed her, and then I carefully slipped into the place that was left behind when she started fighting with Chelsea. And I thought that made us real friends, when, really, we were nothing more than two people who sometimes hung out together.

FRIDAY, MARCH 1

Today was the deadline for mailing out the midyear reports: the ones that would give my updated grades and class rank. Before, Arjuna had been talking about filing an injunction to stop them from sending it. And Mr. Kilming, that guy who wanted to represent me, has been calling me for weeks, saying we need to get on this. But I stopped taking his calls, and today when I looked online at the status of my Stanford application, it said the midyear report had been received.

The irony is that my class rank didn't turn out so bad. Everybody did a little slacking off at the end of the year, especially when they heard about how I had fallen. Chelsea even got her first-ever B. According to my calculations, I only ended up number seven. Maybe that'll be enough for Stanford. I don't know. Is that crazy? I mean, I've looked it up online. They're saying that Stanford almost never rescinds applications: once you're in, you're in. And what am I talking about here? Just one D. That's all. One D in one semester. They never even formally suspended me, so my disciplinary record is still spotless.

Even as I write, a wild, crazy hope is beating away in my chest. I mean, I did what everyone wanted me to do: I stopped fighting. And now life is better, isn't it? I'm at peace with my parents. I'm dating a guy who likes and respects me. Won't this come back to me in a good way, somehow? Is there a chance that Stanford will understand?

Everyone knows Chelsea is the valedictorian, even though it won't be officially announced until May 1, which is the deadline for challenging or altering fall semester grades.

WEDNESDAY, MARCH 6

George and I decided to eat lunch outside today, but we had to watch out: dozens of caterpillars were dangling from tiny filaments. George laughed and flicked one with his finger. It went swinging back and forth like a trapeze artist.

"Had to meet with Alex today to finalize the prom arrangements," he said. "I still can't believe she's the one who outed me."

"Really?" I said. "You can't believe it? She's a total bitch. And we've both seen how she can turn on her friends."

Alex had texted me a few more times, but I still hadn't responded.

He shook his head. "I don't know. She apologized, and I said it was okay, but she kept trying to talk about it. Finally, I was, like, 'Can you keep it down? I don't want *everyone* in the school to know where I really live.'"

"Have you heard anything about that?" I said. "Officially?"

He shook his head. "Nope, and let's hope it stays that way."

"You only have to get through the next two months," I said. "In the meantime, just stay away from Alex."

"Yeah, well." He shrugged. "All the prom arrangements are done. As soon as we find a commencement speaker, we'll be settled."

"So Susan Le isn't going to do it?"

"I don't think so," George said. "She's been jerking us around for months. I honestly think she doesn't even want to come here."

"Good. I think I'd have boycotted commencement if I had to spend a half hour listening to her self-important life advice."

"I don't know," George said. "I wonder what she would've said."

"She'd tell us to work hard, follow our dreams, never give up. . . . The regular bullshit," I said.

"Hey, I believe in that bullshit."

"It's stupid. No matter how hard we work, none of us are going to become Susan Le. A lot of kids have dreamt of becoming a nineteen-year-old billionaire. Many of them probably worked hard. But it only happened for one person. What I want to know is, what happens if you fail? You should invite a real failure to come up. A janitor, or . . . or one of the *teachers*. Someone who tried really hard"—I laughed— "maybe someone who really tried to become a rock star. If that person says that they're glad they followed their dreams and worked hard instead of settling for a safer and easier path, then I'll believe it."

George was looking at me strangely. "Someone? And who might that person be?" he said.

I paused. "What? Did I say something?"

He shook his head. "No, it's no big deal. Anyway, she's not coming. We reached out to get Congressman Chao, and he said that if the dates worked, he'd be happy to do it for free."

"Oh, okay," I said. "As long as you're not mad at me for some reason."

He ran his thumb over my wrist, and when I looked down I was startled to see that a caterpillar had landed on it. I jerked my hand free and shook it until the caterpillar flew off into the bushes.

George had a pained expression on his face. "I was going to coax it onto a leaf," he said.

"Oh, come on," I said. "The caterpillar is fine. Insects are very resilient."

G uess the school isn't as on top of their online gossip as I thought, because it took them until now to find that squib about George. Or maybe it took them a while to consult lawyers and draft a proper response. In any case, my parents got a call last night from the school's general counsel. I listened from the top of the stairs while my dad shouted and threatened to sic Arjuna on them again.

Halfway through the call, my mom came upstairs. "They won't kick out George, will they?" I asked.

She looked at me and shook her head, like, how could she expect anything better from me. "So this is how I'm to hear that you and George are seeing each other?"

I was turning distinctly red. "I, umm . . ."

"Your father will do what is needed," she said.

In the morning, George was gone. My mom woke him up early and drove him to his place in Fremont.

"But how will he get to school?" I said.

"The school district was very gracious in allowing him to finish the school year and graduate," she said. "There are buses and trains that he can take in order to come here."

"That'll take hours! This is so unfair!"

"No. It was unfair to let him stay so long in a household with a teenage girl."

I called him to apologize, but he said, "Yeah, it's no problem. Sorry I'm a bit distracted, I'm trying to sort out the bus schedule."

THURSDAY, MARCH 14

The only time I really see George is when I pick him up from the south courtyard and drive him out to Fremont. I'm willing to bring him to my place, but he doesn't ever want to go back there. So we drive aimlessly for hours . . . sometimes all night. My grades are suffering—I got a 79 on my last chem test—but I don't care. Grades from the final semester of your senior year don't matter. Colleges don't care about them, and they don't count for selecting the valedictorian (although it's not like I have any chance at that anyway).

Now that they've seen my midyear report, colleges are making their choices. Today, I got rejection letters from Williams and UCLA.

My parents took the news in strange ways. My mom has obviously given up on me. She keeps asking about my novel. A few days ago, she said, "Maybe we could help you start a restaurant to pay the bills while you write."

The other day, I finally asked her: "Do you think Stanford will revoke my acceptance?"

"Yes."

"Do you think they should?"

She didn't blink for a few seconds. And then she finally said, "Yes."

"What? Really?" I said.

"You have cheated many times," she said. "You are also litigious. And your test scores and grades are not top-quality anymore. Should they accept you just as charity?"

"Please, Mummy," I said. "There's no one listening. It's just you and me here. And between us, you really don't think I'm good enough? You don't think that I . . . that I have something that's not captured by grades? Some kind of inner fire?"

My mom sighed. "I think you are very hardworking," she said. "And you could have made much of that. But you took a wrong path. And it will take many years to get on the right one."

"But that's not what I asked," I said. "I want to know whether, from your perspective, knowing everything you know about me, you don't think . . . that . . . ." I wasn't sure how to put it, because it sounded stupid even to me. I'd asked the question, and she'd answered it.

All of this is making me remember the time that Alex told me *Stanford student* was just a label. But whatever; guess what, Alex? *Bitch* is just a label. That doesn't make it meaningless. For a minute, I was tempted to text that to her, but I didn't. So far, I'd managed to unfriend her with dignity. But if we started lobbing messages back and forth, I'd be giving her another chance to hurt me.

FRIDAY, MARCH 29

Dr. Wasserman thinks I'm trying to speed up the pacing of my novel by using lots of short, far-apart entries. The truth is: I don't care about this novel anymore. Last week, I got rejected by Penn State, Georgetown, and UChicago. All are selective schools, but with my grades and my accomplishments, I should've been able to get into at least one of them. Isn't there anyone who can see my worth?

I don't know. Sometimes I find myself wishing I hadn't given up the lawsuit. I had a chance. Mr. Kilming said so. In idle moments, I sometimes go back to my old ways. Like the other day I got a bunch of certificates in the mail from some online classes I'd taken, and for a moment I fell back to my old self and started scheming about how to get back on top, but then I stepped back. No. I'm different. I'm not the girl who'd do "anything." Ever since the Marshall Henderson taping, I've somehow become the girl with principles. At least a few of them, maybe. Isn't that worthwhile? I mean, come on, someone out there has to be able to see that I've changed.

But I still have Stanford. Maybe they'll allow me to attend. My whole life, whenever I've done something intelligent or bold, I've always thought, Stanford will appreciate this.

THURSDAY, APRIL 11

From: Linda Montrose <lmontrose@bombr.co>
To: Reshma Kapoor <rtkap@bombr.co>
Subject: Please Send Your Current Draft

Reshma,

Could you send me the current draft of your novel? I'd like to see it immediately. Please reply to confirm that you've read this e-mail.

—linda

MONDAY, APRIL 15

In the last week, Amherst, Brown, Yale, Cornell, Sarah Lawrence, Davis, and UC Riverside have all rejected me. With that, I'm done. Seventeen rejections.

And one acceptance.

It's either Stanford or nowhere. My heart spasms every time they send a letter or e-mail, but it's always new-student stuff: pictures of smiling kids in red T-shirts who're taking a break from their microscopes so they can cheer on their school's best-in-the-nation sports teams. I've filled in my notification card and enclosed my deposit check. I should have accepted their offer of admission a long time ago.

But I'm afraid to mail it. What if they claim they never got it?

. . . .

Stanford's admissions office is down a little hall with tan carpets and blond wooden walls. Stone sculptures—busts of famous people—sit on marble pedestals.

When I arrived, a bunch of young people were kicking back at their desks, laughing with one another. The walls were lined with waist-high post-office bins that were filled to the top with manila envelopes.

I rang the countertop bell, and a girl who was only a few years older than me—she had short hair that sprang outward, anime-style—came to the counter. When she looked at me, her eyes narrowed.

When she didn't speak, I said, "Hi! I'm an admit? I'm here to drop off my notification card."

"Oh." Slowly, she smiled. "Oh, that's great. What did you decide?"

"I'm coming here, of course."

A girl in the back area shouted, "Hey, is that one of our admits? Send her back here!" A little cheer went up in the back. I could see the flash of a television and two feet propped on a leather ottoman.

I was about to yell back at them, but the girl stepped between us and yelled that she'd handle it.

"Sorry," she said. "Now that admissions are over, everyone's a bit more relaxed. Hey, I'm Terry. Now what's your name? I feel like I might've been one of your application readers. We always get very proprietary about the kids in our stack."

"Err, Reshma Kapoor."

"Oh." Her fingers were splayed out on the countertop. "It *is* you."

"You know of me?"

"Let's, uhh, let's get ourselves out of everyone's way."

She led me through snaking halls where exposed pipes hummed above chiseled stone walls. When we reached a dead end, she gave me a smile that didn't involve her lips: it was more of a smoothing out and slackening of her face.

"So, what other schools are you considering?" she said. "I heard that Santa Cruz was thinking about taking you. I know they're looking to raise their profile. Did they?"

We had to scrunch up against the side of the hall as a maintenance man trundled past with a cart holding three huge jugs of water. I, umm, how could I handle this?

I took a breath and said, "I already turned down my other offers. Stanford was always my first choice."

"Oh, wow. Well, thanks." She toyed with the neon-pink, green, and blue rubber bracelets on her wrist.

"I'm sorry, are *you* the one who's making the decision about me?"

"I'm assigned to work on the midyear admissions report that we type up for some students. But, of course, the admissions director makes all the final decisions."

"And are you going to recommend . . . ?"

"I really can't say."

We looked at each other for a few moments. I wanted to throw myself to the ground and grab her knees and scream, *Oh Lord, I am forsaken! Please have mercy on me!*

"I know I'd do well here," I said. "All that stuff I did, it was . . . High school can drive you crazy, you know?"

This time, the smile was only a slight expansion of her cheeks. "What do you mean?" she said.

I opened my mouth. What . . . what did I mean?

Looking into her quizzical, albeit extremely patient, eyes, I had a realization: this girl was a perfect.

"It's . . . I put myself under a lot of unnecessary pressure."

"Reshma," she said. "I was a Stanford undergrad, and I hate to break it to you, but the pressure doesn't end. It's not easy to succeed here."

I was drowning in the sticky sap of her earnestness.

"But I've learned the consequences of taking shortcuts," I said. "Who would you rather have? Me? Or someone who still believes they can fall back on cheating?"

"Umm, Stanford has strict policies about cheating. Professors trust us to uphold the Honor Code. And we return that trust. Out of fifteen thousand undergrads and grads, there are only around forty Honor Code violations every year."

"That's crazy."

"I know! It's insane. But, like, everyone here wants to do their best."

"No, I mean you're crazy to believe that. You accepted *me*. And the only reason you know about my plagiarism is that it got into the newspaper. Do you think no one else in your applicant pool got their perfect GPA by cheating?"

Her eyes flicked up, away from me, as if she was unwilling to endure the sight of so much sadness.

"Stanford cares about more than GPA. We want students who stand out—"

"I know. I wrote a novel. I have an agent."

"Oh, you've found a new one?"

And that's when I knew she must've met with my recommenders. A scene—I was sure it'd taken place sometime in the last week—flashed in front of my eyes: Terry and Ms. Montrose are having coffee together, and at first they spend a few minutes clucking their tongues about me and how my case is really so sad and just so indicative of today's overscheduled, overprogrammed, overparented youth. Maybe Ms. Montrose says, *Honestly, her work showed promise, but it wasn't quite there yet, was it?* And then Terry starts tossing Ms. Montrose a few questions about what it's like to be an agent, and, after they've had such a long and such a lovely conversation, Terry shyly brings up her own novel: a comic picaresque about an admissions counselor who spends her days dodging angry helicopter parents and rejecting their insane type-A children. Montrose asks Terry to send it over, but Terry demurs—it's not quite perfect yet.

"You really don't think I have anything to offer, do you?" I said.

"No! That's not true at all! We know that many—maybe even *most*—of our applicants would do very well here. But we have so few spaces in our class. . . ." She looked at her phone. "Well, I have to get back. So good to actually meet you. Though I'd spent so much time with your file that it was like I already knew you."

All those years, I thought I was gaming the system, but I wasn't.

There's no system. There's only a snap glance by some twenty-four-year-old. You either look and sound and feel right, or you don't. And I didn't. I never had, no matter how much I'd tried to fake it. The moment anyone examines me, the illusion falls apart.

"Wait," I said. She turned back a moment too soon—before she'd had time to reassemble her smile—and I glimpsed her neutral expression: the muscles around her eyes were tight as sphincters. Then her smile rippled back to the surface.

I took her hand and forced the deposit envelope into it. "Please," I said. "I don't know how else to say it. This is my future. You've already admitted me. Just let me attend. . . ."

Her hand snapped close, crumpling the envelope. "Why don't you take another look at those other schools?" she said. "Maybe you still haven't yet found the perfect place for you!"

T he prom is coming up. George keeps saying he might not have
time to go, which is absurd, because as one of the senior class
presidents, he helped to organize the entire thing. Today we were
arguing about it over text message.

> I don't mind paying for everything.

Maybe that was a mistake. He took a while to write back.

> We'll talk later.

> Are you seriously not gonna show up for me
> right now?

> I'm supposed to be working right now.

> Come on if you're stringing me along b/c you're
> afraid to dump me then please don't. Just do it.

> My boss is looking at me. Gotta go.

Can you call?

He didn't call. A few hours later, I broke the silence.

Look, I really can't take this.

It's another burden.

Another thing in my life that's going wrong.

It's not all about you.

That slow-motion argument simmered for days.

I was only dating you for the sake of the novel anyway.

Some of us have to work in order to get anywhere in life.

I know.

And while I was trying to think of some way to tell him that I was feeling vulnerable and that I didn't want to burden him, I just wanted, I don't know . . . I just wanted to see him, he wrote back:

I really don't think you DO know or you'd be cutting me a little slack.

And after that, he didn't respond to any more of my texts.

Prom is in a few hours, and I haven't heard from George since my last entry, so I guess I'm not going. This happened last year, too. After buying a dress and finding a date—the son of one of Daddy's college friends—I backed out at the last minute because I had a paper due on the Monday after.

. . . .

Went to answer the doorbell, but I ducked down and leaned against the front door when I saw it was Alex. She shouted: "Come on out, Resh! The limo's here! Whether you like it or not, we're taking you to my post-prom party!"

After a few seconds, she said, "Jesus Christ, Reshma, are you still mad at me over that gossip site? What do you want from me? I already apologized. You should be over this by now!"

She pounded on the door again, and I must've shifted slightly, because she said, "I know you're there! So please, just listen! You know, my plan was actually not a terrible one. You were worried that you and George were too close for him to think of you that way, so I planted the story in order to get his mind working in that direction.

And it worked! Of course it did. I know him. I know how suggestible he is. And I've already told you a million times that I had no idea that George and your family were trying to trick the school district. If I had, I never would've done it." The door shook again. "Now open up and get out here!"

Then I heard another voice coming through the door.

"I hope she's okay," Chelsea said.

"I guess she's moping about George," Alex said.

"Are they broken up for certain?" Chelsea said. "That sucks. They were so cute together. And such a great story, too."

"Whatever," Alex said. "He was just a guy. It's not the end of the world."

"But she liked him. Isn't that the important part?"

"Yeah." Alex paused for a long moment. "I guess she really did."

Then she rang the doorbell a dozen times more. What was this? Had Chelsea and Alex become friends again? I suppose it made sense. Alex always needed a friend that she could torment and mock and feel superior to, and once she'd lost me she'd gone back to Chelsea.

"I'm glad we're doing this," Chelsea said. "Reshma can be a little abrasive, but she's a good person at heart."

"No, she's really not," Alex said. "Has she ever done anything to help another person?"

There was a muffled shout in the distance, and then a car revved up.

"But if you don't like her," Chelsea said, "then why do you hang out with her?"

"You know, it's so typical that you'd equate 'She's not a good a person' with 'I don't like her.' The truth is that I really don't care how good or how evil a person is. If you're electing a president, then you want a good person. But when you're choosing your friends, you just want someone who understands you. So, yes, Chelsea, I do like her. You're the one who doesn't like her."

"What? No. I love that we became friends with her. I think she needed us."

I could feel Alex roll her eyes. "Yeah, keep feeling good about yourself."

A car horn sounded. Alex held down my doorbell for a long minute, and then she and Chelsea ran off. When I was sure they were gone, I went up to my room and cried until my head hurt and my throat was dry.

SATURDAY, APRIL 20

Dear Reshma Kapoor,

We regret to inform you that your offer of admission to Stanford University's incoming class of freshmen is being rescinded as a result of plagiarism charges that arose subsequent to our initial evaluation of your application. Stanford takes academic honesty very seriously. As noted in your admissions packet, even pre-matriculated students are expected to uphold the intellectual and personal integrity that is embodied in our Honor Code.

Your check has not been deposited. We have expedited your review in order to give you the opportunity to accept any other offers of admission that you've been extended.

We wish you the best of luck in your future endeavors.

Sincerely,

Elaine Nguyen

Dean of Admission and Financial Aid

On the way to school, I stopped at a red light, saw the sun shine through the eucalyptus trees, and thought: I'm worthless.

My sister sent me a link to a YouTube video where a baby panda falls off of a swing set. I watched it once, clicked it to replay it, got halfway through, and muttered: "I'm worthless."

I got an e-mail from a Korean ninth-grader who lives in Indianapolis. Her deepest desire is to be a TV news anchor, and she asked me for advice on how to get there. I started writing a long list of questions she should ask herself and steps she could follow, but, halfway through, it turned into: "I'm worthless. I'm worthless. I'm worthless." Writing those words makes me feel better.

I hit SEND and counted down one, two, three, ten, fifteen seconds until my Bombr account would actually send the e-mail, and then clicked UNDO at the last second. Why bother? She'll learn soon enough. Or maybe she won't. Not everyone is worthless. Just me.

WEDNESDAY, APRIL 24

Heard from someone who hadn't spoken to me in a while.

Hey, how you feeling? I'm sorry about Stanford. =[

Just wanted to tell you to stay strong. Life will go on.

I don't know. I just keep wondering what'll become of me.

You're smart. You'll do fine. Some college will want you.

Smart enough for Stanford?

I waited at my desk, phone in hand. Twenty minutes passed without any reply.

No, I know you don't really think I am. You meant I'll do fine like I'll set my sights lower and find my level.

I waited another ten minutes, then wrote back.

> ???

> Hey, really sorry. Don't have time to talk right now. I'm in the lab.

> You're lucky that I'm too tired to add anyone new to my shit-list. Enjoy playing with your test tubes.

He didn't reply.

THURSDAY, APRIL 25

The worst part is that my mom keeps trying to put a good face on things. She's been talking about how these top colleges don't really give a good education anyway, and saying this way I have a year to research colleges and get some work experience and figure out what I really want from life and then I can really be successful right from the beginning of my college career.

For a while, I humored her, saying, uh-huh, all right, cool, that's good, but when she started talking about how maybe this was the best thing in the end and from now on maybe I wouldn't have such high expectations for myself, I said, "All right, Mummy. I get it: I'm nothing special; I'm not going to achieve anything."

"What!"

I was shocked into silence. My mom had spoken so sharply that I could feel the word reverberating back and forth in my ears. And when I opened my mouth—I don't even know what I was going to say—she yelled again. In all our time fighting, she'd never raised her voice before.

"Why do you think I care about smartness or specialness? No, I don't care about that. All I care about is that you become everything you can be. If you were only smart enough to dig ditches, then I would put you into the finest ditch-digging school in this country and would set you up with some fantastic ditch-digging machinery. And if you dug a particularly long and fine ditch—a ditch that you were proud of, then I'd make sure you took pictures of the ditch and sent them to me, and then I'd forward them to your aunts and your grandparents, and even though others might laugh, I would be proud of you. And that ditch would be special to me."

"Mummy . . ."

"I know that when you had those grades of yours, I never boasted of them, I never called attention to them, and I never praised you for them. But that was because I knew—I could sense—that they were not honest. But you should not use that as a way to say I do not care for your accomplishments."

"I'm sorry for that, Mummy. I wish I'd never done it. I betrayed you, okay? But can we please forget it? And can't you just accept me for who I am?"

But my mom's eyes were hard, and I could tell she hadn't heard a thing I'd said. "You know to work," she said. "That is the most important thing. Meena never worked like you did. I remember how you'd work: nights, days, weekends, twelve hours at a time sitting in front of the dictionary. I still remember one night, after I'd quizzed you for several hours, you kept asking me to give you one more word, one more word, and I thought, My God, she will do great things someday."

"It didn't work, Mummy. My score didn't go up at all."

She shook her head. "No. It didn't. So maybe you will not play around with the dictionary anymore. But the thing that made you study that dictionary is also the thing that makes you special."

I shook my head. My mom had never gotten it. If working hard was all that counted, my parents would be richer than Susan Le. The truth is that in this world, you can either be a winner or a loser, and I am obviously one of the losers.

Today, during the morning announcements, Colson said, "I hope you're looking forward to graduation! It's confirmed: Susan Le will be speaking! Many thanks to your class presidents for working so hard to book her. Your other two commencement speakers—the class valedictorian and salutatorian—will be announced on May first."

I sat so still that I could hear the sound that my eyelids made as I blinked. It felt like everyone was looking at me, but I'm sure they weren't.

I calmly got up, left my bag, left my notebook, left my pen, left everything at my desk in the back row, walked past Ms. Lin, and headed into the hallway to text my parents that I needed to speak with them.

SATURDAY, APRIL 27

It's hard to get my parents into the same room nowadays. My mom has a product launch coming up at Google, and my dad is always down at his little office. I guess they've always worked a lot. And it's not like I minded or anything. But it's different when people are working together. It's different when work means getting excited at the dinner table over some breakthrough with the algorithm or over some new deal that they've made. Now it's not like that. My dad is keen to talk about what he's doing with the remnants of their business, but I can tell my mom's not interested. And whenever he asks about her work, she shrugs and says it's going well.

So the only way to catch them was by waking up very early this morning and knocking on the door of their bedroom. My dad was sitting up, drinking coffee, with an iPad resting on his bare belly. And my mom was typing away at her computer. And it wasn't a dark or gloomy day—the room was full of sunlight—but there was a quietness and a stillness there that I didn't like. And I wondered if maybe I'd made that quietness. Had I introduced the fear and distrust into our house, or had it always been there?

When I told them, "I have something to tell you," I don't even want to describe the look my dad gave me. It wasn't even a look, so much as a tensing up of the body, like he was expecting me to punch him.

"Umm, they announced it at school yesterday. Susan Le is speaking at our commencement. . . . Now wait," I rushed onward. "Believe me. You don't have to go. In fact, maybe I won't even go either. We do not need to sit through her speech."

"Ridiculous," my mom said. "I'm the one who put your school in touch with her."

"Why?" I said. "Why would you do that?"

"Because they asked me. Your obsession with Susan has become absurd, *beta*. Why must you always bring her up?"

My dad put his iPad down, then he pulled himself backward until his hairy back had slapped against the wall. "Why all this fighting?"

I didn't even know what to say. They'd been giving me the silent treatment for months because I'd plagiarized a few sentences in an article, but they were willing to sit and listen to the woman who'd cheated them out of millions of dollars? It didn't make sense. None of it made any sense at all.

My mom and dad exchanged weary glances. The harsh morning light made their skin appear wrinkled and discolored. I wanted to keep arguing, but there was no point.

SUNDAY, APRIL 28

I remember Susan Le, you know. She came over a few times, years ago, when she was thinking about investing in my parents' company. I must've been about thirteen, and she would've been about twenty-seven, and I followed her around, asking her questions and telling her about my classes and my good grades and all the contests I was entering. She smiled and asked me questions. She had the straightest black hair—it came down just past her ears—and every time I met her she was wearing tight black jeans and a plaid button-down shirt with a gold pen tucked into the front pocket.

And I remember thinking I'd never before met anyone like her. Until then, there'd been adults and there'd been kids, and adults were dull and impossibly old and they lived lives that had nothing to do with me, while kids were tiny and powerless and played strange games that I didn't understand.

But Susan Le was something in the middle. She had the ferocity and aliveness of a kid, but she existed in the adults' world. When she spoke, they listened. When she moved, their eyes followed her.

· · · · · · · · ·

All day I've been pacing around the house, getting angrier and angrier. I don't know. I just don't know what it is. Something about Susan Le getting chosen for commencement. My commencement. The one I would've spoken at if I'd become valedictorian. Something about Susan Le standing up at the podium where I was supposed to speak.

It's a coup for Bell High. Most billionaires are boring and obscure, but not Le. She's the It Girl. Le is on the cover of magazines. People respect her. They even made a movie about her. Little girls want to be her. Parents tell their children to be like her. She is everything I am not.

And she is a thief.

It's so hard for me to hold that in my head. Everyone else in the world tells me, "No, what she did was fair and legal. Your parents were the stupid ones. They shouldn't have accepted her buyout."

Even Alex claimed not to understand what she'd done.

> Are you really never going to speak to me again?
> Why do you hate me so much?

And I got so angry that I sent her back a long stream of texts ranting about Susan Le until finally she wrote back:

> Whoa whoa, okay. That actually seems pretty sleazy. I never would've tried so hard to get her if I'd known about this! But I still have to ask why you're taking this out on me? Even your mom doesn't seem that mad. She was the one who helped me talk to Le.

I tried for a long time to compose a text that would explain it to her, but I couldn't think of anything to say. Because that's the worst part! Even my parents have accepted the standard narrative. They don't blame her; they blame themselves!

But that's crazy.

Susan Le knew something they didn't! She made a deal they didn't know about! If that's legal, then legality means nothing.

And whenever I think about commencement, I feel like I've divided into two Reshmas. I'll call them reshma and RESHMA!!! and they're having a dialogue that goes something like this:

reshma: Que sera. *Stuff happens. It's nothing to do with you. Just get over it and move on.*

RESHMA!!!: *Do something.*

reshma: *You'll regret it. Your parents will be annoyed with you. And anyway, you're not really the schemer you thought you were, are you? Your machinations have gotten you nowhere.*

RESHMA!!!: *Do something.*

reshma: *Come on. Take a deep breath. In and out. That's it. Now think about this logically. What can you do? She's a billionaire. You're nobody. Worse than nobody. You're a disgrace. No one will listen to you. No one will help you. Even your parents don't want you to do this.*

RESHMA!!!: *Nope, I still want to do something.*

And that's how it's gone, for hours, just back and forth, in the hallways, up and down the stairs, and then out the front door and looping around the pathways and then in through the garden door. I've picked up my phone a few times to text George, but I've always stopped myself. He wouldn't get it. No one would. The thing no one understands about me is that sometimes, once in a while, I get this feeling like I can do *anything*, and that feeling is so rare and so beautiful that it's really hard not to simply surrender to it.

· · · · · · · · ·

All right. It's decided. I was pacing through my room when I tripped and stumbled on a stack of mail that I'd tossed at the foot of my bed.

As I glanced down, one of the letters caught my eye. I picked it up and read it. Then I read it again. After reading it a third time, I called Mr. Kilming and told him I was formally retaining him to be my new lawyer.

M r. Kilming and I were in the principal's conference room. Colson and Ratcliffe and the school's counsel were sitting across from us.

"This is absurd," Colson said. "We've already put your class rank onto the midyear reports. Everything is done."

"I'd prefer that my lawyer go over the calculations one more time."

Mr. Kilming tapped his toe against the hardwood floor. "My client doesn't want any irregularities," he said.

"Fine. It's very routine. We input your name, and the computer spits out a ranking."

Ms. Ratcliffe spoke up. "I can't help but notice your parents aren't here. They're not angry that you dropped the suit, are they?"

I angled my head and made a noise in the back of my throat, like I was gathering a wad of saliva. Her flinch sent her chair rolling backward.

Colson passed over the transcript. Like I said, I was seventh. I could've been even higher, except that Ratcliffe had given me a D–instead of the C or C+ that she'd hinted was possible. The rest of my grades were all right, though: A+ grades in chem, Spanish, Latin, and econ; and regular A's in art history, calc, and government. My other teachers were so happy I wasn't going to be valedictorian that I didn't even have to argue them into giving me better grades.

"Wait," I said, feigning surprise. "What's this?"

Colson raised his hand to the heavens. "Come now. More complaints?"

"You gave me a D *minus*?" I said. "That's absurd. My final paper was A-plus work."

"Well . . . dear . . . you didn't develop your argument very . . ." Ratcliffe stuttered out.

Mr. Kilming and the school's lawyer exchanged grimaces, as if they were sharing some inside joke.

I forced Ratcliffe to fetch her grade books and the whole class's graded papers. Then I went through and disputed every point on every assignment. When she tried to defend a grade, I'd paw through her graded assignments until I found someone who'd got a higher grade and then I'd force her to explain, in detail, how that paper was better than mine.

Sometimes I'd get quiet for a moment and Colson would start to close his laptop, and then I'd speak up again, and he'd groan very deeply.

The sun went down and a dozen school buses passed our window.

They forced Ratcliffe to do all the talking:

"But, dear, this was for your own good. Your argumentation is simply weak. . . . Your papers don't go deep enough. . . . The rest of your life will be immeasurably better because of the skills you've acquired due to my higher standards. . . . No, I will not show you Chelsea's final paper, but it absolutely was an A-plus paper. It was well-reasoned and well-written. . . . Favoritism? This is absurd. . . . Look, Vice Principal, here's Ms. Kapoor's paper. . . . Everyone can go ahead and read . . . No, it's obvious, it's obvious. . . . I won't have you . . . This is absurd. . . . The quizzes, too? No, this is too much. . . . No, I don't have to do this. . . . No, no, no, you already *agreed* to the settlement. . . . No, you can't back out now. . . . My God, fine. . . . No, it's not up to interpretation. . . . The villain is *clearly* Madame DeFarge. . . . What do . . . This is . . . Fine. . . . Fine. . . . Fine. . . ."

We were well into our third hour. Colson's head was sliding out of his hands. Finally, Ratcliffe screamed, "Okay, damn it! Take a B. My God, you *monster*. Just take it and leave me alone!"

Colson shot upright. I leaned back. "You all witnessed it. I want my transcript changed right now. Wait . . ." I ran through some calculations in my head. "No. You should log it as a C plus. I just want the grade that I earned."

Even my lawyer groaned. Colson logged into the database and authorized the grade change while Ratcliffe hovered in the doorway, shooting me sulky looks.

Colson was about to close his computer when I said, "While you're in there, you might as well register these."

I threw the envelope from Las Vacas College onto the table.

"Five classes," I said. "Organic chem, multivariable calculus, intro to physics A and B, and human biology. Five A pluses. Well, one hundreds, to be exact. All completed before January eighth." That was the official closing date for fall semester grades.

Colson's face twitched. "Errm, that's very nice, but you know that college courses don't register on our transcripts. . . ."

My laughter was drawn up from the bottom of a deep well of hysteria—it went on and on and on. "They don't keep you in the loop, do they, Colson? You should go and talk to Coach Masters. He'll know how to handle these grades."

He scowled at me.

I almost left him in the dark. It was his fault if he didn't understand his own school.

But I couldn't resist showing off the secret history that I'd pieced together:

You see, Bell is a tough school. And that makes it particularly tough on student athletes. Coach has had a lot of players who couldn't take up their college scholarships because they didn't have the grades. So, this year, he quietly went and looked for a college that was willing to make a deal. He'd funnel students into some of their extension classes, if they offered him guaranteed A's. Then, he formed a bridge partnership between the high school and the university—one of their professors was nominally a teacher here and one of our teachers was nominally a professor there. They headed up a joint center that they'd ginned up under some little-known provision of the school district's regulations. That means that LVC's classes count as high school classes and that those grades *can* be factored into our GPAs.

Since most of the perfects and study machines didn't talk to the jocks, we hadn't caught on to the scheme. If we had, we would've immediately grasped its implications, and everyone would've taken these classes. As it is, I was the only one who found out—through George—and I was definitely the only one who was crazy enough to sign up for five classes over the winter break.

Colson called up a spreadsheet on his computer.

"My final GPA will be 4.54," I said. "Chelsea's is 4.55 and Jeremy's is 4.53."

I chewed on the inside of my cheek. It'd been hard to give up on the number one slot, but it was also necessary. What mattered was standing up and telling the truth. And people would be much more likely to listen if they didn't think of me as the person who'd stolen the top spot from their golden child. And, whatever, I suppose Chelsea has put in some amount of work over the years and that, on some level, a person could say she deserved to be number one.

He ignored me and kept punching numbers into the computer.

"Do you think I'm lying?" I said.

Ten minutes went past. Sweat poured down his face, and I started to get a sick feeling in my stomach. That had been a cute trick, going with a C+ instead of a B. But what if I'd calculated wrong?

Ratcliffe was stuttering. "I . . . I'll change it . . . a D plus . . . It wasn't C-plus work anyway. I was—"

"Shut up!" Colson said.

I laughed until my chest burned. "Careful. There are lawyers present."

Colson slammed the computer shut. He took in a number of ragged breaths. And then he flipped open his phone. Half an hour later, we were talking to Coach Masters. Colson did a lot of yelling. We were there until well past midnight. But before I left I watched as the computer printed out my report, and then I took a copy and searched down through all the columns until I saw that they'd given me the ranking I wanted.

I'd finally beaten them.

THURSDAY, MAY 2

I expected the universe to cheer for me. But I was wrong.

I suppose this novel confused me. I am the hero of this novel. Well, antihero. Still, I know that if you've gotten this far, then you can't help being pleased at my success. Also, you've heard about Colson and Ratcliffe and Susan Le, and you know that they're awful.

But, in the real world, everyone is hungry for me to fail.

I was in Latin when they announced the valedictorian and salutatorian over the intercom. Some people shrugged and went back to picking at their nails. But, in the back, a clot of smart slackers with lip rings and colored hair muttered sarcastic comments about how they were sorry they'd graduate before the new Reshma Kapoor wing got built onto the school. As I listened, I realized they actually thought my dad had bought the spot. I broke in and tried to explain what I'd done. I figured that if anyone would appreciate how I'd fought the power, it'd be these vaguely punkish kids. But one girl rolled her eyes and said, "Oh. Well, I'm sorry I didn't know there was an award for 'most fake A pluses.'"

Even the perfects have grown colder. When we meet, it's always in the courtyard—never in the cafeteria. The other day, I walked past the old table, just for nostalgia's sake, and saw a pack of juniors—they were obviously their class's version of the perfects—sitting there, chattering away while they looked down on everyone.

When I saw Chelsea, she smiled her beatific smile at me and shrugged, as if to say, *Oh well*. Stanford had wait-listed her in the regular decision period. She got into six out of the ten schools she applied to, but none of them gave her much money, so she's probably going to end up at Berkeley.

Ray went into open rebellion: he kept grousing about how I was a cheat. At one point, I saw him closeted in a corner with Aakash. They both glared at me as I passed. Then, one day, Ray cornered me in the parking lot. We were right between my SUV and a white sedan. He wedged himself in behind me and said, "Look, are they gonna do any more investigating about grade stuff?"

I beeped my door lock. "I don't know. I think they only wanted to untangle the LVC thing."

He put his hand out to stop the door. "Are they going to hand-verify the grades from the computer system? I need to know."

His hand was shaking.

"Oh my God. You altered your grades."

"It's no big deal." He pulled the door open and leaned into the car. "I guessed an administrator's password, then turned a few B's into B pluses, B pluses into A minuses. . . . Stuff like that."

"Jesus. For how long?"

He whispered. "Long enough."

"You could've been first."

He shook his head. "Being first is how you get caught."

"Wait. Without the alteration, what would you have been?"

"I'm smart. Smarter than you. I deserve my rank."

I rapidly blinked my eyes, trying to clear the fogginess. He bowed his head and, no matter how long I stood there, he stayed silent. Eventually, I had to get into my car.

Today, during first period, Colson went on the speaker system and announced a change: this year we would elect our own graduation speakers, rather than having the top-ranked kids speak. He said we should think very carefully about which of our fellow students was most representative of the values of this school, and then fill out the nomination ballots on the school's website.

I knew they'd strike back, but I hadn't expected them to be so blatant.

Before he'd finished, I'd stalked out into the hall and was already dialing Mr. Kilming. This was obviously retaliatory. I'd get an injunction, and then I'd tie them up in so many lawsuits. At the back of my mind, I wondered how long Mr. Kilming would keep working before demanding some money and at what point he'd realize that my parents weren't going to foot the bill for this, but I shoved that thought aside.

I felt a tap at on my shoulder. Alex was standing behind me.

"I'll take care of it," she said.

"What?"

"You can start writing up your speech. I'll take care of it."

"I don't . . ." I looked all around, trying to see if maybe there was an audience, but we were in a completely empty hallway.

"For whatever insane reason, you refuse to believe that I'm your actual friend," she said. "So I will make sure you get elected, and then I'm going to need you to forgive me for that thing with the gossip column. And the thing with Le, too."

"Hmm. I think I will pass on that offer."

"Fine," she said. "Don't trust me. But in a few days I'll expect an apology."

Then Mr. Kilming answered my phone call, and I walked down the corridor to make sure Alex wouldn't hear.

From: Linda Montrose <lmontrose@bombr.co>

To: Reshma Kapoor <rtkap@bombr.co>

Subject: RE: Where are you?

Dear Ms. Kapoor,

I apologize for failing to return your latest call. It's been a very busy time for me at the agency. Actually, that's what I wanted to talk about. I'm afraid that I over-estimated my abilities and took on too many new clients in too short a time. After realizing that it had become impossible for me to zealously advance the interests of everyone who I represent, I was forced to make some hard decisions.

Reading your draft has convinced me that it was a mistake to take on a book that was at such an early stage of revision. Your book needs room to grow and flower without an agent constantly pressuring you to finish. I think your novel will benefit from a long, unforced period of revision, perhaps while you're in college, to give it the maturity and insight that this story deserves.

I sincerely apologize for whatever false expectations might have been inspired by my offer to represent your work. However, given these concerns, I find that I am forced to terminate our agency agreement.

I wish you the best of luck in completing this fascinating book and, eventually, finding an agent who's right for your needs.

Sincerely,

Linda Montrose

I have absolutely no idea how she did it.

. . . .

Results of Election for Student Commencement Speakers:

1. *Kian Gupta (129 votes)*
2. *Reshma Kapoor (101 votes)*
3. Travis McNell (55 votes)
4. Jeremy Ozick (43 votes)
5. Chelsea Blahnik (21 votes)

Congratulations to your two class speakers: Kian Gupta and Reshma Kapoor!

AN INTERVIEW WITH SUSAN LE
ENTREPRENEUR MAGAZINE

Q: And what's next for you?

A: I'm going back to speak at my high school's graduation!

Q: Wow, that must be a trip.

A: You bet. Bell is and was a crazy place. I love it to death: it made me what I am. But it also drives people insane. Remember that girl who spit in her teacher's face? She's the salutatorian at Bell.

Q: Didn't she lose her case?

A: Yep. But she pulled some mysterious shenanigan and got the slot anyway. I'm looking forward to seeing her: she'll be speaking, too.

· · · · · · · · · ·

After reading that snippet of Susan Le's interview, my mind made strange clicking sounds all day. It was so strange that Susan Le, of all people, was the only one who was excited to hear me speak.

TUESDAY, MAY 21

E very time I talk to my parents, there's a weird silence underneath. I told my mom I was going to be speaking at graduation, and she said, *"Acha, acha,"* but I don't know if she really understands what happened.

Honestly, I don't know if I really get it, either. I got caught up in some titanic impulse, and, oh God, it felt amazing to sit across from Ms. Ratcliffe and batter her until she cracked. That was the first time in months when I really felt like myself.

But now what? School is basically over. I sat for my final exams. I probably failed everything, not that it matters. I mean, my almost-perfect grades didn't get me into any colleges, so why should—no, even as I write that, it feels wrong. Too self-pitying, you know? It's something the old Reshma would've said.

I looked up the final exam schedule for George's classes, and I waited for him outside the door of his last final: an American history class. It was the last day of school for seniors, and it felt like we were already halfway through the summer. Air was blowing through the courtyards and corridors, and even though it wasn't that hot, I was sweating. Except the sweat didn't feel dirty or gross; it evaporated instantly in the breeze, and left behind a faint dampness, as if I'd been freshly washed and hung out to dry.

And as I stood outside that door, a stream of people put down their pencils and handed in their tests and grabbed their backpacks. They came out and milled at the edge of the courtyard, standing back so they'd be in the shade of a nearby apricot tree, and chatted with each other. A few nodded at me; I'd seen them at some party George or Alex had taken me to. But they were mostly there for one another.

I could feel life tugging them away. They would keep edging outward from one another, but then someone else would come out, and they'd press tighter together. They weren't even friends, I think. Not mostly, anyway. But they were smiling and laughing, because they felt something. An ending. They'd never be here together, again. One girl, a black girl with poofy, natural hair grabbed a white guy, leaning up to hug him, and the way he stiffened and waited a long second before putting his arms around her made me wonder if they'd ever even talked before. But it didn't matter, because right at that moment they had a connection.

And I felt so . . . desolate.

After my last final, I'd run out without talking to anyone. Alex and I were friends again. I'd gone over to her house a few days ago, and she'd told me how she'd stuffed the online ballot box with fake votes for me. She was unhappy that I hadn't told her sooner about the real situation with Susan Le and my family.

And then we had a nostalgic moment, I guess, where we regretted how it'd taken us so long to become friends.

But even that was . . . I don't know. It was a closed friendship. It was an alliance against the world. It was shared jokes and secrets and mutual enemies. It wasn't anything like what I was seeing in the courtyard. Those kids laughing together and hugging. That sense of community was something different I'd never experienced here.

And meanwhile, I waited for George to come out. He stayed at his desk until the very end, even though he spent the last fifteen minutes staring at a blank question and chewing on his pen. But after the teacher began collecting tests, he wrote a rapid string of words in that empty space and kept writing until she snatched the paper away.

When he emerged, there was a little cheer, and two of his track teammates rushed him and grabbed at him. I waited there at the edges while they wrestled with him, and I thought maybe he was going to let them carry him away from me, but finally he tapped them on their shoulders and asked to be let down. And then he came over to me, and he said hey, and I hugged him, and it felt really natural, except that I hugged him for too long, and when I laid my head on his shoulder, he pulled away.

"I'm sorry," I said. "I shouldn't have pressured you like that."

"Yeah," he said. "It's okay."

Then he looked over his shoulder. His teammates were staring at me like I was an enemy.

I don't know what I expected to happen, but this wasn't it. All I wanted was to feel connected to him again. When he looked away from me, I frowned and said, "Is that it? 'It's okay'? That's all?"

He shrugged. "Come on, Resh."

"I just don't get it," I said. "I made some mistakes, yeah, but you knew who I was. I told you all about myself. You . . . you even read my book. And you said you were okay with that. And, when, you know, you said that stuff about how I'd never had to work for anything . . . well . . . I thought you were the one person who could see the real me."

He blinked his eyes a few times, as if I was a speck he was trying to wash away, and then he stood there in silence for a bit, before he said, "Yeah, I don't know . . . I guess I'm sorry, too. You . . . you maybe need someone a lot different from me. Someone who . . ." He shook his head and shrugged.

"Wait," I said. "What were you going to say?"

"Nothing, it was stupid."

"Come on," I said. "You had something to say." I pointed to his teammates. "You'll probably say it to *them* later. So why won't you say it to me?"

"Resh, I just . . . you're too intense for me," he said. "I'll admit that I liked it at first. But after a while I felt like I spent more time worrying about your problems than about my own, you know? But, hey, that shouldn't . . . that doesn't mean you need to change. I really mean that. You're special. And there's something really . . . it's hard to describe. When I talked to you, nothing felt impossible. And I think you'll eventually find a guy who loves that invincible feeling so much that nothing else matters to him."

And then he hugged me and mumbled about how he was looking forward to hearing me speak at graduation. And then he was gone. Afterward, I went to my car and cried a bit, but not as much as I could have.

It's funny how some things hurt more than others. I suppose I'd always suspected that my real self would be too much for any guy to handle, so when George said those things, it wasn't that bad. Instead, I was like, Oh yeah, I already knew that.

FRIDAY, MAY 31

Graduation is tomorrow, and I still don't know what I'm going to say, but last night I banged out a copy of my speech and today I brought it in so that Colson could review it.

The speech was full of contrition and hope and joy for the future, and when I wrote it, I felt absolutely nothing. I sat there as he read through it, and I expected him to be suspicious about it, but he looked up at me and blinked a little bit and said, "Wow, Reshma. This is . . . Thank you."

I'd included a part in there, just for him, about how happy I was that the school had always had my best interests at heart.

I don't know. It's a good speech, I guess. Short and emotional and true in its own way. And maybe I'll deliver it. But I also have another speech. And another plan. One last plan.

Susan Le is a public figure now: a CEO. And she can't afford to be embarrassed. What would happen, I wonder, if I was to threaten to unveil all of her machinations? What would she give me in order to make that potential embarrassment go away?

Sometimes I can hear myself standing in front of my mom and saying, *I would've done anything.*

There's something very appealing about the word *anything.*

Anything. Anything. Anything. I am capable of anything.

SATURDAY, JUNE 1

My cap and gown were a bit too large. They'd belonged to my sister, although I'd had to take off the valedictorian's fringe that Meena got to wear. Even though it'd been a good tactical move, I still sometimes regretted giving up the number one slot.

A bunch of teachers were ushering the grads into the auditorium. Jumbled together, we streamed through doors and hallways. It was so weird for the whole class to be in the same place.

I bumped into someone, looked up, and noticed that it was a guy whom I'd spent an hour talking to during the first week of school, four years ago. I think his name was Greg. It was a wonderful, deep conversation (by ninth-grade standards). We talked about how weird it was to go from a middle school where we'd been the eldest to a high school where we were the youngest. I left it thinking that I'd made a friend for life. I don't think I ever saw him again after that.

Greg said, "Oh, hey, Reshma! Remember me?"

"Of course!" I said.

We walked abreast for a few moments. "So, we're graduating," he said.

"Yeah," I said.

Silence. Then I sped up and pulled ahead of him.

Alex was wandering around with a cup full of peanuts, and for the first time since I'd known her, she looked distracted and anxious. When I said hello to her, she shook, as if startled, and said, "Oh, hi."

"Those are for her, aren't they?" I said.

Alex nodded. "Room one twenty-eight," she said.

We'd never talked about what I was going to do at graduation, but Alex obviously had her suspicions. She shoved the cup of peanuts into my hand, and we locked eyes. We were standing in the corridor behind the auditorium, and people in caps and gowns were walking everywhere around us. A girl shouted some sort of greeting, and Alex flashed her an automatic smile before turning back to me.

"You, umm, you probably shouldn't do whatever you're planning," Alex said.

"Come on," I said. "You're telling me to back off? You? Really?"

"I'm kind of serious," she said. "I mean, I love the idea of jamming up Susan Le. In fact, I'm a bit annoyed that you haven't included me in the plans, whatever they are. But—"

"Well, I think I'm about to commit a crime. And I thought that with your political aspirations . . ."

She shrugged. "Sure. I appreciate that. But doesn't the same thing go for you? You could be a huge success someday, too. Do you really want to risk that by pissing off a billionaire?"

The cup of peanuts rattled. My hand was shaking. Her confidence meant a lot to me, but I'd gone too far to back down. So all I said was "Thanks," and then I went in search of Susan Le.

. . . .

It wasn't hard to find the room. The vice principal was hovering around just on the other side, like some combination between a prison guard and a butler. He stepped in front, blocking me, but when I waved the peanuts at him, he sighed. "Don't be in there for too long," he said. "We're about to start seating everyone."

The handle to the door of room 128 had a strange heat to it, as if the room beyond was on fire.

A voice screamed, "I can hear you breathing out there, bitch!"

I threw open the door.

Susan Le was a tiny woman—no more than five feet—whose graduation gown billowed around her like the shroud of a ghost. She was sitting in one of the dressing rooms that I guess they use for school plays. She was on a stool in front of a white countertop. And when I came in, she didn't turn around or anything, just kept staring at her own reflection in the mirror. She had a broad metal band on her left wrist. At first I thought it was just jewelry, but then I saw bright text scrolling across its interactive case.

"Where's the twit? I want my fucking peanuts."

I closed the door behind me. "Do you really want them? Or is this a test?"

"Ahh, the spitter," she said. "You came to see me. Isn't that sweet?"

As she spoke, her mouth made strange pouting shapes. She wasn't talking to me. She was talking to her own reflection in the mirror.

"Yeah," I said. "But this isn't the first time we've met. You know my parents, too."

"Of course," she said. "I think I knew that. You're one of *those* Kapoors. Yes, yes, yes. They're good people. Good engineers. I bet they hate you."

"I'm not their favorite person."

"No." Le shook her head. "No, no, no. I bet you're not."

She smiled. Which, of course, meant her eyes drifted to the mirror. She grinned at herself for a moment. Her black hair was cut even shorter now, and it clung to the curve of her skull.

Colson's voice called through the doors, "Excuse me, Ms. Le . . . how's it coming? I'm afraid we only have ten more minutes before . . ."

"Well," I said. "I thought I'd give you a little advance copy of my speech."

I hiked up my graduation gown and pulled the printed-out sheets out of the pocket of my jeans.

"I'm speaking right after you," I said.

Le took them offhandedly and was about to toss them onto the countertop, but her hand paused while her eyes scanned across the page. Then they went across again. She unfolded the paper and began to read. This wasn't the speech I'd given Colson. That speech had been sweet, but this one was venomous.

It was all about the hypocrisy of slamming me for cheating, and then inviting a thief and a cheater to speak at graduation. It detailed exactly what Le had done to my parents and pulled together a few other things I'd found online: cases where she'd forced out founders or violated contracts. Her entire fortune was built on broken promises.

Halfway through, she glanced at me. "None of this is secret."

"No," I said. "But there are cameras out there. And they're going to film you sitting next to the podium while I say this stuff."

She looked at her wristband.

"Colson's right outside," I said. "And we're starting in three minutes. If you escape, I'll give the speech anyway, and everyone will know you ran."

"You think I can't take being embarrassed?"

"I think you don't love it," I said. "In fact, I think you're afraid of it."

She laughed. "Oh, I get it. You know me better than I know myself? Well, come on then. Tell me. What happens now?"

I gulped. I'd gone in there thinking that all I wanted was for Le to give my parents their company back. But in that moment, something very different came out of my mouth.

"I want you to give me a job."

I still can't believe I said it. I have no idea where that came from. I swear that I hate Susan Le. I've always hated her. Even now, when I think about her, hatred boils up out of the edges of my mind. But in that moment, all I wanted was her approval.

"Any job," I said. "Executive assistant. Trainee. I don't know. But something where I can learn from you."

She held my speech between the tips of her thumb and forefinger, as if it was something dirty and smelly. "Really?" she said. "After all this, you want to work with me?"

"I read that interview with you in *Entrepreneur*. You see a bit of yourself in me. And I think it's the part of yourself that no one else sees or acknowledges. They all want to pretend you're a visionary or a hard worker, and maybe you are. But there's another part: the ruthless part."

"This is pathetic."

"I know. I'm sad. I'm pathetic. I'm stupid. But I'm also ruthless. And that counts for more than the other stuff. You're the one who taught me that."

As I said the words, they sounded so right, like I'd finally unlocked the secret of myself. You know, you write a whole novel, trying to figure out who you are, when really it's so simple. The only thing that makes me better than other people is the fact that I'll do anything, and they won't. I tried being noble—tried sparing my mom—and all I created was a vacuum. The absence of being. Without my ruthlessness, I was nothing.

Susan Le ripped up my speech and ripped it up again and again and again until it was a collection of inch-long squares that she very carefully deposited in her purse.

"You know," Le said. "When I went here, I hated everyone.

Every single person. They were so stupid. So compelled by petty bullshit. Even the smart ones were stupid. And I hated them the most, because they spent all their time and all their brainpower doing exactly what they were supposed to do. That was the most annoying thing about them. The sheer waste of it all. And I kept thinking that as soon as I got out of here, it'd be different, but it wasn't.

"Your mom and dad were just the same. I told them they were sitting on a billion-dollar idea, but they didn't believe me. They thought it had no commercial applications. They were good engineers, but they had no vision. They kept going behind my back, trying to unload the company before I could build a demand for what we were selling. If it'd been up to them, we'd all have made pennies. So yes, I forced them out. It was one of the best decisions I ever made. And if you want to bring it up again, I'll be happy to defend myself to whoever wants to know the details."

She turned back to the mirror and tucked a strand of hair behind her ear.

"Please," I said.

Her wristband lit up, and she tapped a short message into it.

"You're lonely," I said. "I know you're lonely. Can't you see what a concession I'm making? You harmed me and my family, but I'm willing to overlook that, because I can see that we need each other. And yes, maybe I'm not as brilliant as you. Maybe I'm asking for something I don't deserve. But you have to see that you're not going to find another person like me."

"Hey, get in here!" she shouted.

The door flew open, and I whirled around. Did she have security somewhere?

"I don't need her anymore," Le said.

And Vice Principal Colson grabbed me by the arm and escorted me out.

· · · · · · · · ·

The crowd filled the auditorium. Some kids had brought their entire extended families: there were whole little sections that stood together and chattered together and dressed alike. I'd avoided looking for my parents in the stands. I didn't want to think about them watching as people booed me.

Kian was sitting on one side of me and Chelsea was on the other. Chelsea caught me looking at her, then reached over and squeezed my hand. Hers was clammy and cold. In fact, her whole body had a pale sheen.

When Colson began talking, the room fell quiet: I could hear the commuters honking at each other out on El Camino.

I was about to graduate.

I still couldn't believe I'd asked Susan Le to hire me. And I couldn't believe she'd turned me down. How could she do it? What I'd wanted was so tiny. She even could've lied and made nice in that moment and reneged on her promise later. But she hadn't bothered. To her, I wasn't even a monster; I was completely insignificant.

Susan Le came onstage to applause that went on and on and on. The vice principal ran out and put a step stool in front of the podium. When she clambered onto it, there was a spurt of laughter. A smile oozed out of the corner of her mouth as she surveyed the room. She was silent for a moment too long, and the applause started again. It was only when this second burst died down that she began telling us a bunch of anecdotes about amazing people who'd changed their lives. The whole thrust of it was that willpower and drive could make anybody into a huge success. The subtext was that Susan Le was rich because she deserved to be: she hadn't been born intelligent and dedicated; she'd made herself that way.

People laughed at the right places and applauded at the right places. When she left the podium about half the audience stood up. I remained sitting, but Kian and Chelsea both stood. She didn't go back to her seat, though. She kept going, retreating backstage. Even Colson seemed nonplussed. What was happening? She was such a coward! Was she really going to dodge my speech entirely?

I tried to convince myself that it didn't matter. She'd see it on YouTube. Or she'd hear about it.

Kian's speech came next. The moment he began, the room wilted. Somehow, the master debater wasn't comfortable speaking from the heart. The delivery was perfect, but the speech was long and full of clichés: the wonderful people he'd met; how much he'd always miss the place; the things he'd learned; the difference we all needed to make in this horrible world.

By the end of the twenty-minute speech, the crowd was restless: its slight sideways motion resembled water coming to a boil.

My turn was coming up. I hoped they'd boo me. Since I couldn't have approval, I at least wanted havoc.

Despite his horrendously boring speech, Kian sat down to a sustained round of applause. I suppose a lot of people in our class really respect him.

When Colson called out my name, there were scattered hisses. I got up, and the booing rose. But, then, somewhere between my second and third step, it fell away. By the time I got to the podium, a few people had started to clap their hands. The spotlight caught me. I blinked, dazzled. The microphone was still warm from Kian's fingers.

A moment passed, and one long *hisssss* echoed through the room. It went on for a very long time, maybe five seconds, but I think it was only one person. Eventually, even that died away.

Someone shouted, "I wanna marry you, Reshma!"

I still have no idea who that was.

Then, in the front row, someone yawned. His gaping mouth was a tiny black hole. When he'd reached the apex of his yawn, the person next to him yawned. Without meaning to, I let out a long yawn as well. And then the crowd was a winking starscape of open throats: everyone was already pretty tired.

The parents were mostly up above, in the back rows and mez-zanine. Their faces were pink dots. My parents were in there somewhere. And so were George's and Alex's and Chelsea's. Every-one I knew, pretty much, and all their parents, too. Standing there and watching me.

I looked down at my phone, which was displaying a copy of the speech Susan Le had ripped up, and then I started to speak.

My voice had that low, strong quality that I think I've described before, and the room went absolutely quiet. I went on like a bull-dozer, feeling the anger build up inside my throat as I said, "Yes, I cheated. I admit it. And I deserve what I got. But there's a person here who's cheated on a far grander scale."

No one applauded. No one made a sound. The sun streamed in through windows all along the top of the auditorium, and the only people who moved were the ones baking away inside the hot little spots of light that it made.

Something about their silence was so awful. If they had booed me, I could've disregarded them. I could've called them idiots and fools. But they didn't boo. They listened. A few times, they even clapped. And that was . . . it was the worst. After a minute, I knew I'd made a terrible mistake. I wanted to sit down and stop talking, but I couldn't. Something forced me to keep going, to keep that anger in my voice, and keep glancing back at Susan Le as I spewed out insult after insult.

My insides clenched, and I saw, at that moment, what George had been trying to tell me. I was selfish. That's what it came down to. I wanted everything from him, but I never gave anything back. Even when he was in trouble, I never . . . I can't even say that I disregarded his trouble. It's more like I never even saw it. I never opened up my heart to it. I was selfish. I was so selfish. Oh God, how could anyone bear to be in the same room with me? I was absolutely terrible.

Today was an unforgettable day in the lives of thousands of

people. It was the culmination of years of study. Some of these kids might be the first in their families to graduate high school. Some of the parents probably didn't know English. They couldn't even understand the speeches. They were down there beaming away, so happy to be here. Others were getting awards. Or, you know, why even think about it that way? Some of them had done nothing in high school. They'd smoked pot and skipped class. But they'd still been here. Something had happened. Even when they were seventy years old, this would be a major part of their lives.

And instead of doing something to honor that moment, I spent ten minutes telling them about some sordid drama involving my parents and the cruel, lonely woman who was probably already back at her house in Palo Alto by now. And why did I do it? What did I gain? No one wanted me to do it. And there was so much else to say, too. Like . . . these were good people in front of me. I know at some high schools it's not that way. I know some high schools are full of cruel and petty-minded kids who make life hell for those around them.

But not at Bell.

I hadn't known that, you see, because I spent so many years avoiding them and trying to be better than them. But any one of them would've been a better choice to be graduation speaker than me. Like Alex, with her weird sense of right and wrong. Or Chelsea, who never let the mask drop, no matter how hard I pushed her. Or Aakash, with his incredibly methodical nature. Or George, with his quiet determination to do the right thing by both me and his parents.

When I ended my speech, there was no applause. A few camera flashes went off as I walked to my seat, but otherwise I had complete silence. Even Chelsea refused to look at me. I sat there with my hands folded in my lap as Colson made his final remarks, and the moment it was all over, I dashed offstage.

I still can't believe what happened. I had so much to say and so much love in my heart, and all I had to do was end my harangue and switch my speech over to something happier and more heartfelt. I had the podium, and I had the moment. But I didn't take it.

. . . .

I just e-mailed my last entry to George. I don't know. Maybe it'll stand in for the apology that I didn't know how to give him.

MONDAY, JUNE 3

There was a furor, of course. My speech got a million views on YouTube and was featured on a few news programs. Susan Le issued a statement trying to explain herself, but her company is publicly traded now, and her shareholders don't need the negative publicity. The chairman of her board issued a statement saying they were looking into reports of these irregularities.

This morning, a lawyer called my parents to offer them a settlement. Le would admit that they had developed the image-recognition algorithm and would give them a small stock grant. They haven't mentioned exactly how much stock they'll be getting or how much it's worth, but when my dad told me about it, his eyes were wide and he spent all his time looking out the window.

The only requirement, of course, was that I needed to recant my story and say that I'd exaggerated everything. My mom wasn't around when my dad asked me to do that. I think she didn't want me to. I heard them shouting about it last night. But I said okay, and this morning I signed and released the statement that Le's people had sent over to us.

So now the world considers me a plagiarist *and* a slanderer. Apparently, I'm the poster child for a spoiled and entitled generation.

Which is fair, I suppose.

THURSDAY, JUNE 6

From: Leo Wasserman <leowas68@hotmail.com>
To: Reshma Kapoor <rtkap@bombr.co>
Subject: Can you take a look at this for me?

Dear Reshma,

My novel is finally done! Attached, you'll find *Dr. Nathan West and the Case of the Strangled Teacher*. Would you mind reading and giving your comments? In about two weeks, we're having a little critique discussion of the novel, and my wife and I would love for you to participate. Thanks so much for your help!

Sincerely,

Leo Wasserman, PhD (Doctor of Philosophy) and M.W. (Mystery Writer)

Sent a text to George, telling him I miss him.

Yeah. I guess I miss you, too.

Did you read my note?

Yeah.

That stung a bit. I wanted to text him a million more apologies. But what did that matter? Nothing I said could make his life easier.

How's your mom? Is she proud of you?

Don't even ask. She's out of control.

Was there a party?

More like did the party ever stop? Every time I come home she's on the phone bragging to some old auntie about how I got a scholarship to Berkeley.

So she finally came to terms with the sports thing?

> Oh you know Indian people. Once we realize there's money in it we're fine with anything.

> LOL. So you think she's convincing the people back home that "running track" is the new "programming computers"?

> That is very possible. I've already had one cousin call and ask if I can coach him.

We went back and forth, lightning fast, for two hours. Neither of us wanted to call the other, I guess. But finally I wrote:

> Hey you want to hang out? I'm free any and every time.

There was a long pause.

> This'll sound like a lie, but I can't.

> Ever? Not even for an hour?

He told me that he was working three jobs now: nights at a restaurant, days at the shoe store, weekends at a farmers' market. He was trying to save up as much money as possible so that he wouldn't feel like a bastard if he chose to live near Berkeley's campus instead of commuting there from his home.

> Bus is getting close to my house.

> Nice talking to you. I miss you.

Our entire conversation had taken place during one of his circuitous bus-to-Caltrain-to-BART-to-bus journeys back to his home.

MONDAY, JUNE 17

As a condition of the settlement, Susan Le's PR people booked my parents for a segment on a morning show. I offered to go on the show, too, but everyone looked at me like I was crazy: nobody trusts me to stay on-message in front of a camera.

But I went along for the taping, and I sat with them in the green room as Le's lawyers gave them prepared statements in which they carefully delineated the role that Susan Le had played in the development of their company and their ideas, and then, just as carefully, thanked her for everything she'd done. In it, they acknowledged she'd committed no wrongdoing, and that they were grateful for the completely voluntary compensation she was giving them, out of a sense of fair play, for what she felt were their contributions to the company.

My dad stroked my mom's hand as they look at their statements. We were all alone in that windowless room, except for a blond-haired woman wearing an earpiece. My mom had recently dyed her hair, but the fluorescent lighting brought out all the gray in the fringe of hair that surrounded my dad's bald head.

Then my mom's phone buzzed, and she said, "Ahh, Jim wants to move the Sequoia Capital meeting up a few hours."

"Will they invest?" my dad said.

"No, they're too focused on social. I doubt they'll get into tech."

"But we have social applications, too! I forgot to tell you! I've been working on creating plug-ins for Bombr that . . ."

My dad flipped over his paper and started scribbling on the back of the sheet. My mom shoved her prepared statement into her purse and leaned in to my dad so she could see better. Meanwhile, his pen was slashing across the back of the paper, and he was talking very fast. My mom's eye furrowed, and her finger stabbed out to call attention to some mistake. Their heads bent closer together.

I still couldn't believe I'd asked Susan Le to hire me. It seems insane to me, but I know that if she'd said yes, I would've abandoned my speech and gone into business with my parents' worst enemy.

I must've made a noise in the back of my throat, because my mom looked up at me, and we locked eyes.

My mouth opened. I was about to confess everything and apologize to them and beg them to forgive me.

Then she frowned at me, and she blinked a few times, like there was something about me which was a bit blurry, and I decided not to say anything.

THURSDAY, JUNE 20

Dr. Nathan West examined the body with a tremendously exacting amount of excruciating care. He'd seen a hundred dead bodies in his career as a part-time consultant for the San Francisco Police Department, but this body was just about the most dead body that he had ever seen. Its skull had been smashed open, and its brains were leaking all over the floor. The murder weapon: a silver trophy—bashed into a leaden lump—lay by the side of the brainless and thoroughly brained teacher.

Dr. Nathan West was as brilliant a detective as he was a psychologist, but this time he was truly stumped. The door of this office had been locked from the inside. How could anyone have possibly got in to kill this teacher?

At his side, the student said, "We all loved Ms. Manfred. She was our favorite teacher. Who could want to do this?"

Dr. Nathan West turned to her. The student was named Laila Azadian, and she was the one who had found the corpse. As stage manager of the school's amateur theatrical society—the one that was managed and directed by Ms. Manfred—Laila was one of the teacher's closest associates amongst the student body.

Laila's dense eyebrows came close to joining above her nose

and her somewhat overlarge hands gripped and tangled with each other. "You don't think it's a student, do you?" she said.

"It can't be," Dr. Nathan West said. "If it was a student, that would make a terribly predictable case. And they only call me in when the case is an excellent and unpredictable one."

. . . .

Dr. Wasserman's house was a Craftsman cottage on the edge of Mountain View. Apparently, he collected images of lighthouses: they were emblazoned on sculptures, figurines, tapestries, throw pillows, carpets, and plates. I sat in the Wassermans' narrow living room in a recliner that'd been turned around so it faced away from the TV. The two of them sat next to each other in the love seat. Her hand was intertwined with his, and his head was bent down so his scalp was pointed at me: it was pink, with a coating of fuzzy white hair, like a blooming dandelion. His breaths were almost gasps. He looked like he was ready to receive a beating.

"Sorry this gathering is so intimate," his wife said. "But all the rest of Leo's writer friends said they couldn't make it. You're such a dear for coming."

I grimaced. Their couch was sagging underneath them. I had a mental image of them sitting here at night, holding hands and exchanging chaste kisses during the commercial break of a *Law & Order* rerun.

I had the whole huge printout of his novel in my lap. I was about to open my mouth to begin talking, but he interjected: "How's your novel coming? Are you done?"

"I'm not sure. It's puttering along."

"Oh, that's okay. The important thing is to let the ending breathe. Too many writers forget that the novel can't end right at the big climax. There has to be a falling action, where the tension is slowly released. And then a dénouement, where all the final threads get wrapped up."

"Come on, now," his wife said. "This isn't therapy, it's a critique circle. Why don't we pull the bandage off? Reshma, what did you think of my husband's book?"

I rifled the pages with my thumb. Sure were a lot of them: almost four hundred sheets of paper. Every single one was filled with words. "This novel is . . . not very good," I said.

Wasserman let out a slight hiss.

I waited. The hiss stopped.

"Umm, dear," Mrs. Wasserman said. "You're supposed to give reasons. And, you know, in a critique, Leo usually doesn't get to speak to defend his work. So please talk until you're done."

I shrugged. "I don't know what to say. This is unreadably bad. You obviously know a lot about stories. And this follows all your rules: there's rising tension and internal/external arcs and third options and it's got the Hero's Journey and . . . is there something a little extra, too?"

"Five-act structure," Wasserman muttered. His wife looked at him and jerked her head from side to side. "Sorry," he said. "I'll be quiet."

"But I didn't enjoy reading it," I said. "Almost every sentence is clunky and ugly. And the characters and plot are silly. It doesn't feel like it has a reason for existing."

The noise that came out of Wasserman's mouth was strangely akin to whale song.

"I'm sorry," I said. "I don't enjoy saying this. You've been writing for so long, though, and your work is still so bad. Have you ever considered quitting? I mean . . . I normally wouldn't recommend that, except . . . it's clearly not making you happy. I mean, you were always a bit wifty, but you used to be tall and confident and funny.

And now you're this little nervous guy. Come on, Mrs. W, you see it, too, don't you?"

Her nose was scrunched up and her eyebrows were twitching. She looked like she wanted to reach across the expanse of carpet and strangle me.

I stared at the ground. "That's, umm . . . That's all I have to say. . . ."

He looked up. His face was stained with tears. "Thank you for your critique," he said. "I'll try to keep your comments in mind for the next draft."

"You're really going to try to rewrite this?"

"Thank you for your . . ." His voice broke. "This is all I've ever wanted to do!"

Then his wife threw her arms around him. "It's okay," she whispered. "You can do it. I know you can."

I tried to make as little noise as possible when I snuck out, but Wasserman croaked: "Wait."

I'd almost made it to the door. I looked over my shoulder.

"Don't forget the falling action and the dénouement," he said.

I almost wished I'd lied. But . . . maybe he will recall my words someday, when he's close to the edge of despair, and they will make him realize that his true calling lies elsewhere.

In a way, I was elated. Ever since giving my valedictorian speech, I've been trying to be less selfish, and sometimes I wonder if maybe that means I'll also have to be nice and sweet and fake all the time. But you know what? Sometimes the most selfish thing to do is to be nice when your friend really needs you to be honest.

MONDAY, JUNE 24

The back room of the shoe warehouse was a nest of metal shelves, packed so close that we had to walk sideways to get through them. Even though it was over eighty degrees outside, I was chilly in here amongst the concrete and the piping.

George's mouth dropped when his manager introduced him to me:

"This is Reshma, our newest hire," he said. "She's going to be shadowing you for the day."

He snapped off some quick instructions and then left us there, in the back, surrounded by mountains of new shoes.

"How did you . . . ?" he said.

"What, I'm not qualified to sell shoes?" I said. "I'll have you know that I am a high school graduate."

"Stock shoes, for now. You're in the back."

"Oh," I said. "And is there anyone else back here?"

I leaned on one foot and tapped the other on the concrete floor. His face was just a few inches from mine. He swept a strand of hair behind his ear, and I thought the nervous gesture might be a cover for how uncomfortable he was, so I started to back away, but then his hand was on my waist, gathering me closer to him.

"Hey," he said. "Can I kiss you?"

FRIDAY, JULY 28

I enjoy seeing George at the store. Since he works in the back and I've been transferred to the front, we don't butt up against each other too much. The whole store laughs at how much time I spend in the stockroom, but it's a gentle laughter. I don't know what it is about me that's changed. I feel like I'm acting exactly the same, but no one here hates me.

The working world is so clean and simple. Your boss might say, "Good job," but you don't get a number—a grade—that you can use to lord it over other people. I work as hard as anyone. We don't work on commission, but I keep my own private set of sales figures: I sell a third more shoes than the next-best person. When I try to show my tally to the manager, he looks over the numbers and says, "Hmm, interesting," and doesn't act on this information at all. He only cares about making sure that the corporate office doesn't get on his case.

Okay, you're not interested in this. You're waiting for the novel to be over. And . . . well . . . maybe this is the ending?

MONDAY, JULY 29

No, wait, it can't be!

TUESDAY, JULY 30

T he last time I ended this novel, I was *sure* I'd gotten to the end because I had everything I wanted. This time, all I've got is a job in a shoe store.

Err, and I'm no longer quite so insane. When did that happen? How did it happen? Everyone says I seem ten times nicer and happier nowadays, but I still identify so strongly with the girl who sat in that basement a year ago, bubbling with so much anger and resentment. I feel like I owe her so much, and I'd be sorry to discover that I've killed the most dynamic and interesting part of her.

THURSDAY, AUGUST 1

Today Alex let slip that she was going to be helping Chelsea move, so I decided to head over to her place and see if I could catch her in time to say good-bye.

It's not that I like or care about Chelsea, but the two of us have been through so much together, and I don't know . . . I suppose I also wanted her to acknowledge that I could've taken her number one spot away from her if I'd wanted.

I've never been to her house before, and now I know why. Chelsea lives in East Las Vacas, in a strip of bungalows on Swamp Road. Her house has a little lawn and a wooden fence, but it's tiny—only five rooms—and huge trucks are constantly barreling past on their way to the highway.

Alex and Chelsea were out front, watching an older man in a T-shirt and cargo shorts try to maneuver a bicycle into the backseat of Alex's beamer.

"This thing is so tiny," the man said. "How do you fit any people in here?"

"Oh, well, I think it's not, like, a real backseat," Alex said. "It's just there for the insurance. For some reason, two-seaters cost way more to insure than four-seaters, you know?"

The man frowned. I don't think he did know.

"Hey!" I said. "How's it going?!"

Chelsea kept her back to me for a moment, and I thought, Oh my God, this is it. This time she won't be smiling. This time she won't be nice. This time she'll show what she really thinks of me.

But when she turned around, the grin was as wide as ever, and she said, "Oh wow! Great to see you here, Resh!"

Alex clapped her hands. "Perfect timing, Resh! You've got an SUV, right? So much more room!"

Chelsea glanced over at Alex and then back at me. The man finally gave up heaving at the bicycle and said, "Look, let me get a wrench. I'm just gonna take the wheels off, okay?"

He trotted indoors and left us standing out there in the heat. The air was still, and the only sound was from the cars passing behind me.

"Hey . . . I, actually, umm . . ." I looked pointedly at Alex to signal that maybe she should leave me alone with Chelsea.

"No, I'm gonna stay for this," she said.

"Fine." I looked at Chelsea. "I just wanted to say that I'm sorry. You know, nothing I did was personal. But . . . you were the one who suffered. It was your name in the newspapers next to mine. And you were the one who didn't get to speak at graduation and didn't get in early to Stanford. You were the better person."

Okay, yeah, I know I went there to make her thank me, but I changed my mind. I don't know. I guess I realized it was silly to want her to be honest with me when I'd never been honest with her.

Chelsea pointed her face at me, and I stared into her oversized sunglasses. The big black lenses made her look like a praying mantis.

"An apology," Alex said. "This is so sweet, isn't it? And to think that after all these years of mutual loathing, you—"

"Shut up, Alex," Chelsea said. Then she rubbed the tips of her fingers against the side of her skirt. "Thank you, Reshma. I appreciate that. But there's nothing to apologize for. It's been wonderful getting to know you this year. I'm only sorry you won't be there at Berkeley to make sure I keep my nose to the grindstone. Oh, and I know that you could've been valedictorian if you wanted to, and I'd like to thank you for letting me have it. The title really meant a lot to my dad."

Behind Chelsea's back, Alex made a face like she was gagging, but I shook my head.

Chelsea is amazing. She is one of the marvels of the universe. Even when there was absolutely nothing to gain, she remained completely self-possessed. Wow. I don't know. I guess I'm just not fated to ever know or understand the real Chelsea.

Then Chelsea said, "Well, I better get back to packing," and Alex said, "So . . . I'll see you later tonight, Resh?" and I realized that the window had already closed on the possibility that something meaningful would arise from this interaction, so I glanced at my phone and said, "Oh! I have to go," and, with a flurry of hugs and waves and good-byes, allowed myself to be shepherded back to my car.

MONDAY, AUGUST 12

Okay. This is the dénouement. Get ready, because nothing comes after this.

Aakash has been spotted making out with Kate Erickson. She was a girl in our class who was hella into computer science: she commercially released two iPhone apps during our senior year. I looked on his Bombr account to see what he was saying about her, but saw that almost 75% of his bombs are being thrown to @Kateerickson14. They're always sharing links with each other and arguing about philosophy. It's a bit disgusting,

Raymond Lodge's dad is really into Indian classical music, so I pretended to be interested in the topic and went to talk to him—as part of a mission to reclaim my cultural heritage, you know? After a few minutes, I slowly steered the conversation over to Ray's grades. And, before I knew it, his dad was showing me stacks and stacks of Ray's old report cards. I took surreptitious photographs of some of the high school grade reports. Soon enough, I will acquire a copy of Ray's final transcript. This will hopefully contain a number of discrepancies with the quarterly score reports. Thus, I will be provided with reams of blackmail material to deploy should that bastard ever achieve a position of high responsibility after he graduates from Brown.

Tina Huang got into Columbia, regular decision, and is going to attend in the fall. I feel like I should've worked her in a bit more. Maybe I should've combined her with Cecily? But whatever, I hate when you read a high school novel, and it's like there're only six kids in the whole school.

Kian and Alex kept making out all summer, but they never started dating. They're both too smart to get tied down before college starts.

Yesterday, Mummy said that maybe the shoe store is interfering with my writing productivity. She thinks I should quit and focus on being a full-time writer. When I told her that the novel had zero chance of being published, she looked at me sternly and told me not to give up: if this was something I wanted to do, then I needed to pursue it.

I'm still not sure whether to destroy Linda Montrose. Some days I think, Yes, she is certainly worthy of being destroyed! And on other days, I think, No, you know, she was doing her job. Why should she rep a book that she doesn't believe in? Nowadays, I try not to destroy people unless I am at least 90% sure that they deserve it. So I guess she's safe. For now.

I tried to schedule another appointment with Dr. Wasserman, but his wife called me back and said he didn't think he could see me anymore. That sent me into a shame spiral that lasted for days. I still wonder whether I could've phrased my criticism a little better.

Anyway, I know it's traditional to dedicate your first book to your parents, but none of this would exist without Dr. Wasserman. I hope that when he reads this, he finds himself able to forgive me. In the meantime, I gave him super positive reviews on Angie's List and on Yelp. I'm still not sure what was wrong with me, but I think he cured it, right? And I'm sure plenty of other screwed-up writers are looking for talented therapists and editors.

One day, I e-mailed Ms. Lin to tell her I was sorry I'd abused the trust she'd placed in me. When she gave me that amazing recommendation letter, she'd been so confident that this plagiarism thing was an isolated fluke. She wrote back:

You are forgiven. Now go forth and forgive.

Sometimes, George looks up at me and says some very nice things. I have slowly learned to say some nice things back to him. Like, he's very kind. And decisive. Good to have around for when you overdose on prescription amphetamines. He's going to Berkeley in a month. Since I'll still be in the area, we're going to stay together, but . . . well . . . I don't know. Berkeley is fifty miles away. He's moving forward and I'm staying behind.

. . . .

I don't know what to do with Alexandra. She's such a major part of this story, but she's got no plot or resolution. When I was revising it, I e-mailed the book to her along with the note:

Can we maybe talk about your character arc?

She wrote back:

Sure!

I spent a day or two being afraid that maybe she'd be mad over something I'd said in the book. When I went into her house, she was sitting on a cushion on her living room floor, and she had pages from my book spread all around her.

"Oh my God, your novel is so meta," she said. "Are you, like, are you going to write this conversation into the book? Maybe I ought to say something so unspeakably foul that you're forced to cut this scene. . . ."

"All the other major characters have an arc." I paced back and forth in the narrow corridor she'd formed between the stacks of pages. "Wasserman descends into this weird madness. Ms. Ratcliffe's bohemian façade slowly cracked, and we saw that she's the sort of racist who can't look at a pair of perfectly fine Indian parents without assuming that they're abusing their child. George and I fell for each other. My parents and I reached some kind of détente, and—"

"Okay, okay, I understand."

I couldn't face her, so I kept my head down. "But have you and I finished our arc? I mean, weren't you going to tell me that you admired me and wished you could be more like me?"

"Umm, Resh," she said. "I didn't want to draw too much attention to this, but I'm pretty good at life. I have friends, grades, fulfilling activities. I mean, I like you, but I think maybe *you* should have learned from *me*."

"You definitely changed, though. You drifted apart from Chelsea, for one thing."

"Oh, I could never really talk to her. Not like I can with you," she said. "Except, hold on. Reshma, what was the deal with this amphetamine overdose? That is crazy! You should've called me. I would've been there for you, right? Yeah. I'm almost sure I would've. Come on, you shouldn't have hid that from me." She gritted her teeth. "I just . . . I guess I never thought about what I might be doing to you by—"

"Don't be silly," I said. "If I hadn't gotten the pills from you, I'd have gotten them from someone else."

She shook her head. "Maybe that's my arc. I've finally realized that drugs are bad!"

"Have you?"

Alex flung a few of the pages up into the air, and we both

watched them flutter down. "Hmm . . . no. Maybe I'm done dealing, though? That's progress, right?"

"I really don't get it. You and the perfects were mean to me for years. How did it all change?"

"First of all, you're, like, the only person who still calls us 'the perfects.' That's so sophomore year, Resh. Get with the times. Second, we were not mean to you, you were mean to us. Third, if we're such 'friends,' then why has your novel portrayed me in such an extremely unflattering light? For instance, right now the novel seems to imply that I leaked a gossip item about you in on online blog, which is completely false. All I did was plant a very judicious rumor that was designed to force George and you to acknowledge your nascent feelings for each other. Everything would've worked fine, and nothing would've blown up, if it wasn't for the fact that he was illegally pretending to be your relative! So really all the fault here belongs to you."

"Oh please," I said.

"No, no, no," she said. "It was a Machiavellian scheme. I am a Machiavelli. I'm like twelve Machiavellis, in fact."

"You are no Machiavelli. You are one gossipy little bitch."

"I am offended, I think that our arc ends here! Now!"

I leaned against one of the arms of the couch. "Hmm, I guess it could work if we drifted apart as inexplicably as we came together. . . ."

"Ugh, no. You cannot write that." Alex looked down and started sweeping the pages together into one big pile. "Come on, Resh. You know, reading about all that stuff I said and did to you . . . it really does hurt. I don't know. In school, I always hated you. I mean, for years whenever I'd talk to you, you'd glare at me like I was interrupting. And God forbid I ask what you were doing for the weekend, because you'd just snap, 'I'll be studying.' It just . . . it really felt like you had no soul. How could we have ever been friends? What could I have said or done to get past that wall?"

That wasn't really how I remembered things.

"No," I said. "Don't you remember? Freshman year? You . . ." My voice was cracking, and it was so embarrassing, because why should I still care about some tiny little thing from four years ago? "You . . . you wouldn't let me sit with you at lunch."

"Fuck," Alex said. "I . . . I remember making those stupid rules. I was so excited about how *real* we were going to be. How we wouldn't talk all the time about grades and school. How we'd be so much *better* than everybody else at school. I can't believe how awful I was."

"We . . ."

Both of us had wasted so much time.

"Anyway!" She took up the big pile of paper—my novel—and slapped it down onto the coffee table. "Guess it's good that you decided to write this thing, huh?"

I felt a little frazzled, because if there was ever a moment to resolve everything, then it was right now.

"Alex," I said.

"What's next on the agenda?" she said. "Do we have an agenda? What I've learned from this experience is that you just can't have fun unless there's an agenda, so I think maybe our first agenda item is to create a system for agenda creatio—"

I shouted, "Oh my God, stop saying *agenda!*" and then Alex broke down laughing, and ever since then she's stymied all my attempts at book discussion by saying she'll add that to the agenda.

So there it is. Maybe the problem is that I'm trying to slap an ending onto a friendship that only began like six months ago.

Wait, I guess one more thing has happened:

Today, my phone chimed while I was helping a customer. It was an e-mail from that media agent, Amy Zazo, saying she'd asked Linda to send her the latest version of my book and was there a good time for Amy to call me? My heart started to pound. Was this it? Was I going to be back on top? As I sized the customer's foot and brought out three boxes of sneakers for her to look at, all the fantasy scenarios spun themselves out in my head: She'd found a publisher! Someone in Hollywood wanted to option my book! They needed me to go back on TV to promote it!

Finally, the woman took her shoes to the shiny sales counter—it's covered in yellow and blue stripes—at the front of the store, and I sent an e-mail to Amy, telling her to call me whenever she had the time.

Afterward, I went home and read my manuscript. And, maybe this is strange, but as I went through it, I started crying. Every word felt so much like me. Normally, I think of myself as having a very cold heart, but I could feel the warmness and the desperation oozing up through the text. Did Amy really think it was worthwhile? And what draft had she read, exactly?

I looked back: the last version I'd sent Linda had been right after

I was named salutatorian, but before I'd given my commencement speech. Amy had loved the book even though she didn't have the full ending.

The next morning, Amy called me at the start of my shift, and I ducked out into the warehouse area to take to the call.

She started off by giving me a very warm "It's so wonderful to finally get a chance to chat with you!" and went on to say, "I know Linda didn't think this book had a future, but I have to say that, while she is a very fine children's lit agent, I don't think she sees the full potential here."

Then she praised my book's gracefulness and insight and explained that she'd been following my whole case very closely, and that now she had my side of the backstory between Susan Le and my parents, she thought there was a wonderful opportunity to turn this into a really gripping, plot-driven memoir.

"It's the kind of story people love!" she said. "You knew, all along, that a wrong had been done to your family, so you struggled against all odds to correct it, and you finally succeeded! I mean, I obviously don't have those chapters, but I can just imagine that sense of triumph when you're delivering that speech to that silent audience. You know, that's really the capstone: all through the book it feels like you're always asking permission from your parents to speak out and defend their rights, but in that moment, you're finally *taking* permission. It's the moment when you come into full moral consciousness."

Even though we were on the phone, I was smiling desperately. "Yes, although it was actually very complicated. . . ."

"And sitting next to Susan Le . . . what was that like? Did you ever speak to her? What were you thinking? What did you feel when you saw her? You know, in many ways, she's your shadow self here: a version of you that grew up without the strong, instinctive moral center that grounds you."

The only thing I could feel was the metal superstructure of the shelves that I was leaning against.

Last night, when I was reading my book, I realized that I didn't really write it in order to get into Stanford. Or, well, I did, sort of. But actually writing the novel and getting into Stanford were two aspects of the same desire: I just wanted someone to love me. And at that moment, while I listened to Amy praise me, all I could hear was my own voice begging Susan Le to see that she'd never find another person like me.

I let Amy talk to me for a few more minutes and found myself promising her that I'd send her the rest of the chapters as soon as possible.

After ending the call, I felt weirdly empty. I had a decision to make. I could either write the chapters the way Amy wanted, or I could send her the real manuscript.

The only problem was that both of those options felt completely repulsive.

Then I heard a rattling noise. Someone had banged a dolly into some of the metal shelves. I turned, and then the dolly clanged again and boxes rained down. I heard George curse.

I forced myself to smile, then walked around to where he was scrambling around on the ground, trying to assort the shoes back into the right boxes.

"What's going on?" I said.

"Damn dolly," he said. "It's too wide to fit in these aisles. I keep complaining to the manager about it, but he doesn't do shit."

"Why don't we just move the shelves?" I looked around. "Look, all we'd need to do is move this shelf so it's flush with that wall, and then we'd have more than enough space."

The ventilation clicked off, and suddenly my voice sounded way too loud.

George was still crouching on his heels, but he looked up at me and then brushed his hair out of his eyes. "Wait, what's wrong?"

"Come on," I said. "Let's do it."

"Resh, what's wrong?"

I started wrestling a shelf out of position. That, unfortunately, made even more boxes rain down. Finally, George and I realized that we'd need to unload each shelf before we could move it. As we worked, I kept looking over my shoulder, hoping that the manager wouldn't notice I wasn't out on the floor. But I guess it was a pretty slow day. George kept complaining, saying no one was even gonna notice that we'd done this, but I tossed him a few kisses whenever he looked ready to quit.

When we finally finished, the room looked almost exactly the same. George started kissing my neck while my back was against a metal shelf, but I broke free and made it out to the sales floor.

I suppose the manager missed me—or maybe he noticed how flushed I was—because he rolled his eyes and said, "Come on, Resh. I know it's slow, but you can't just be disappearing to the back whenever you're working the same shift as George."

I glanced at the floor and tried to look contrite, even though my heart was pounding. When my manager turned away, I rocked up and down on my heels.

And that's when I realized that this novel was finished. No need to name it. No need to give it a tidy wrapping-up. Maybe someday I'll send it to Amy, and maybe I won't, but for now it's going to sit on my hard drive.

I grabbed an old sales invoice and a pen and leaned on the sales counter. In between customers, I outlined my plans for the future.

My store really was abominably managed. Any healthy competitor could've run it out of business in a month. And, since my store remained in business, I could only conclude that the entire field was equally sick.

This whole retail sector was ripe for conquest.

By sunset, the back of the invoice was covered in thick squiggles: the arrows were overlapping and running into each other. And each arrow had a label so tiny that I was reading them more by memory than by sight. But I can tell you this: the words *hook* and *admission* and *school* were nowhere on that page.

ACKNOWLEDGMENTS

First, thank you for reading my book.

Second, I have to apologize to my mom and dad. I was totally going to dedicate this entire book to you, but then I started wondering if maybe it'd be uncool for my very rebellious teen book to have "For my parents . . ." as its first line. But don't worry—your thank-you is on its way.

Still, before I circle back to you guys, I want to thank my agent, John Cusick. His editorial comments were transformative. When he told me that I ought to cut twenty thousand words from my initial draft, I was skeptical, but he was absolutely right. Without him, you'd be reading a much slower-paced novel. And as if that wasn't enough, he's also been a tremendous advocate and career counselor. He is this book's other father.

A number of editors have made their mark on this book. Thanks to Lisa Yoskowitz for purchasing the book. Thanks to Emily Meehan and Julie Moody for providing the first round of comments; without them, Reshma's relationships with the men in her life would've been much less substantial. Aakash, in particular, grew and grew thanks to their influence. Julie's also been with the book this whole time and, at this point, probably knows it better than I do. It's hard sometimes to piece out her individual contributions (the curse of being an assistant!) but any comments that've come to me with her name have always been spot-on.

Thanks to Jody Corbett for her copyediting. She's made a number of excellent catches—it's been invaluable to have a fresh pair of eyes on the book during the latter stages of the publication process.

Thanks to Kieran Viola for adopting the book and being so enthusiastic about it. She's been everything I could've hoped for in an editor. In terms of comments, she's more responsible than anyone for fine-tuning Alex and Reshma's relationship. In my initial drafts, their friendship was inconsistent and unsatisfying. Kieran is responsible for any warmth that eventually crept into it.

Thanks as well to Kathy Dawson for that one-hour phone call wherein she completely destroyed my conception of the book. Kathy explained, very carefully, that Reshma had no character arc. In initial drafts, Reshma was much more focused on competing with Chelsea. It was Kathy who helped me realize that the heart of the book was in Reshma's relationship with her parents. Without her, this book would've been much colder and crueler.

Thanks to Rebecca Fraimow for reading an initial draft and advising me on "girl stuff," and for being such a wonderful friend over all these years. I don't think I could have imagined, when the two of us were involved in that play together during our freshman year of college, that someday I'd be thanking her in print.

Ever since I sold this book, I've periodically reminded myself, "You have to thank Valynne! You have to thank Valynne!" So here I am, thanking her. This all started because she won a writing contest and then e-mailed me—the first runner-up—with an offer to introduce me to her agent. I don't know anyone who's as thoughtful and generous as Valynne Maetani. She is the person that I e-mail whenever I have questions or concerns about the world of children's book publishing. I can't thank her enough.

Thanks as well to Courtney Alameda, Kelly Loy Gilbert, Christian Heidicker, Michelle Modesto, Tess Sharpe, and Erin Summerill for their support and advice on my debut author journey.

Thanks to Nick Mamatas for being an electrifying instructor and a no-nonsense mentor. Thanks to Prof. Brad Leithauser for admitting me to the MFA program at Hopkins, even though I was writing about flying houses and spaceships and things like that. Thanks to Prof. Jean McGarry for being my fellow traveler in all my reading adventures. I still remember how excited I was to find someone who shared so much of my taste. And thanks as well to Profs. Matt Klam, Alice McDermott, Eric Puchner, Mary Jo Salter, Glenn Blake, Yvonne Gobble, Amy Lynwander, and the rest of the staff at the Johns Hopkins University Writing Seminars. The first draft of this book was written during the winter break of my first year at Hopkins, and I know that it would not have been possible without the unique mix of freedom and instruction that my professors offered.

Okay, I promised myself that I was ONLY going to thank people who directly impacted the writing of THIS book, but I am going to make one exception. I'd like to thank my first boss, Ernesto Sanchez-Triana. He hired me right out of college, tolerated my incompetence, and created an environment in which I could learn how to be a functional human being. Working with him has taught me so much about time management and how to communicate with others, and I'm extremely grateful for the day that our paths crossed.

And, finally, I'd like to thank my parents: Sonalde Desai and Hemant Kanakia. There it is. You know this book is forevermore going to be on the results page when people Google you, right?

Anyway, thank you so much, parents of mine, for your wisdom and your faith in my abilities. If I've accomplished anything in life, I'm pretty sure that 90% of the credit belongs to you. If parents were assorted and ranked like high schoolers, you two would be perfects.